available by Bailee Abbott

Paint by Murder Mysteries
A Brush With Murder

Kill T

W

Ca

Kill Them With Canvas

A PAINT BY MURDER MYSTERY

Bailee Abbott

CROOKED
LANE

NEW YORK

Copyright © 2022 by Kathryn Long

All rights reserved.

Published in the United States by Crooked Lane Books, an imprint of The Quick Brown Fox & Company LLC.

Crooked Lane Books and its logo are trademarks of The Quick Brown Fox & Company LLC.

Library of Congress Catalog-in-Publication data available upon request.

ISBN (hardcover): 978-1-63910-104-7
ISBN (ebook): 978-1-63910-105-4

Cover illustration by Rob Fiore

Printed in the United States.

www.crookedlanebooks.com

Crooked Lane Books
34 West 27th St., 10th Floor
New York, NY 10001

First Edition: October 2022

10 9 8 7 6 5 4 3 2 1

To my sister, Joanne Naragon, whose strong belief in me as a writer helped give me the courage to take this journey and never quit.

Chapter One

"Hush, Max. You're scaring away the ducks."

I tugged at his leash and led us both to a bench situated in the shade underneath an oak tree. The view of Chautauqua Lake calmed me in ways few places could. Sailboats floated across cobalt blue water that glistened with the sun's rays. In the distance, trees sketched in splashes of green, gold, red, and orange bordered the shoreline. Both local folks and tourists rushed to soak up the sunny days and mild temperatures of late October before winter forced them to store their vessels and switch their recreational activities to cold weather sports like skiing in Ellicottville's Holiday Valley Resort.

Max stuck his nose in a pile of dry leaves and sniffed. As if satisfied with his search, he lay down at my feet. He was twelve pounds of fluffy white fur with a sassy, energetic personality that matched his Maltese and poodle breeds, and the perfect pet for me. After coming back home to Whisper Cove and feeling anxious about my new venture, I depended on Max for the kind of support only a dog could provide. Lots of cuddles, wet kisses, and unconditional love, no matter how bad my day turned out to be, always cheered me up.

"Here you are." Izzie plopped down next to me on the bench. She leaned her head against my shoulder. "So beautiful, right? I love Whisper Cove this time of year. I think our town has the best fall view in all of western New York."

Since Izzie was only a year younger than me, it always seemed like we were twins. She and I told everyone we were as close as siblings could be. Though sometimes, I think we worked too hard to prove that claim. We were opposites in so many ways. She was tall and willowy with long brown curls while I possessed a short, curvy figure and black hair that was cut in a straight bob. Izzie tended to be a worrier. She wanted everything to turn out perfect, and she carefully calculated her every move. When opening up the paint party shop this summer hadn't gone as smoothly as expected, she had turned into a tangle of frayed nerves, and her cranky, bossy nature snuck up and took over. Planning the events and pushing the agenda to the point of micromanaging had become obsessive. I took her mood swings in stride because I knew she never meant to hurt anyone. Mom advised her to take up yoga or seek guidance from a spiritual counselor. Izzie had given both those ideas a thumbs-down. Besides, since the business was doing well now, and there wasn't a murder investigation to put a snag in it, she had mellowed and relaxed, at least somewhat. She was trying. The need for validation and praise overwhelmed her at times. I knew that. No doubt, insecurity was her Achille's heel.

I, on the other hand, was impulsive, ready to take risks and make mistakes. Obviously, praise for my efforts rated low on my list of concerns. Sure, I felt great when someone complimented me, but I wouldn't worry or think less of myself if no one did. I was constantly changing or giving up on my goals, like my attempt to become a successful artist in the Big Apple or my colossal breakup with a guy who wasn't perfect, but then again, who was? Maybe avoiding commitment was *my* Achille's heel.

"Aunt Constance will be arriving any minute now." Izzie tapped her watch.

I scratched Max behind one ear. "You know this is overkill. She's checked the agenda for tonight's event five times. I worry about her. No one in their sixties should stress so much."

"Please." Izzie rolled her eyes. "Dad told us she's been going to her fitness center three times a week, and recently she bought a bicycle to ride every morning. I wouldn't worry about her."

I pointed. "That's because her doctor advised her to get in better shape."

Constance Abbington was Dad's widowed sister-in-law who got on his nerves at times. *Spoiled, self-centered,* and *obnoxious* were a few of the words he used to describe her, but only in his moments of frustration. She spent money, her share of the Abbington family trust she'd inherited, like there was no end to it. When pressed, though, Dad admitted she had made his brother happy and proved time and again to be a loving aunt who showered us with praise and attention.

Right now, that attention leaned toward irritating rather than loving. Like Izzie's worry over her business venture, Aunt Constance felt pressure to succeed. She was counting on this event being a success. She was, after all, the president of the Chautauqua Sisterhood's local chapter that covered towns from Mayville to Whisper Cove.

In truth, we had a lot riding on this venue too. As Izzie had stated more than once, in order to succeed, our painting event business had a reputation to uphold. I had to agree. Afterall,

I'd become an equal partner. I was counting on this career choice being a success because I was tired of do-overs. Maybe my risk-taking days were over. Twenty-six might be young, but I was determined not to rely on a trust fund inheritance. Izzie felt the same way. We both had something to prove and accomplish on our own.

Even though our parents lived comfortably in their unconventional, carefree lifestyle, it hadn't always been this easy. In their younger days, they had worked hard on their art careers, making a name for themselves. They'd struggled to earn a living. After Granddad Abbington died over a dozen years ago, the trust fund had passed down to our father Joe and his older brother, our uncle David. Only then had the lives of both our families changed and become much easier.

"Yoo-hoo! Good morning, my favorite nieces. What a fantastic morning! I don't blame you for getting outside to enjoy the weather." Aunt Constance pressed a hand to her chest and caught her breath. She squeezed her ample form in the tight space to sit on the bench next to Izzie.

"Hi, Aunt Constance. You're right on time." Izzie smiled, but her voice strained just a bit. "Let's go to the shop. I'll show you that everything's in order." She stood, then led the way across Artisan Alley.

Our shop was at the end of the Alley, along with several craft businesses that skirted the lake. The inviting cottage structure was painted a cheery yellow, and sketched above the door in bright blue letters was the name "Paint with a View." A huge picture window faced the lake.

I tugged at Max's leash and quickened my pace to catch up with Aunt Constance and Izzie. "I'm sure the event will run smoothly. You'll be on the front page of the Chautau-qua Sisterhood's newsletter." I wrote in the air with my finger: *"President of local chapter is praised for her efforts raising money for charity by arranging a paint party event with Whisper Cove's very own Paint with a View."* I grinned. "A sure bet, Aunt Constance. You'll see."

Constance fanned her flushed face with the paper she was holding. "Let's hope so. I haven't told you, but the pressure is on me more than ever. The director of the Sisterhood's northern district, Viola Finnwinkle, called me this morning. She plans to attend our painting event to observe how things go." Her brows curled. "Come to think of it, the visit is unusual. She's never attended any of our functions before, even though I've invited her. She's a very busy lady with all her duties as director."

While I held open the door, both Izzie and Aunt Constance passed through into the shop. "Maybe she wants to see firsthand the great job you're doing. Or could be she loves the idea of a painting event and wants to recommend it to other chapters. A win–win for your chapter and our shop."

"I'm all for that happening," Izzie said.

Constance sat in the closest chair. "I don't mean to burst our party bubble, but Viola never drops by on a whim unless she has a more serious agenda. She's up to something. I can feel it in my bones." She squirmed in her seat. "I swear. It's bad enough she's coming this evening, but she insists on taking the ferry across the lake to Whisper Cove and leaving her car at the dock while I play taxi driver and take us to the lodge. Why she makes things so difficult is beyond me."

I set a bowl of water on the floor for Max, who imme-diately lapped up most of it. I ignored Aunt Constance's complaints because feeding her sympathy only made things worse. "Would you like something to drink? We have water, soda, or maybe you'd enjoy a cup of chamomile tea. Nothing like the soothing, medicinal power of chamomile." I pulled out of the cupboard a metal tin filled with tea bags. I sensed Aunt Constance was headed into either a downward spiral of depression or overwhelming anxiety.

"Tea would be nice. Thanks." Bending her neck side to side, she then lifted her chest and breathed out. "There. That's much better. Now, Izzie, sweetheart. Let's go over my list." She pressed a hand to smooth out the creased folds of the paper she held.

I shoved the mug of water into the microwave and pressed "Start." It was the same paper with the same list she'd brought with her the last several times. By tomorrow, the check-ins with Aunt Constance would be over, and once the word got out, they'd hopefully be replaced with phone calls from others wanting to schedule events. We did a decent amount of business with the paint parties that took place here in the shop, usually two or three times a week, but Izzie's idea to expand by offering on-site events like the one at the lodge had been brilliant. That's why this evening was so important. Word of mouth to spread news proved successful in small towns like Whisper Cove and Mayville.

Izzie opened boxes filled with supplies for the event while Aunt Constance peered inside each one and counted.

"Check, check, and check." Aunt Constance drew marks on her list with a pen. She shoved both paper and writing utensil in her bag. "Now, you'll arrive at the lodge an hour early like we discussed?"

Izzie and I both nodded, and Max let out a sharp bark.

"Excellent. I'm thinking it's wise in case you get a flat tire or something that makes your drive longer, you know. Call me if there's any problem." She snapped her fingers. "I'll come right away. Nothing can go wrong this evening."

Max bit into one of our supply boxes and chewed.

"Good grief. Please get your poochie away from our precious cargo. Why is he here at the shop, anyway?" Her voice took on an edge.

I snatched Max up in my arms and set him behind the counter with me. "Mom scheduled to have their new furnace installed today. Max freaks out over strangers and loud noises." The microwave dinged. "Tea's ready."

"Maybe next time, dear. Sorry, but I need to scoot. My Silver Sneakers class starts in an hour, and I have to change before heading to the fitness center." She waved while stepping outside. "Six o'clock. Don't be late."

Izzie plopped down in the chair next to the wall. "Thank goodness. Do you know how many times I've had to stop myself from saying things that would've struck a nerve?"

I sat on the bar stool and sipped the tea meant for Aunt Constance. "I do know. I was repeating 'patience is a virtue' over and over in my head to keep from snapping at her. What's wrong with us? We've always known Aunt Constance is like this. Why is it bothering us now?"

"Because we're as anxious as she is about this event. It means everything to all of us. Like I've said, we have a—"

"Reputation to uphold. Yes, I believe you've mentioned that once or twice." I laughed.

"Well, it's true." Izzie lifted her chin.

"I agree." I set the mug aside and hopped off the stool. "I need to let Max out. Do you want to start loading the Rover with these boxes? I can carry one outside now."

"How about taking the painted canvases out first while I tape the boxes shut?"

I walked to the rear wall of the shop and stepped onto the stage. Though our space was small, we made the most of it. We had three long tables and places for at least thirty customers. A large projector screen hung above the stage, and one of us would sketch drawings as we gave step-by-step instructions for people to follow. Nearer the front and next to the register, we'd added a display of small items such as painted bookmarks, miniature picture frames, and brush sets. Izzie had come up with that idea to take in more profit. Along the side walls, several hand dryers hung from hooks. They helped to dry the canvases quickly. Scents of turpentine, linseed oil, and paint filled the shop. I loved those smells. Like everyone in our family, I wouldn't be happy if I wasn't doing something with art. This craft was part of my existence.

I picked up one of the paintings and studied the ghostly image. The Lady of Chautauqua Lake, as she was known, floated above the water while ominous clouds darkened the sky. In the distance, candlelight shone with an eerie yellow glow through the eyes and mouths of jack-o'-lanterns. I turned and held up the canvas. "Do you believe in the legend?"

"I do believe the part about Abigail Bellows dying tragically over a hundred years ago. But the idea that she haunts the lake every Halloween is nonsense." Izzie shook her finger. "Please say you agree. I can't handle another fan with a ghost story. Not today or this evening."

"Why? If you don't believe in the haunting, then you shouldn't be scared." I teased. Covering my mouth with one hand I groaned. "*Wooo.* I'm the ghost of Abigail Bellows. Beware on Hallows Eve. If you wander outside, I'll drown you in the lake and steal your soul. *Wooooo.*"

"Stop it, Chloe. You're being silly. I'm not scared of ghosts. I just don't want any distractions this evening." She shrugged.

"Uh-huh. We'll see in a couple of weeks." I juggled the three paintings in my arms and headed toward the door. "Come on, Max. Time to scoot."

Izzie zipped around me and opened the door. "Try not to trip over any ghosts on your way to the car, please."

"Not a chance. They only come out at night." I shifted the paintings to one side so I could see the path leading to where we'd parked the Land Rover. With eyes on my feet rather than straight ahead, I bumped into someone's solid chest. One by one, the canvases slipped from my arms and tumbled to the ground. "Crap."

"You shouldn't be so clumsy, Miss."

I heard the familiar voice and deep laugh that followed and snapped my head around. "And you should've stepped out of the way. Or maybe your reflexes are too slow." My face split into a wide grin. I tapped my lip and tipped my head. "Hmm. Now what's your name? I can't seem to remember, since it's been so long." I studied the familiar muscular frame, tanned skin, and warm brown eyes while Max sniffed at his shoes before hurrying next door to explore our neighbor's property.

Detective Hunter Barrett had investigated a murder in Whisper Cove this past summer. In a short time, we'd gotten to know one another. Since most of our encounters had dealt with his case and my snooping, I had no clue what our relationship meant to him on a personal level. Friends, maybe, but I got the feeling he thought of me as a pain in his behind. Someone who interfered with his investigations had to be on his naughty list. There had been a brief moment, though, at the party to celebrate me becoming Izzie's partner. An exchange that hinted at something more. I wasn't sure, though, because I'd only heard from him once since then. A short call to ask how I was doing. He'd left the conversation with a suggestion to meet for a drink sometime, but that's where it had ended. Until now.

He picked up the canvases. "I'll carry these to your car, if that's where you were headed."

"Sure." I dug my heels into the sand-covered path and led the way. Reaching the Rover, I popped open the tailgate, then moved several steps away as he placed the canvases inside.

"I just closed a murder case up in Jamestown. Double homicide that took up every ounce of energy I had to give. Lots of footwork and so much time involved . . ." His voice trailed off into silence.

"I was only teasing. You don't owe me an explanation." I closed the tailgate.

"I know I should never have suggested meeting, not if I wasn't going to follow through. I meant to. I'm really not the kind of guy to say—"

"Stop. It's fine. Trust me." I touched his arm, then quickly pulled away. "So, what brings you to Whisper Cove?" I led the way back to the shop.

"Robbery. A couple of store owners reported thieves broke in last night and stole items. One of them was along Artisan

Alley. No damage to their shops, which is a good thing." He cleared his throat. "I came here to warn you to be on the lookout. You should make sure your door is locked in the evening, especially if you're here alone."

"That's awful. Who was robbed? I should stop by and see if they need anything." My heart raced. The weeks following the murder this summer had been without incident, and peaceful in a reassuring way. Now this.

"Your neighbor at Go Fly a Kite, for one." He opened the door of the shop for me to step inside.

"Poor Gwen. She doesn't handle stress very well. I can imagine how upset she must be." Gwen was a divorced, older woman who tended to be a bit flighty. She'd nearly suffered a nervous breakdown earlier this year over trouble with a few unsavory residents. Thank goodness she had found someone to bring joy into her life. Winston was kind and gentle, the opposite of her ex-husband.

"Who's upset over what?" Izzie walked out of the storage room. She brushed stray Styrofoam bits off her shirt. She nodded at Hunter with a smirky grin. "Hello, Detective. It's been a while. Must be bad news if you're here."

I winced and moved the conversation along before she could add another teasing jab. "Gwen was robbed." I turned to Hunter. "What did they steal? I hope nothing too valuable."

"That's the thing. There was a bank deposit bag full of cash from the previous day's sales left in a drawer underneath the counter. Gwen says she planned to deliver the money to the bank the next morning. The robber took kite spools, string, and a bolt of white kite material." He sat in one of the chairs and crossed his arms. "The other robbery happened at the general store on Whisper Cove Boulevard. Rope, tape, nails, wire, and a hammer were stolen."

"Sounds like supplies for a school project. Maybe some kids in town are too poor to buy the materials they need, so they just took them." I shrugged.

"Makes sense." Izzie grabbed a bottle of water from the mini fridge.

"Just as good as any motive I've come up with." Hunter stood. "I should be going. I want to pass the word around to the other business owners before I leave town. 'Course I wouldn't be surprised if most all of them have already heard." He reached the front and turned. "Like I said, keep a close eye on things. Whoever did this could come back. I wouldn't want either of you to get hurt." He nodded his goodbyes, then opened the door.

Max scampered inside. Landing at my feet, he opened his mouth and dropped whatever he'd found, sending it rolling across the room to where Hunter stood.

Staring at the floor for a second, Hunter then grabbed a plastic bag out of his pocket and picked up what looked like a flashlight, not much bigger than a felt-tipped marker. "Never can be too careful." He stuffed the bag in his jacket pocket.

Max licked my leg. I smiled and scratched the top of his head. "He probably found it somewhere near Gwen's shop. Are you thinking it belongs to the robber?"

"At this point, anything becomes possible evidence, even a tiny flashlight. You two have a good day and stay safe."

"Bye, Hunter. See you in another . . ." Izzie turned and winked at me. "How long has it been? Oh right, in three months, give or take."

"You're hilarious, Izzie Abbington," Hunter called out.

I gazed through the picture window as he stepped off the porch and then jogged across the lawn. "Will you stop giving him such a hard time?" I turned and slanted my chin.

"Sorry." She shrugged. "I'll stop. Promise." Holding up her arm, she crossed her fingers, as if that promise would be a challenge. "He's just so easy to tease."

I pulled my chair closer, almost touching, knee to knee, when I sat down. "Tell me." My voice lowered.

"Tell you what?" Her brows lifted.

"What exactly happened between you two in high school?"

She stood and pulled back her chair. "Let's take this conversation in another direction. Did you see how Hunter was looking at you?" She covered her chest in a dramatic pose and fluttered her eyelashes. "Oh yes. Love is in the autumn air."

I stood and walked to the counter. Grabbing the paper towel roll resting on top, I threw it in her direction, but it bounced off the wall instead of hitting her. "There's nothing going on between us. No love. Not even a spark." Even if there could be something, I wasn't sure I was ready yet.

"If you say so." She picked up the roll of paper towels and tossed it into a utility basket. "Maybe we should load the car with these boxes."

I wagged my finger. "This isn't over. One of these days you'll have to tell me the story."

"*Have* to tell you? No. *Will* tell you? Yes, one of these days." She handed me a box, then grabbed another.

I whistled for Max, who trotted along behind me as I followed Izzie to the car. After making one more trip to grab the last of the easels, I locked the door. Hunter's words sounded in my head. I turned to glance at Go Fly a Kite. The items stolen made me curious, but still, my stomach rippled with a twinge of fear. I gripped the easels tighter, remembering what had happened this past summer, then took hurried steps to the car.

* * *

"We're right on time. Thank goodness." After a twenty-minute drive east, Izzie passed the sign welcoming visitors to Willow Shores, then eased into the drive alongside Bellows Lodge. Our neighboring towns shared the building to hold all kinds of events—club meetings, social functions, and the occasional fundraiser. Even Whisper Cove's high school prom had taken place at the lodge one year, after plumbing issues at the school flooded the gymnasium. Ironically, the lodge was named after Carter Bellows, the father of Abigail Bellows. People claimed her spirit hid inside the lodge when she wasn't busy haunting the lake. Nothing like spinning a wild ghost story to scare folks.

I slipped out of the car and gazed across the empty lot. "We even beat Aunt Constance. Ten points to us for promptness."

The lodge had been built in the late nineteenth century. Carter Bellows had made his fortune, while living in New York City, by investing in whatever products the market demanded, furs and lumber mostly. Later, he settled in southwestern New York, along Chautauqua Lake, and led the effort to build Willow Shores. He became known as the town's founder as well as its benefactor. When Abigail, his only child, drowned in a boating accident at the age of twenty, Carter blamed himself for neglecting the one person he cared about the most. After that, he became a recluse and drank away the days and nights until the alcohol killed him a few years later.

The exterior was built of bath stone shipped from England. The warm, honey coloring had faded over the decades, but the stone had held up well. Etched in letters above the archway and front entrance were the words "Bellows Lodge—1896." Lilac bushes grew and flourished on either side, like bookends to the archway. They'd been Abigail's favorite flower, and it had been Carter's dying wish that they be cared for by the townsfolk.

"Hey, can you give me a hand?" Izzie spoke from behind me.

"Oh, sorry. I was thinking how sad their story was. No amount of money can keep tragedy from happening."

"You're talking about the Bellows family?" Izzie opened the tailgate and removed one of the boxes, handing it to me. "It's sad that people reacted by spinning some crazy ghost legend. What an awful way to respect the dead."

"People can be cruel and insensitive. That's for sure." I hefted the box and frowned. "Did Aunt Constance give you a key?"

"No, but we might as well stack these by the door. She should be here soon."

Aunt Constance's black SUV pulled into the parking lot as we finished. She stepped out of the vehicle. From the passenger side, a tall, slender woman with long red hair exited. She wore a full-length dress, in a deep crimson shade, that reached just below her knees. Draped over one arm was a navy-blue wool coat, and hanging from the other was a red leather bag that matched her outfit. She'd come prepared for the autumn evening, as the temperature would drop several degrees after nightfall. Aunt Constance, on the other hand, looked armed for a winter blizzard, clad in a fur-trimmed coat, knit hat, and gloves.

"That must be Viola. She's younger than I expected." I studied the woman as she gracefully walked across the lot without so much as a side glance at Aunt Constance, who hurried to catch up.

"Hello, ladies. I take it you're the artists who'll run this event?" She tapped her watch and added, "I don't have much time this evening, but I'd love to chat about hiring you for dates in the future. My nephew's birthday is next month, and this would be the perfect entertainment for his party." She waved Aunt Constance on to unlock the door. "And two of our chapters north of here are interested in having paint parties as well. With your talent and my contacts, I can guarantee your calendar will be booked well into next year." Not waiting for a response, she grabbed one of our boxes and entered the lodge behind Aunt Constance.

I blinked and turned to Izzie, who pumped her fist in the air before leaning closer to me.

"I think Viola Finnwinkle might be our fairy godmother," she whispered.

By now, Viola stood at the front of the room, unpacking the box she'd carried in and setting items on the front table near the projector screen. I had to admire her pitching in to help us. I grinned as Aunt Constance must've had the same thought. She shrugged off her coat, hat, and gloves, then dug into the box for more supplies. It seemed totally out of character for her. She was usually more the kind to bark orders while others did the physical tasks.

"Maybe wait and see. We don't know this lady. She might be full of promises but fall short on the delivery." I scolded myself for sounding negative. Given the scowl on Izzie's face, she must've taken it that way. I hurried with a quick recovery. "Still, the idea of filling our calendar is exciting."

We set up the easels and blank canvases for nearly fifty guests. At our small shop, thirty was a tight fit. The instruction for this event would be challenging. I added sets of flat, round, and liner brushes next to the easels while Izzie distributed the cups, paper plates, and paper towels.

"I wish Willow were here. We really need the help with this number of people, most of whom I bet haven't held a brush to paint a picture since elementary school." Izzie sighed.

Willow was the young, talented assistant Izzie had hired before the shop opened. After the events of this past summer, she'd decided to take some time off to spend with her family, promising to return before Whisper Cove's Hallows Eve celebration.

"At least we have these." I held up the canvases for this evening's paint theme. There were two sets of paintings done in stages, from rough sketches to finished artwork. The brilliant idea had been one of Willow's that proved very useful. While Izzie and I were busy helping others, a guest could take a look at these canvases for guidance. Especially this evening with a huge crowd, they were a blessing. I situated the canvases around the room while Izzie finished pouring water into the cups.

The chatter of voices coming from outside the door signaled guests were arriving. I glanced around at our setup. Every detail was staged perfectly. I stood next to Izzie, waiting while the sisters shrugged off their coats and gabbed.

Constance approached. A tight-lipped expression hinted at her nervous state. "The evening will go smoothly, right?" She tugged at her collar. "I mean, you've set up everything so well. I'm proud of you. I know my David would agree, if he could be here." She sniffed and plucked a tissue out of her dress pocket. Dabbing at her eyes, she turned and headed toward a group of ladies huddled around the coffee maker and snacks.

"Does she seem more emotional than usual?" Izzie's brow wrinkled as she chewed on the corner of her lip.

"It's obvious. Putting on a show for Viola tipped her over the edge. The best way we can help is to make sure this evening goes off without a hitch." I squared my shoulders as if ready to do battle.

"We got this." Izzie tapped the microphone sitting on the podium in front of us and spoke. "Good evening, ladies. Are we ready to have some creative fun?"

Murmurs and nods of agreement threaded through the group as the women scattered to take seats. Only two of them seemed to squabble over a spot nearest the front. A tall, rather stocky woman with snow-white hair, dressed in a red sweater three sizes too small, cast a steely glare and squeezed into the seat, leaving the shorter and frailer one to stare, with her fists clenched. The winner of the coveted seat ignored her by fingering the brushes and repositioning the paper towel and cup.

I pushed my tongue against one cheek and exhaled. "Only takes one or two to make things awkward," I said to Izzie under my breath.

As if accepting defeat, the woman standing looked around the room for an empty seat. In an instant, Aunt Constance hurried forward and wrapped an arm around her shoulder. She guided her to the back of the room, where the only vacant spot remained. Patting her shoulder, Aunt Constance smiled and mouthed a few words before rejoining Viola at the front.

"That was strange. Do you recognize either one of them?" Izzie spoke out of the side of her mouth while flipping the projector switch to light the screen.

"Nope, but I'll bet they aren't living up to the Sisterhood's stellar reputation. Just look at the scowl on Viola's face." I nodded in her direction.

Izzie shuddered. "Fairy godmother has a thorny side. Poor Aunt Constance. She'll get an earful from the director, and none of it will be nice."

"Okay, ladies. Let's take a look at what you have in front of you. Three kinds of brushes that you'll soon learn how to use, cups of water to rinse off the paint, and paper towels to dry the bristles." I held up each item.

Izzie explained the process of our class while I walked over to point at the canvases of the painting in stages. "Any questions?" When no one raised a hand, she added, "Great! Let's paint our ghost."

The event was going along without a hitch. Izzie and I managed to circulate through the room, answer questions, and give instructions. We were in sync and worked without interruption.

When there was a brief lull in activity, I took advantage of the break to find the restroom. The muffled sound of voices echoed from the hallway. I slowed my steps, not wanting to intrude on what might be a private conversation. At once, the volume lifted, and the tone of the conversation became angry. Words snapped and soon both voices were shouting.

I leaped around the corner, prepared to do whatever it took to defuse the situation. I refused to let some silly quarrel between guests ruin the event. However, I got no farther than a couple of steps. My mouth gaped open at the sight of Aunt Constance and Viola. Both were red-faced, and their eyes practically bulged. My heart pounded, and I swallowed hard, ready to wedge myself between them before either of them did something rash like throw a punch.

"After all I've done, all our *chapter* has done, to contribute to the Sisterhood." Aunt Constance poked a finger at Viola. "And this is the thanks we get?" She waved an arm. "You all sit in your offices, gather around some table in your meetings like you were royalty dictating the fate of others. It's disgusting and disgraceful."

"I'm sorry, Constance. We have to consolidate in order for the Sisterhood to survive. In fact, two other small chapters are being merged with yours. This will help make the chapters more effective. You'll see." Viola quieted down, tipped her chin, and pursed her lips. "This isn't up for debate. The decision is final, whether you agree or not."

"But I'll lose my position as chapter president," Aunt Constance screeched, loud enough for those in the room behind me to hear, and the chatter dissolved into silence.

"You'll have until the end of the month to submit your chapter's financial statement for the last quarter. All minutes from meetings, the calendar of events you've scheduled out until the end of the year, and other items I'll be asking for will be in the memo I'm emailing to you this evening." Viola pulled on her coat and turned to leave. "I'll call for an Uber. No need for you to take me back to the ferry dock."

"I'm not through with you, Viola." Aunt Constance grabbed her coat and hat. "You won't get away with this. You hear me?"

In seconds, both women stormed out of the building. I flinched as the door slammed, and the only thought in my confused mind was how, in one second, the evening had fallen apart.

Chapter Two

Pivoting on my heel, I found myself face-to-face with several ladies who'd obviously been curious to see what and whom the argument was about. A nervous titter escaped my lips, but I cleared my throat to speak. "The show's over, ladies. Just a minor disagreement. Nothing more." I waved a hand to motion them back to their seats. "We have paintings to finish, don't we?"

Releasing my breath, I slowed my pace to cross the room and stand alongside Izzie, whose expression appeared stunned—her wide eyes, dropped jaw, and blanched complexion were almost as scary as our ghost lady, Abigail. I pointed to my lips and widened them into a smile.

She got the hint, immediately snapped her jaw shut, and nodded. "Everyone ready for the next step? Great. Let's finish our ghosts. We'll be using both white and blue paint to give her a translucent appearance. First . . ."

Izzie's firm, reassuring voice seemed to work its magical charm as everyone concentrated on painting. The chatter had dwindled to a hushed whisper here and there, but as I circulated through the room to help with the painting, I overheard most of the comments that voiced concern about their chapter's future and Aunt Constance losing her position. I couldn't stop my worrying about Aunt Constance either. She'd been a part of the Chautauqua Sisterhood for as long as I could remember. Working so hard to campaign and win the seat as local president meant everything to her. Some older members even claimed she was the best their chapter had ever had. She worked tirelessly on organizing events, and the Chautauqua Sisterhood's local fundraisers often raised more money than any of the other chapters'. It made no sense to me why the people in charge would want to dismiss all that commendable work she and her members had done. I didn't blame her for getting so upset, and suspected she wouldn't let it go without a fight.

Within an hour we were finished, and the last of the guests strolled out to the parking lot, their paintings in hand. I pulled my phone out of my bag. "I'm calling Aunt Constance."

Izzie peeked over my shoulder. "I hope she's okay. I can't believe Viola and her accomplices are dumping the chapter. Such a cruel thing to do. I mean, Aunt Constance talks about how much money her group raises and how their membership keeps growing every year. You know, I wouldn't be surprised if Viola has some other reason for doing this, something she wants to keep a secret."

"If there is something underhanded going on, Aunt Constance will find out." The call went straight to voicemail. I shook my head at Izzie and shrugged, waiting for the beep. "Hi, Aunt Constance. It's Chloe. You rushed out so quickly. We wanted to make sure you're okay. Please call me as soon as you can." I pressed the button to end the call.

"Should we contact the authorities?" Izzie chewed on her nail.

I blinked. "Why would we do that?"

"I don't know. She's old. What if she's lying somewhere having a heart attack? You heard the way she was screaming." Izzie's voice edged up.

"Let's not go there. She probably went straight home because she's too upset and maybe too embarrassed to come back and face the other sister members. That seems logical." I scanned the room. "What we need to do is pack up and leave. It's late and I'm exhausted. If we don't hear back from her tonight, I'll call again in the morning."

We loaded boxes into the Land Rover, then worked on cleaning up the room. I pulled out a sweeper from the utility closet to vacuum while Izzie wiped down the tables. Traveling to the hallway, I stopped. Leaning against the wall was a canvas. "Hey. Someone left their painting." I shouted over my shoulder.

Izzie came into the hallway, carrying a bottle of cleaner and a dishrag. "Maybe the person left it after using the restroom."

"Makes sense." Once I picked up the canvas, I gasped. Sure enough, the painting was one from this evening. Abigail's ghost hovered over Chautauqua Lake, and jack-o'-lanterns glowed with eerie smiles in the background. What I didn't expect to see was the body, floating facedown in the water. The disturbing scene sent a cold chill through my body.

"What in the world?" Izzie's warm breath tickled my neck. "Is that . . .?"

"A body. Yes, that's what it looks like." I leaned closer and peered at the image. Red hair floated around the head that rested against what looked like a fallen tree trunk. She was covered to her knees in dark clothing, leaving the milky white skin of her legs exposed. Her arms lay limp at her sides. My gaze traveled up to the ghost of Abigail. I hadn't noticed the difference in the tiny detail of her expression until now. The mouth gaped open, as if she was screaming, while her slender finger pointed at the water and body below.

Izzie gripped my shoulder. "Who would paint this?" she whispered.

"Not only who, but why?" I set the canvas against the wall and stepped away. Wiping my hands on my thighs, I took a breath. "Maybe this is just someone's idea of a joke." My voice quivered.

"Someone with a cruel sense of humor." Izzie hugged me to her side. "Well, it is the Halloween season, after all."

"Yeah. Trick-or-treat." First, the bad news Viola had delivered, followed by one horrible argument, and now this. What else could possibly happen?

* * *

"Your aunt isn't exactly the reliable sort." Dad spooned some of Mom's breakfast quinoa onto his plate and added a toasted wheat bagel. "She probably stopped to have a drink or several at her country club on the way home, to calm her nerves, and is sleeping off a hangover."

"Joe. That's not a nice thing to say. The girls are worried about your sister-in-law. You should be too." Mom kissed the top of his head, then sat next to him at the kitchen table.

I stared at them over the top of my coffee mug. Kate Abbington possessed the kindest and most generous nature a

25

daughter and husband could wish for, but she was a warrior too. She was ready whenever her family and friends needed her to fight for them. Tall and willowy, like Izzie, she moved with grace and dignity. Her thick auburn hair, often plaited in a braid, now hung loose around her shoulders. No one else in our family possessed those flaming red locks. My only claim to her looks were those green eyes and fair skin. I was short like Dad, and we both had black hair, only his was now peppered with gray.

"You're right." After hugging Mom, Dad glanced my way. "I'm sorry, Shortcake. Your aunt has a kind heart, even if she does spend the Abbington inheritance like there's no end to it. Ouch!" Dad rubbed his arm where Mom had pinched it. "Enough. I'll stop if you will."

Izzie shuffled into the kitchen, stretching her arms and yawning. "What's going on? Sounded like someone was taking a beating." She winked at Dad before grabbing a plate from the cupboard.

"Nothing but a minor disagreement." Mom poured more coffee into Dad's mug. "We've settled the matter, though. Haven't we?" She tipped her chin while waiting for his response.

"Yes, we have. Now, it's nearly nine o'clock. I bet if you give your aunt another call, she'll answer," he said.

Izzie sat at the table with her fruit and bagel. She held a hand over the plate when Mom tried to add a spoonful of quinoa. "We will, on our way to pick up an order in Stow." She scooped some fruit into her mouth.

"That's this morning? After the crazy evening we had, I completely forgot." I gulped the rest of my coffee and carried the mug, along with my plate, to the sink.

We'd told our parents about the argument between Aunt Constance and Viola and how they'd both stormed out of the lodge without a word to us, but we decided not to mention the canvas with its disturbing scene of a body floating in the lake. There was no point in upsetting them over something that was probably nothing to worry about. I wished I could convince myself that was the case. After a fitful night of sleep, I had failed to think of a reasonable explanation for the painting. Instead, I awoke with an uneasy feeling in my gut, like the ghost lady had delivered a sign that something bad was going to happen.

"Can you be ready in twenty minutes?" Izzie chugged an entire glass of juice.

"You should take the ferry. According to my phone app, road construction is starting this morning. With one lane closed, traffic along the lake road to the bridge overpass will be at a snail's pace," Mom interrupted.

"Let's hope Dewey is running the ferry, then." Izzie rinsed her dishes. "What do you have planned today?"

"Oh, we promised to instruct a class of young artists at the nature center on the north end of the lake this morning." Dad smiled. "The director offered us lunch in return. Can't turn down a deal like that."

"Especially when we have the pleasure of introducing all those little ones to the world of art." Mom waved her arms outward with palms up.

I laughed. "What are you painting?"

"Jack-o'-lanterns, of course," Dad said.

"Well, you two have fun. You want us to pick up something for dinner?" Izzie asked.

Mom shook her head. "Chicken stew is already in the slow cooker."

We waved goodbye as we hurried down the hallway.

Max's nails clicked across the hall floor as he followed me upstairs to my bedroom. Sitting up, he pawed the air and whimpered.

"Not this time, buddy." I scooped him up in my arms and kissed the top of his head. "I'll be back soon. Just a quick trip across the lake."

I set him on the floor, then hurried downstairs to meet Izzie. We took my car this time since it was a short two-block drive to the ferry. I'd had the air-conditioning fixed last month, but Jake Marino, who owned the only car repair business for miles around, had advised me to have the brakes replaced before winter. Fortunately, I wasn't planning any long trips in the near future.

"Still no answer." Izzie tossed the phone in her lap. "Maybe Dad is right. She tied one on at the club and is sleeping it off."

I laughed. "I doubt it. Her doctor also told her to cut out alcohol. She admits there are too many calories in those fruity cocktails with the pink umbrellas she enjoys drinking."

"Then where could she be?" Izzie sighed and leaned back against the head rest and closed her eyes.

"I'm sure we'll find out soon enough. She has to come out of hiding eventually." I glimpsed sideways out my window. Dark clouds hovered in the sky to the west, and they were moving our way. With any luck, we'd miss the thunderstorm predicted to shower down on Whisper Cove later this morning.

At the end of Sail Shore Drive, I turned left on Whisper Cove Boulevard and parked in the lot next to the dock. Near the shoreline, a dozen or so geese were pecking at the ground for crumbs left by visitors. As we stepped closer, they squawked and flapped their wings before scattering to the south end of the lake. The giggles of children erupted as they played several yards away from the dock, scooping sand with their shovels and buckets.

I lifted my head as a cool breeze stirred the dry leaves lying on the ground. A slight chill ran through me. I pulled my arms through the sleeves of my jacket and zipped the front. No one stood on the ferry deck. Besides ours, only one other car sat in the lot. "I don't see any sign of Dewey. Maybe we're out of luck." I groaned. Being late to pick up an order wouldn't look good for business. I took several steps away from my car, and my foot landed on something soft. Looking down, I found a knit hat. Hesitating only a second, I picked it up. Dewey kept a lost and found box on the ferry since passengers sometimes left behind personal items like this. At the end of the year, anything unclaimed was donated to a nonprofit organization like Goodwill.

"Wait." Izzie pointed. "I see him. He's standing at the far end, looking over the edge of the deck."

Dewey Sawyer was the attendant and pilot of the ferry. Of course, the available times to use this transportation were limited. He was the only employee the town could afford to pay. A confirmed bachelor close to forty, he lived alone just outside town. The story was that he'd inherited his widowed mother's house and her modest stock investments. With that and his meager pay to run the ferry, Dewey got by. He kept mostly to himself, and his only weakness was indulging in drinking his favorite beverage, Yuengling Premium, preferably in the bottle. The real advantage, and what made the ferry so popular, was passengers being able to bring their vehicles across the lake with them. If there wasn't enough room, you'd have to be patient and wait until the ferry returned for a second trip.

As we stepped up on the deck, Dewey was drying his damp face and hair with a towel. The sandy blond curls sprang out like corkscrews when he shook his head. He rubbed his face with one hand and leaned over to peer at the lake water again, as if he hadn't noticed or heard us.

Izzie whistled. "Earth to Dewey. Are you running the ferry across the lake this morning anytime soon?"

Dewey gasped and sprang to attention. His hand and fingers splayed across his chest. "About to give me heart failure, you did." His gaze flitted sideways for an instant and straight again to us. "You want to take the ferry?"

"Uh, that's what we're here for, and I expect you're here to take us." Izzie planted both fists on her hips. "What *do* you keep staring at, Dewey Sawyer? Your face looks pale and almost white." Izzie inched closer to him.

I walked alongside her. With a frown puckering my brow, I squinted. "And your hands are shaking like you overdosed on caffeine. Are you on that diet again? The one where you eat next to nothing? I remember last time you ended up in the hospital eating your meals through a tube. Not a smart thing to repeat." I shook my head. Dewey was as thin as the stem of a rigger paint brush. He couldn't afford to lose any weight.

As we came to within a few feet of him, Dewey backed away from the edge of the deck and sobbed. I turned for a second. He stuffed his fist in his mouth, and his eyes bulged, as if they could pop out of their sockets at any second. Something had upset him, which wasn't so unusual. Everyone in town knew he was prone to hysterical episodes.

Puzzled and curious, I shifted my attention from Dewey to the lake water. I leaned over, searching exactly at the spot where he had been looking a moment ago. My insides lurched like they'd turn inside out, and I clutched my stomach with both hands. "Good lord." I strained to speak.

Izzie gripped my shoulder and let go of a low, feeble cry. "Is that really . . . is she . . .?"

Even though my brain told me to look away, I couldn't tear my gaze away from the horrible sight. A body was floating facedown in the water near the shore, a woman with long red hair, spreading like tentacles around her head. Her blue wool coat was snagged on a huge tree trunk that had landed in the lake and been left there after lightning struck it down in a summer storm. An inch or two of her red dress showed along with the bottom half of her legs, which had turned white and wrinkly. This image was almost exactly like the one in the painting we'd found left behind at the lodge, only this scene was terrifyingly real. Viola Finnwinkle was dead, and she'd been left floating in Chautauqua Lake. As if my mind had finally caught up to what had happened, I fumbled in my pocket to pull out the knit hat. I gasped as the hint of what it could likely mean hit me. The knit hat with a narrow brim was purple, and it looked exactly like the one Aunt Constance had been wearing to our event.

Chapter Three

The echoes of thunder drew closer together, nearly overlapping, and the sky darkened with each passing minute. I covered my head with the hood of my jacket and stood to the side as medics hurried past to load the body into the emergency van. An hour had lapsed since Hunter and the crime team had arrived. Dewey sat huddled under a blanket in the corner of the deck, near the back gate. His vacant-eyed stare, the look of someone lost and disconnected from everything around him, made my heart ache.

Hunter insisted Izzie and I should wait in our car until he was ready to question us, but I refused to leave. I'd brought along a thermos of coffee for our morning trip. Thinking he could use something hot to drink, I'd offered Dewey some. While he sipped coffee, I had rattled off reassuring comments, but none of them had seemed to matter. Dewey was spiraling down into one of his hysterical episodes. After Hunter approached to question him, I left.

Izzie remained in the car, with the phone slapped to her ear. Her mouth moved like it was spilling a thousand words a minute. She was calling about the pickup order in Stow.

Hopefully, the business owner wasn't too upset. Anyone should understand that finding a dead body pretty much killed a person's plans. No pun intended.

I hadn't forgotten the purple knit hat tucked away in my pocket. How could I? The idea of turning it over to Hunter curdled my stomach with guilt, but I had no choice. The hat was evidence at a crime scene. I heaved my chest, taking in a deep breath. Puckering my lips, I released a mouthful of air. "You got this."

I marched over to Hunter, who was talking to the coroner and a couple of the crime team members. Within a few feet, I stopped. I could wait until they finished. Besides, I worried what I might overhear, like some evidence of what the coroner or Hunter's team had found that would confirm the horrible thought I was having about Aunt Constance. I didn't think I could handle that, not while my insides were still churning over the sight of Viola's body.

All at once, the coroner walked toward the parking lot, and Hunter glanced my way. His team members spoke before leaving to search the grounds. His tight jaw clenched, the muscles working back and forth. I fingered the knit hat in my pocket. Putting off what I had to do only piled on more anxiety. I walked with long strides to reach him, then removed the hat from its hiding place. Without warning, my voice caught, and no words came out. Screams of laughter rippled through the air. I turned to watch the kids running along the shoreline, splashing water with their feet.

"Chloe?" Hunter said.

I blinked and followed that with a stiff nod. I'd overheard one of the team members say they couldn't find any ID for the victim.

Viola had carried an oversized bag to the event. If they couldn't find it, maybe this was a case of robbery and assault. I clutched the hat. "I found something in the parking lot. Not sure, but . . . I thought maybe you'd . . ." I shoved the item at him. "Here."

His eyes narrowed as he examined the hat. He looked up. "There's something you're not telling me, isn't there?"

I lifted my shoulders without saying a word.

"Out with it." He shook the hat. "What do you know about this?"

"I don't *know* anything. I found the hat on the ground near my car." My hunch wasn't proof of anything. Clothing shops and online retailers sold items like that one by the hundreds—thousands, even. Why should this particular hat belong to Aunt Constance? I groaned. Hunter's scowl puckered his face like it would swallow him whole.

"Hey. What are you doing with Aunt Constance's hat?" Izzie spoke over my shoulder.

This time, an eyeroll accompanied my groan.

Hunter cocked his head. "Who's Aunt Constance?" He pulled a stick of gum from his jacket pocket and unwrapped it slowly. Popping it in his mouth, he chewed and remained quiet while he stared, at me in particular.

"She's our aunt. Obviously." I pointed. "That hat isn't necessarily hers. Anyone who traveled on the ferry could've dropped it. Or someone walking by the dock." I pivoted on my heel and pointed at the children who were still playing along the shore. "Like one of them."

Hunter's foot tapped. He brought the hat closer, to examine it, and grunted. "With the letters *C A* embroidered on the inside?" He held up the hat, the letters facing out so we could see. "What about the victim? Is she a relative of yours too?" He chewed harder.

"What? Hey, no need for snarky comments." Izzie crossed her arms, and now her foot was tapping.

"Yeah. No need for that." I tipped my chin. "Her name is Viola Finnwinkle. She happens to be, or was, the director of several chapters of the Chautauqua Sisterhood."

"The Chautauqua what?" Hunter's left eyebrow curled like a question mark.

"It's a women's organization. You know, like the Elks Lodge is for men? Anyway, she attended the paint party event we hosted last night at Bellows Lodge."

He plucked his notepad and pen from his pocket and scribbled some words. "Bellows Lodge. That's a fair distance from the ferry. Why would her body end up here?"

"She took the ferry to Whisper Cove and left her car here while Aunt Constance drove them the rest of the way to Bellows Lodge." I pointed to the vehicle parked close by. "That must be hers, and we have no idea how she got back here, do we, Izzie?

"She did say something about calling for an Uber before she left the building," Izzie added.

Hunter scribbled. "I'll have a deputy call local services to see if any has a record of giving the victim a lift." He then waved to the team member closest to him. "Check inside that car. Maybe you'll find her purse or items in the glovebox that could help us."

I braced myself for what I was planning to say next. No point in keeping anything back. "You should also know that our aunt and Viola had a tiny disagreement during the event."

Izzie pinched her finger and thumb together. "Tiny."

"Mm-hmm." He tapped his pen against the notepad. "Did you happen to hear any part of their tiny disagreement?"

Just then the team member who'd checked the car jogged to where we stood. "No purse. The glovebox has a registration in the name of Viola Finnwinkle."

Hunter nodded then refocused his attention. "The disagreement?"

Izzie shrugged. "I heard nothing—not directly."

I cleared my throat and scratched behind one ear. "I was in the hall, going to the restroom, and, um, you see, Viola was explaining to Aunt Constance that her chapter was being dissolved, and she would no longer have a job as president."

"I take it that information didn't go over well with your aunt?" Hunter scribbled more notes.

Izzie interrupted. "Not the point. Aunt Constance is as kind-hearted as they come. She was upset and probably rushed out to go straight home."

I squeezed her arm. Too much information, and by the look on Hunter's face I guessed where his mind was going, and a sudden thought came to me. "Someone from the party left a painting. It has to be a clue, and whoever left it must know something about Viola's death." I described the gruesome details on the canvas and where we'd found it.

Hunter shifted his weight. "Where's the painting now?"

"At the shop in the storage room," Izzie said.

"I'll send a deputy around to collect it."

Izzie pointed. "What if one of the sister members left it because she witnessed Viola's death?"

"Or that person is the killer who murdered her. That would mean Aunt Constance is in the clear, right?" I urged.

"Let's not jump to conclusions." He held up the hat between his finger and thumb while his other hand retrieved an evidence bag from his jacket. Carefully, he slipped the item inside and zipped the tab closed. "Right now, I'd like to hear what your aunt has to say about this hat." He stared. "Where did you say she lives?"

"I didn't." I scrunched my nose. "She has a house in Mayville."

"We can show you," Izzie jumped in to add. "Just follow our car." She grabbed my arm and dragged me across the parking lot, not waiting for Hunter to respond.

"That's not necessary," he called out. "I've got a GPS in my car and you shouldn't—aw heck."

I heard him mutter some colorful words that cut off when I slammed the car door and fired up the engine. "I know what you're thinking, but it won't work." I glimpsed Izzie for a second, then glanced in my rearview mirror before pulling out of the lot. Hunter hadn't reached his car yet, giving us maybe a five-minute head start.

"Even so, do you want her to face Hunter all by herself? We need to be there." Izzie buckled her seat belt. "You know how lippy she gets when she's scared and uncomfortable."

I pressed harder on the gas pedal. "Maybe a heads-up wouldn't hurt?" I nodded at her phone resting in the cup holder.

"Good idea." Izzie pressed a button, then leaned back and waited. "If she'll even answer this time." After nearly a minute, Izzie tossed the phone in her lap.

With another nervous glance in my rearview, I turned onto Whisper Cove Boulevard and headed north along the lake, toward Mayville. Once we got into town, I'd take a shortcut through Aunt Constance's neighborhood, one that I hoped Hunter's GPS wouldn't use for his route. "Thank goodness he isn't close behind." I relaxed my fingers a bit to release the stiffness.

"Not yet, anyway." Izzie picked up her phone again. "What's the name of that man with the beady eyes and flat nose who lives next door to Aunt Constance? You know, the one who brings her some kind of dessert once a week, ever since Uncle David passed away. Cute but fattening way to flirt, right?" She giggled.

"Alvin or Theodore or maybe Simon is his first name. I remember thinking of the chipmunks cartoon when I first heard him introduced." I tapped the steering wheel. "And the last name reminded me of a town we used to visit as kids. Mom and Dad would take us to that interactive art museum where we'd paint stuff." My gaze shifted for an instant to spot a blue sedan passing a car several places behind us. "We've got company." I sang out the words. Seeing the yellow caution light several yards ahead, I stomped on the gas. With no cars in front of me, I sped through the intersection just as yellow flipped to red.

Izzie snapped her fingers and twisted in her seat. "Bennington."

"Yes! Simon Bennington. That's it." I frowned. "Now what?"

"Just wait." Izzie tapped another button. "I need the number of Simon Bennington on Regal Circle." In seconds, she was clicking numbers with the tip of her fingernail. "This has to work," she whispered. "Hi, yes. This is Izzie Abbington,

Constance Abbington's niece. I'm concerned about my aunt. Did you happen to see if she came home last night?"

A few seconds passed, and Izzie nodded at me. "Okay, thank you, Mr. Bennington. That is such a relief to hear." She set the phone in her lap once again and chewed on her bottom lip. "She's home, but . . ."

I flipped the turn signal and turned into Emerald Estates, where Aunt Constance lived. "No time for 'buts' or 'what-ifs,' Izzie. We're a minute away and about to find out what's going on." I cursed under my breath, viewing my mirror. A blue sedan sped down the road. "GPS is getting too damn smart, and we're out of luck."

I spun the steering wheel to take the next corner, then pulled into the cul-de-sac. Aunt Constance's house sat near the far end of the circle. Her backyard had a private view of the lake. Built in the late nineteenth century, the two-story home was spacious, with clapboard siding and limestone accents. Way too much house for one person, but the truth was my aunt regarded her home as a status symbol of sorts and somehow worked comments about it into her conversations more often than not.

"You go on. I'll stay back to see if I can stall Hunter," Izzie said.

I pressed my lips into a thin line of skepticism. Hunter on a mission seemed impossible to stall, even for a few minutes. I hurried to the front door and rang the bell. Tension surged through me. I took a couple of deep breaths and jiggled my arms. After a few seconds of silence, I leaned sideways to peer through the door's glass pane. Aunt Constance shuffled in slippers across the hallway.

As she opened the door, her mouth widened in a yawn. See-ing me, her eyes blinked and her head reared back. "Chloe?" She tightened the belt of her housecoat. "What are you doing here?"

I stepped around her and tugged at her arm, then slammed the door and turned the lock. "I don't have a lot of time before he comes to ask you questions."

"Who comes? What questions?" She crossed her arms and shoved them against her chest. "Chloe Abbington, have you been drinking?" She leaned closer to peer at my face.

"No." I scowled. "Detective Barrett is coming here to ask you where you were last night, after leaving our paint party event."

She rubbed the side of her neck, then rested her hand on her throat. "I don't understand."

The loud pounding on the door interrupted any further explanation. I bit down on my tongue and heaved a sigh. "Just tell him the truth, and please don't throw a fit or yell or faint. Okay?" I squeezed her hand before turning to flip the lock and open the door.

Hunter hurried inside, with Izzie on his heals. His lips were pinched with annoyance while his eyes sparked.

I skipped to the side and braced myself for a lecture. By the grim look of dejection on Izzie's face, she must've taken a hit with round one. I wouldn't cave so easily. "Before you fire off all those questions exploding in your head, let me say that Aunt Constance and I had a talk, and she is fully ready to cooperate and answer your questions." I tipped my chin while my eyes shifted to gaze at her. "Isn't that right, Aunt Constance?"

"Oh yes. Fully and truthfully." She leaned closer to whisper in my ear. "What am I agreeing to?"

I cleared my throat and mumbled out of the corner of my mouth. "Just listen."

Hunter grimaced, then turned his attention to Aunt Constance. "Good morning, Mrs. Abbington. I'd introduce myself, but I have a hunch you've already been told who I am and why I'm here, so let's get to it. All right?" He glanced side to side. "Maybe we should sit?"

"How about the living room?" Izzie led the way.

Constance sniffed and bunched the collar of her robe around her neck. "I really don't think he'll be staying that long since I haven't much to say."

I gave her a nudge toward the room. "Be nice."

"What do you mean? I'm always nice," she snapped. The fiery glint in her eyes emerged. She sank into a chair across from Hunter. "Look, Detective . . . Barrett, is it? I can sum this up in a couple of sentences. I had a disagreement with one of our guests at the party, which I'll admit upset me. So, I drove straight home and went to bed"—she switched her gaze to me—"where I was sleeping peacefully until the doorbell rang."

I squirmed in my seat. The lippy attitude Izzie had mentioned was creeping its way into the conversation. "Lippy" might reach a higher level when Hunter told her about Viola.

"So, you didn't see or talk to Viola Finnwinkle after you left Bellows Lodge? No phone call or rendezvous to meet somewhere?" Hunter massaged his finger against his thumb.

Constance tilted her head and blinked. "What's this about? Has something happened to Viola?"

Izzie stood and quietly stepped closer to Aunt Constance.

I gripped the arms of my chair. "Aunt Constance, I'm afraid something horrible has happened. Viola is dead." The words tumbled from my lips.

"Oh. Oh goodness."

On that note, Aunt Constance's eyes closed, and she swayed to the right, then to the left, then right again, while Izzie stepped in a zigzag motion to follow her moves, ready to catch her as she fainted dead away.

"There she goes." I threw up my arms and gave Hunter my own critical stare. "Let's head to the kitchen, and I'll brew some coffee. She won't come to for a while."

"She won't? How long's a while?" He cocked his head and looked doubtful.

I shrugged. "Maybe ten or twenty minutes. Whenever something frightens her, she gets prickly or passes out from stress. Congratulations—you were treated to both."

"Fine. Lead the way." He thumped the arm of his chair and stood to follow me to the kitchen.

Luckily for Aunt Constance, the ten minutes she took to stir awake was enough to relax everyone. Even Hunter laughed once or twice at my attempts to tell a joke.

I tapped my watch. "Almost to the second, as predicted." Pushing away from the table, we followed the murmur of Izzie and Aunt Constance talking. I carried a cup of hot tea and handed it to the recovering patient. "Here you go. Your favorite."

"Chamomile? Thank you, Chloe." She sipped from the cup while peering over the edge at Hunter. "I have to apologize. Too much alarming news in the past twenty-four hours has put me on edge. Maybe we could postpone our little talk until tomorrow?" she said in a whiny voice, and pouted.

"I'm afraid not, ma'am. The sooner I have answers, the quicker I can solve this case, which might not have been an accident." Hunter pulled out his notepad and pen and sat across from her.

"You mean murder?" Aunt Constance shuddered and took several sips of her tea.

"But you don't know for sure." I rubbed my aunt's shoulders.

He shrugged. "I wouldn't be surprised if that's what it turns out to be. Now, did you talk to or see anyone who can verify your whereabouts after you left this party? Like a neighbor or friend? Any detail to establish your alibi would help both of us."

Constance sagged in her chair. "No. No one. I was tired and annoyed, and just wanted to hurry off to bed."

"Wait!" I gasped and snapped my head around. "Izzie, didn't you say Mr. Bennington saw Aunt Constance pull into her drive last night?"

"That's right." Izzie snapped her fingers and pointed at Hunter. "He told me exactly that. You can go next door and talk to him and settle this whole matter."

I leaned my head around to grin at Aunt Constance. "See? No more worries." In the next second, though, my grin wobbled and fell from my lips. She looked anything but happy. I couldn't understand why, but the twitch at the corner of her mouth told me she was concerned.

"I'll do just that—in a minute." He positioned the tip of his pen, ready to add more notes. "Next question. Do you own a purple knit hat, Mrs. Abbington?"

Her eyes flittered first to me, then to Izzie, and finally to Hunter. "I do. Why?"

He scooted forward in his seat. "Can you bring it to me? I'd like to see it."

My breath hitched. If she couldn't, that meant only one thing, and the frown deepening the creases in her forehead wasn't a good sign.

"I don't know where it is."

"Are you sure, Aunt Constance?" Izzie whispered. "It's really important that you show it to the detective."

She tapped her fingers against the teacup. "I must've lost it in the parking lot at the lodge. I was in such a hurry to get home, you see." She pointed. "I always hang my coat in the hall closet and place my gloves and hat on the top shelf. Only I couldn't find my hat. I even went outside to check the front walk and the car. My husband gave it to me the last Christmas we were together. I'd hate to lose it." She shifted in her seat. "What I don't understand is why you're asking about a hat."

"A purple knit hat was found in the parking lot next to the ferry in Whisper Cove. Near where Viola Finnwinkle was found floating facedown in the lake." Hunter tented his fingers under his chin. "I'm not much for coincidences, Mrs. Abbington. So, I'll ask you again. Did you go straight home from Bellows Lodge last night? Or is it possible you followed the victim to the ferry to confront her? After all, she had just gotten through firing you, taking away what you loved. Perhaps things got ugly and you fought. Maybe you hit her with something, and she fell unconscious into the water. Is that what happened?" He leaned back straight in his chair and held up two fingers. "Motive and opportunity."

"Good heavens." Aunt Constance cringed, and her eyes bulged. "That's a horrible thing to say. I could never harm anyone, not with a push or shove—or anything."

"All right, then." He slapped the notepad closed and stood. "I'm sorry, but I had to ask. It's my job. Anyway, I'm sure when I talk to your neighbor, your alibi will check out." He walked toward the front door but turned to face us at the last second. "You'll be available if I need to ask any further questions, won't you?" Without waiting for an answer, he left.

"He can be such a tool," Izzie huffed.

"He's doing his job, even if those questions were a bit harsh. Sorry, Aunt Constance. I was the one who found the hat." I winced. "I didn't think I had any choice but to hand it over."

"Don't apologize. You did the right thing." She set her teacup on the end table, then stared out the window as if deep in her thoughts. "Do you still keep in touch with that attorney you dated?" She twisted around to gaze at me. "He handles murder cases, doesn't he?"

I tensed. "Yes, he does, but I haven't spoken to him in a while, like two or maybe three months." If she was taking this where I didn't want to go, I had to squash the idea—and quick. Asking Ross for any more favors made me uncomfortable. I didn't want to owe him anything. Besides, he was the one who had promised to return in August but ended up making excuses not to. For that reason, among many others, I certainly wasn't crazy about bringing him back into my life.

"Please, Chloe. You could reach out to him. You'd do that for your auntie, wouldn't you?" Her eyes moistened. "I don't like to beg, but this is serious." She lifted her chin and cast a wizened expression at me. "If I'm charged with murder, this could ruin the Abbington name, maybe even your little paint shop business." She pulled a tissue from her pocket and dabbed at her eyes. "The way your detective looked at me, and all those questions . . . I'm in serious trouble, girls."

I sank in my chair. A sense of dread shivered through me. Maybe a bit of guilt, too, for thinking only of myself. She was right. The entire family would suffer. I stole a glance at Izzie, whose face turned pale, then looked back at Aunt Constance, who'd torn her damp tissue into tiny bits. If Hunter had looked at me that way, with his steely-eyed glare, and talked in a voice that chilled a person to the bone, I would beg for help too. I nodded. "Okay. I'll give Ross a call today."

Constance pressed a hand to her chest. "Oh my. That's such a relief. Thank you, dear."

"I can't promise you he'll say yes. Ross is always busy with a heavy case load." I grimaced, thinking of all the times he'd canceled dates and worked most every evening past mid-night. The apologies had gotten old and worn by the time I left New York.

After we exchanged some consoling hugs, Izzie and I left. The skies had cleared, the thunderstorm having moved on to the north. I shook out my wet jacket before getting into the car. "Do you think she'll be okay alone?" I started the engine and let the car idle for a minute.

"If *she'll* be okay? What about us?" Izzie's voice cracked. "I'm sorry. I didn't mean . . . what I wanted to say is we all should take a moment to breathe." Her chest heaved. She puckered her lips and slowly let out the air.

With a gentle touch, I laid my hand over hers. "Izzie, it will be okay. If someone caused Viola's death, Hunter will find him or her, and that person won't be Aunt Constance. You'll see. Now, let's go home." I put the car in gear and backed out of the drive.

"What if he can't? What if all the evidence points to her and nobody else?" Izzie gripped my arm. "We have to help her."

"We are. I'm making that call to Ross, remember?" I slowed the car to a stop at the intersection. Saying that aloud unsettled my stomach. "Maybe there's another option?"

"Chloe, Ross is one of the best criminal attorneys in the state. You said so yourself. We have to ask him for help. While he keeps Aunt Constance out of jail and off Hunter's radar, we do our part and find the clues—all that evidence Hunter is so in love with—and point him in the right direction." She grinned. "You and I are back in business as snoops."

Chapter Four

After three attempts to get a hold of Ross that night, I had given up. Aggravation fueled my mood, and the next morning, before seven o'clock, I tried again. Unless his routine had changed, he'd be in the shower and would rush out, sopping wet, to answer his phone, which he typically left on the nightstand. I smiled at the image of him dripping all over the floor. Childish as it might be, that gave me satisfaction. On the sixth ring, I pulled the phone away from my ear, ready to hang up.

"Hello? Chloe?" He cleared his throat and muttered a curse word. "Sorry. I was in the shower and—why are you calling? I mean, it's good to hear from you."

I pulled a brush through my hair. "Oh, I apologize. If you'd like me to call back later—"

"No, of course not. Just let me . . ."

I listened to his footsteps and the rustle of a towel being pulled off the rack.

"What've you been up to? It's been quite a while since we last talked."

"Really? I hadn't noticed. Things are as crazy as ever around here with work and stuff. How are you? Busy with an important murder case, I imagine." I smoothed strawberry balm on my lips while staring in the mirror.

"Actually, I'm presenting my closing argument today on a case. Should be a slam-dunk decision. In my favor, of course."

I rolled my eyes. "Of course. So, the reason I'm calling is to ask for a favor." I gripped the phone tighter. "Do you have time to talk?"

"For you, always."

I stifled a snort at his use of the word *always*. "It's about my Aunt Constance." I spilled the details as quickly as possible and got to the finish line by asking if he'd consider representing her. "If it comes to that, and if you have time between your cases, and if you don't mind traveling this far, and—"

"Chloe, stop. I can rearrange my schedule, call in a few favors from coworkers who owe me." His voice lifted with an upbeat tempo. "Then maybe while I'm in town, we can catch up over dinner, have a nightcap—whatever you like."

A moan rolled out of my mouth. I slapped the phone to my chest before he had a chance to hear. I should've expected his response, but it still left me surprised, or gobsmacked, as Granddad used to say. I took a breath and skated right by his comment. "Thanks, Ross. I'll call as soon as I know for sure Aunt Constance needs your help."

"I miss you, Chloe," he blurted out.

"Okay. Bye." I spoke in a hushed tone then hung up. My heart pumped while I struggled not to lose it. "Seriously, what's with men? They say one thing and do another."

Max whimpered and sat on his hind legs to beg.

I laughed and folded him into my arms. Kissing the top of his head, I snuggled with him in my chair. "Not *all* the male species, of course. You are definitely an exception."

He answered with a bark and sloppy, wet kisses before I set him back on the floor. "As much as I'd love to cuddle with you all morning, I have to work." I shoved my arms through the sleeves of my wool sweater, once more falling deep into my thoughts. No wonder I didn't trust relationships. Ross had led me to think I was the most important thing in his life, then carried on with his job like always, leaving me on the sidelines. The saddest part was that in some ways I still cared for him. More than he deserved, but I did. Maybe the fun we'd had when he'd visited this past summer had something to do with it. I was reminded how things had been in the beginning of our relationship. Before returning to New York, he'd promised to come back in August, but then work on a case had grabbed his attention. I guessed the new and improved version of him couldn't last.

"So much for promises."

"Hey, up there. Are you ready to go? Our next event is this Friday. We've got a lot of work to do."

I hurried across the hall and paused at the top of the stairs to look down.

Izzie stood on the bottom step, wearing her coat, hat, and gloves.

"Did you grab the sketches?"

"Right in here." She patted the oversized bag that hung at her side. "Better wear your winter gear. It's nippy out this morning. Believe it or not, I spotted frost on the lawn."

I hustled downstairs. "Are Mom and Dad doing their yoga?"

"Yep. Mr. and Mrs. Bixby are with them. It's cute how their generation is so into yoga. Anyway, I promised them we'd be home for dinner. Mom even set out Grandma's china and crystal goblets."

"Oh? What's the occasion?" I zipped up my parka and hefted the strap of my bag over one shoulder.

"Does she really need one?" Izzie chuckled and opened the front door.

"Ha. No." The chill stung my cheeks. I tucked my chin into the knit scarf wrapped around my neck and hurried to the Land Rover.

The Bixbys, Tod and Joanna, were our next-door neighbors. They spent a lot of time with our parents, whether playing a late-night game of Pictionary or sailing on the lake to a local winery.

We sped down Sail Shore Drive toward Artisan Alley. As we passed Spill the Beans coffee shop near the intersection, I spotted Gwen and her boyfriend, Winston, exiting arm in arm. The two of them made such a cute couple. Nothing like a golden age romance to spark warmth in your heart.

"Chloe, the suspense is torture. When are you going to tell me about your conversation with Ross?" Izzie squeezed the vehicle into the only spot left in the lot.

"Nothing much to tell. I asked, and he said if Aunt Constance needs him, he'd clear his schedule." I stared out my window to view the lake. A couple sat on a bench, tossing breadcrumbs to the ducks. The birds pecked at the ground and reminded me of bobblehead dolls on car dashboards.

"Oh please." She turned off the engine. "The Ross I met this summer had the eyes of a man who hasn't gotten over you." She poked my arm. "Admit it. You enjoyed the attention."

"Like a pain in my rear." I laughed. "Maybe I enjoyed it a tiny bit, but that's over. All I'm saying is he agreed to help, if necessary. Now, let's get to work." I shoved open the door and made hurried strides to the shop front.

"Fine. I won't push." She threw back her head to laugh.

"Thank you." I readied my key to unlock the front door, but it swung open. "Willow," I gasped.

"It's really me." She lifted her arms and swiveled back and forth.

Her dimples punctuated her smile. She'd changed her spiked hair color from purple and blue to shades of green and bright orange. Her tiny frame and short height would fool people into thinking she was younger than her early twenties. However, it was her immense artistic talent that astounded me. Without formal training, she rivaled many experienced artists I'd known in New York.

"Hey, welcome back. We've missed you." Izzie stepped around me to squeeze her in a tight embrace.

Willow slipped out of her arms and turned in a slow circle. "The place looks great. Looks like you managed okay without me."

"Don't even think that for a second." Izzie pointed at me. "Chloe, tell her. How many times have we said, if Willow were here, she'd know how to fix this or do things better?"

I nodded. "Dozens. Maybe hundreds."

"If that's true, then you won't mind if I start work today? I could use the money." At once, the smile dropped.

Whatever had caused the change in mood, I was sure it had something to do with her family. After years of running away to avoid her overbearing parents and their attempts to control every detail of her life, she'd gone home this summer to see if any part of their relationship could be saved.

"Sure you can. You look like you could use one of Bob's Fizzy Orange drinks. Let me get one for you." Izzie skirted around the counter and pulled open the mini fridge.

"How was your visit?" I turned away to place my coat on the rack and give Willow a moment to decide. Either she wanted to talk about it or would change the subject.

She hopped up on the stool. "Well, not much is different. Almost as soon as I walked in the house, my parents brought up going back to college. No—wait. They *insisted* I attend college and major in business. I tried to be patient and kind and understanding, but after a week, I gave up and went to stay with my brother." She sipped the bottle of Fizzy Orange and ran her tongue along her lips. "So good. I've missed this. I'm glad Bob still makes it. What about his barbecue with greasy fries? I can't wait to order some." She sighed.

"You won't have to wait too long. Bob has offered to deliver orders to guests during Friday's event. We get to try out his new drink—Fizzy Pumpkin—and he has a new item on the menu. Barbecue puffs. He breads and deep-fries them. To die for, I tell you. Anyway, we're hoping the weather will cooperate. It's supposed to warm up. Otherwise, we can bring the activities back inside the shop," Izzie explained.

"So, you've been staying at Grayson's. How is he? Keeping out of trouble, I hope." I fiddled with the hem of my sweater.

"I can't say since I haven't seen or spoken to him in months. I crashed at my other brother's place, the one who lives in California." She finished the drink and tossed the bottle in the trash can. "Anything new happen in Whisper Cove while I was gone?"

I stared at Izzie, who shrugged her shoulders. "You better hold on to your stool for this story," I said, and launched into an explanation about Viola's body, and how Aunt Constance was a person of interest. "Not a prime suspect. Yet."

"Let's hope it stays that way." Izzie pulled out the drawings from her bag and spread them across the counter. "Meanwhile, Chloe and I plan to do some snooping on our own. Knowing Hunter, he'll keep dogging our aunt's trail, which will certainly stir up attention. In a small town like ours, even rumors could destroy the Abbington name."

"Does he think Viola was murdered?" Willow peeked at the drawings and picked one up, then set it aside.

"Not yet, but *if* it's murder, Aunt Constance could end up his first and only suspect." Izzie followed Willow's moves as she set another drawing aside. "You don't care for those two?"

Willow shook her head. "Those are the ones I like. The others have too many details. Better save those for a more advanced group." She lifted her head and blushed. "I read the Autumn Sizzle event is for beginners. I've been following the shop's website every day."

Izzie grinned. "Dedication. I love that in an employee."

"Oh, and there've been a couple of robberies. Gwen's shop, for one," I added. "Hunter came by and warned us to be careful."

"Wow. This town is like a magnet for trouble. I hope you two don't find yourselves in the middle of it. Snooping around could be dangerous." Willow held a drawing in each hand. Her gaze bounced from one to the other. "This one." She slid the drawing across the countertop to Izzie. "No fussy details, and the lines aren't too complicated. The fall colors will make it pop. It'll be the perfect scene for your painting group."

Izzie studied the drawing. "I'm with you on this one. Could you do your magic and paint three canvases?"

"One for each stage, along with some directions? You got it." Willow hopped off the stool, then paused. "If you decide to go looking for clues and evidence, let me know what I can do to help."

"Just be here to run the shop if both of us are gone. That would help the most," Izzie said.

Willow gnawed on the tip of her thumb, then grabbed the box of drawing pencils from the shelf and juggled three blank canvases in her arms as she headed to the back room. Without a word, she'd left the conversation and put her mind on the project at hand. A second later, she peeked around the doorway. "Sorry. Whenever you need me, just holler."

"If we're going to do this amateur sleuth gig, we should make a list of who to talk to." I pulled out my phone and opened the Notes app.

"Dewey Sawyer, obviously." Izzie pointed at my hand and circled around the counter to stand next to me. "I like Dewey too, but what if the way he behaved when we found him wasn't about seeing Viola's body, but about him killing her? I mean, anyone who commits a murder would be shaken up, right?"

"True. I guess that's how Hunter would think of Dewey." My finger moved over the keys. "What if we visit some of the local businesses and ask around to see if anyone happened to be walking along the lake that night?"

"Don't you think Hunter is already on it? He probably assigned a deputy to question people in town." Izzie shrugged.

"The thing is, not everyone is comfortable talking to the authorities." I scooted forward in my chair. "In fact, some won't talk to strangers either. We, on the other hand, are Whisper Cove townies. Most everyone knows us." I smiled and batted my eyes coquettishly while pointing to my face. "I ask you, who could resist this?"

"Yeah, well, it's worth a try, but we need to be smart and not let Hunter find out." She stood and grabbed her laptop. "While you brainstorm who else to put on the list, I'll send out email and text reminders to guests about Friday's event. Do we have any flyers left?"

"Maybe twenty. We handed out and mailed plenty the other day. Remember?" I flexed my toes at the mere mention of it. Two hours burning up the pavement as we'd covered the entire town on foot, stopping at every business to drop off a stack of flyers. Not to mention sending them to everyone on the mailing list of residents in Whisper Cove and neighboring towns. Worth the effort, though, since not everyone got on the internet to view our website. The "yes" responses filled twenty-eight reservations out of thirty we had space for.

"You're right. We've done all we can with the flyers." Izzie tapped on the keyboard.

"Smart move to include details about the Trick Your Pumpkin event coming at the end of the month. People are already signing up." I snuggled into my seat and willed my brain to think of other people to add to the list. "What if we go at this from a different angle and find out who Viola's enemies were?"

"That will take forever. My guess is she had plenty of those." A flush inched across her face. "Sorry. Shouldn't speak ill of the dead."

"True, but in a way, you're right. She was the director and had to make difficult decisions that could've angered the people who had the most to lose." I set down my phone in the empty chair next to me.

"You mean like Aunt Constance." Izzie groaned.

The chimes over the door tinkled. "Good morning." Megan greeted us with an arm wave. Her blonde curls bounced along with her curvy frame as she approached and gave each of us a hug before plopping herself in the closest chair.

Megan Hunt owned Light Your Scent, a candle shop located a few doors down from ours, and she was Izzie's best friend.

"You won't believe who I got a call from last night." Her eyes gleamed. "The owner of a popular craft gallery in Buffalo wants to include me in their upcoming event to promote local artisans. He's even filming interviews of us that will stream during the event. I'll be able to showcase my candle designs and hopefully gain new customers. Isn't that exciting? My luck is finally changing."

"Hey, that's awesome news." Izzie gave Megan a fist bump. "No one's gonna keep you from becoming a success." Her eyes widened as she sank slowly into a chair. "Not that you aren't already a success, because you are. This will make you an even bigger success."

Megan chuckled. "Stop. I know what you meant."

"You deserve every bit of success that comes your way, Megs," I said, and winked at her.

"Say! Did you hear about the body found in the lake the other day?" Megan shivered and tucked both hands under her legs. "Dewey Sawyer found her. Poor guy can't take that kind of stress. Word around town is she was murdered, and Dewey is the number-one suspect. Isn't that awful?"

I exchanged glances with Izzie, who covered her mouth as if stifling any comment itching to come out. I drummed my fingers on the arms of my chair. Megan didn't know about Aunt Constance. In my mind, that tidbit of information should remain a secret for as long as possible.

"All right." Izzie sprang out of the chair and threw up her arms. "We know. We know about the body found in the lake. We even know who the victim is."

"You know who the victim is? How could you know who the victim is?" Megan shoved a curly lock behind one ear while her brows inched together. A gasp escaped as her jaw dropped. "Were you there? Did you see it happen? Did somebody push her in the lake? I want details." With each question she scooted forward in her seat until finally she was standing.

"Whoa, there." I fanned my arms. "Let's take a breath and start over. We know the victim because she was at our paint party event at the lodge the other evening. You know, the one our Aunt Constance hired us to host?"

"And she is—or was—the director of several of the Chautauqua Sisterhood chapters, including the one Aunt Constance runs," Izzie jumped in to explain.

I nodded in agreement. "Viola Finnwinkle is her name."

"But we weren't there when Viola went into the water. We arrived at the ferry the next morning and found Dewey on deck, staring at the lake." Izzie wrung her hands.

"If she was at your event, which you told me was held at Bellows Lodge, what was she doing at the ferry dock?" Megan blinked.

"She took the ferry and left her car at the dock parking lot. Aunt Constance drove them to the lodge. We think she took an Uber back after she left the event," Izzie explained.

Willow stepped out of the storage room, holding one of her paintings. "You might as well tell her the other news. It's bound to get out soon enough. Small-town gossip always wins."

"She's right." I shrugged and stared at Izzie.

"Aunt Constance and Viola had an argument at the event, you see," Izzie said.

"Viola told her the chapter was being dissolved and she'd lose her job as president." I shook my head. "It was an ugly scene. Both of them flew out of the building, and we didn't see them for the rest of the evening."

"Oh. Oh wow." Megan's face paled. "But that means—are you saying your aunt killed Viola?"

"No!" Izzie and I answered together.

"She denies having anything to do with Viola's death, and we believe her." I pointed at Megan. "We would appreciate it if you didn't say anything. Hunter is investigating, and we're sure he'll figure it out."

"They haven't even determined if there was foul play. For all we know, she could've passed out, hit her head on the deck, and fallen into the lake and drowned." Izzie bobbed her chin. "It's possible."

Megan ran her tongue across her top lip. "Yeah, I guess so. Don't worry. I won't say a word, but Willow's right. The rumors will fly and, before the weekend, everyone in town will know." She grabbed keys from her pocket. "I should get back to my shop. I have to decide which candles I'm including for the Buffalo event, and email photos to the gallery owner by Friday."

"You should stop by the lake shore Friday afternoon if you have time," Izzie said. "Our event starts at four thirty. Bob is delivering his new Fizzy Pumpkin beverage and barbecue puffs."

"Yum. Can't turn down anything from Bob's. I'll come as long as you don't put me to work like last time." Megan winked. "Just kidding. I'll lend a hand if you need one. Mom's been helping out at the shop. She can cover for an hour or so. See you Friday." She waved and walked outside.

"I think we should speed up our timeline to snoop." Izzie swiped her hair back into a ponytail.

"Like starting this afternoon." I tapped more notes in my phone.

"While you're gone, I'll finish checking off items on our Autumn Sizzle to-do list." Willow clipped the painting of stage one to the wall.

"Thanks. I'll give Clark Andrews a call to reschedule that pickup order in Stow. This time I'll make sure to be there. Not even another murder will stop me." Izzie huffed and slapped the phone to her ear. "Yeah, I know. 'Be nice, Izzie. Be sensitive and considerate.' I hear Mom's words in my head. Maybe yoga isn't such a bad idea." Her hand teetered side to side. "Oh, hello, Mr. Andrews. How are you today? This is Izzie Abbington. I thought maybe we could reschedule the pickup order?"

As she glanced my way, I motioned to the door to indicate that I was stepping outside. A cool breeze drifted in from the lake. The crisp, heady smell of dry autumn leaves mixed with the scent of pumpkin and cinnamon spice macrame ropes hanging from Gwen's porch awning. I hugged my arms to my chest to keep warm. Megan's words had rattled me, but Izzie's comment worried me even more. What if the coroner confirmed that Viola had been murdered? And what if Hunter decided Aunt Constance was the killer? Like Izzie predicted, he might stop searching for any other suspects. As for the situation ruining our business, I had my doubts, though the rumors about Aunt Constance's involvement, even if she was never arrested, would hurt Mom and Dad. I shuddered. People staring, whispering when they walked into a store or restaurant, or casting scornful looks—that's what concerned me more than anything. I rubbed my arms and gave my head a hearty shake. "You're letting this get the better of you."

A loud shriek brought me to attention. I shaded my eyes with one hand to block the morning sunlight and get a clear view of the shoreline. A group of teens were lining the boat docks with pumpkins and cornstalks. No doubt, our Halloween tradition excited folks. During the last week or so of October, everyone, young and old, came out to decorate Whisper Cove, especially along Artisan Alley. Merchants adorned their shops with the most festive colors—oranges, reds, and yellows along the front walkways and in their display windows. A pumpkin carving contest was even included in our festivities, and the winner got a choice of free advertising in the *Whisper Cove Gazette* for a month or a year's subscription to the paper, compliments of the owner, Wink Lawrence.

I turned to step back inside, but spotted two teenagers standing by a tall oak tree. A boy balanced his female companion on his shoulders. She wrapped a rope of sorts around a limb and attached a white sheet. Taping strands of what looked like cornsilk on the top, she then moved her hand as if drawing something. With a nod, she let the sheet flutter back and forth in the wind. Scrambling down off the boy's shoulders, she stood alongside him and laughed.

As they walked off toward the dock to join the others, a strong gust kicked up, making the sheet spin around and face my way. I tensed. A mouth was agape, and eyes wide with fear stared at me. The ghostly image of the Lady of Chautauqua Lake flashed in my head.

"Kids today aren't much different from when I was young. Halloween and the curse of Abigail Bellows's ghost always excite them."

My head snapped around to see Gwen standing on her front steps. Dangling from her side was an orange kite painted with a jack-o'-lantern face. Even her outfit matched the Halloween season—bright orange pants and jacket with a maize-colored blouse underneath. The skeleton earrings she wore swung back and forth.

"I was sorry to hear about the break-in. I hope they find whoever did it." I tried to add a smile of encouragement.

"I do too. I'd hate for that to happen to anyone else." She lifted the kite. "Well, I better get back to making these. I have twenty more orders to fill by Halloween."

"Good luck." I waved as she took a step to go inside. Shifting my gaze back to the shore, I watched the makeshift ghost swinging from the rope. If what had happened to Viola was a curse, Abigail had outdone herself, and our aunt was stuck in the middle, like being cast as the villain in one of Shakespeare's tragedies. Whoever had painted that picture and left it hidden in the lodge room that night must be involved some-how. My gut told me the anonymous artist had to be the killer or a witness to the incident. Either that or else someone with psychic powers who had predicted what had happened. I shiv-ered and hurried back inside the shop.

Chapter Five

I threw my jacket in the back seat and powered down the car window. The afternoon was uncommonly warm, with a cloudless sky, brilliant sunlight, and no breeze. We'd left Willow in charge and headed toward the Cove's ferry. Dewey usually stayed at the dock until five or six, depending on how many passengers he had. With any luck, the ferry would be resting at the dock, and he'd be available to answer questions.

"Izzie, I think we should go easy on Dewey. If we press him too hard, he'll panic and clam up. You know how nervous and emotional he gets." I tapped my fingers on the center console. "We need him to talk."

"I know that." Izzie blinked as she flexed her fingers on the wheel. "There he is, scrubbing the deck, and he's alone." She pulled into the parking area and killed the engine. "Perfect timing."

I hopped out of the car and wiggled my arms to loosen the tension building. Talk about nervous—all at once, I was worried about a lot of things. We could botch this and get nowhere with Dewey. Or we'd get somewhere and learn more than we could handle. There was no way to be sure

64

Dewey was an innocent bystander who'd happened to find a body floating in the lake. He could be a murderer. Crimes of passion hit the news all the time. I shoved on my sunglasses and braced my shoulders, then followed Izzie onto the deck. "Maybe this isn't such a wise idea. We aren't professional investigators."

"You weren't a professional investigator this past summer either, but you found Fiona's killer," Izzie argued with a sigh. "What's up with you? Normally, you'd be the brave one leading the way, and I'd be the one holding you back."

"I'm worried because . . ." I threw up my arms. "Never mind." I was overthinking the situation and steering it into the worst possible outcome. Not to mention, thinking about Hunter. I pictured his face turning red and his chest puffing out while he lectured us about how we had botched his investigation. I definitely needed to push that image out of my head and find my confidence.

"Look. It'll be fine. No pressure at all. We'll ask a couple of questions and have a friendly conversation." She sent me a pointed stare. "Just be sure to watch for any signs. Nervous gestures, like a facial tic or stuttering. Something like that will show he's guilty of something."

I scoffed. "Dewey does all those things most of the time, which means they'll tell us nothing, but hey, why not try? Two twenty-something ladies armed with nothing but the gift of gab and decent looks might have a chance to charm him into confessing he killed Viola." I laughed and poked her shoulder.

"Come on, Chloe. This is serious." She scowled. "Aunt Constance in an orange jumpsuit for the next twenty years is a terrifying thought."

"You're right. Sorry. Humor is my defense when I'm anxious. You know me." I cleared my throat. "I'll start by asking him to tell us how he found Viola."

"Perfect. Now, put on your detective face and let's get to it." Izzie stepped onto the ferry and waved. "Hi, Dewey! Looks like you're working hard and doing a great job cleaning the deck."

Dewey raised his head to stare. With the back of his sleeve, he swiped his forehead. Sweat dripped down his face, trailing like narrow streams through the deep creases in his skin to reach his neck. His Adam's apple moved up and down as he swallowed without comment before he looked down once more. "Thanks," he muttered.

"Not too many passengers crossing today, I imagine." I scratched behind one ear. "Of course, the numbers usually drop off in October, don't they?"

"That's true. Building the bridge overpass in 2005 so folks could drive across the lake was what changed it." He brought his head up again and rested his chin on the handle of his mop. "Before the bridge, we had three men on the ferry. We'd take shifts. Me in the mornings, Jack in the early afternoons, and Paddy covered the rest of the day until nightfall." He stared out at the lake and chuckled. "Those were the days."

"What an experience. I bet you have plenty of stories to tell," I said, nodding encouragingly.

"I could fill a book or two with all those." He straightened and tipped his chin. "Started my job in 2001. I was twenty and laid off from the plant in Buffalo. My brother talked about this ferry and how the town needed to hire a pilot. I had some experience, canoeing, sailing, boating. I became a proud ferryman and will most likely be the last if progress and that darned bridge have their way." His mouth turned down at the sides, and his gaze seemed to drift somewhere other than here.

"You *should* be proud. It's a wonderful legacy," Izzie added.

I licked my bottom lip. Putting off why we'd come here wasn't helping my nerves any. "I bet one story you could never tell until the other day is finding a body in the lake. That must've been scary."

Dewey's grip on the mop tightened. His jaw worked back and forth while his mouth clamped shut.

I suspected the conversation was heading for that brick wall, and we'd get nowhere. I racked my brain to think of who would be the best to question next.

"Scared me out of my wits, I'd say. Felt my heart about to burst." He raked his fingers through his hair, straightening the curls into spikey tufts. "My mind was so muddled, I couldn't think straight enough. Just staring at her body like that." He heaved and the breath shuddered out of his lungs.

"I'd have reacted the same way. No one's prepared for something like seeing a dead person." Izzie took a step closer to me.

"No one, I'd say." He glanced up at the sky as a red-tailed hawk screeched and flew over the lake.

Slipping my hands into my pockets, I took a few seconds to think. "You arrived at the dock that morning, right before we got here, I'm guessing."

He shook his head. "Night before. I slept in my shack from dusk 'til dawn. I was tired to beat heck. My cousin borrowed my vehicle for his trip to Mayville and was too late to come pick me up."

The shack he referred to was the tiny ticket booth he'd turned into a place for him to rest and take shelter when the weather turned ugly. It was situated on the deck and at the far side of the ferry.

"You must've taken a dip in the lake when you woke up? I remember you were drying your face and hair with a towel, but I overheard you telling the detective you hadn't gone in the water. Maybe you forgot or were confused." I paused again. His brow had scrunched together in a frown. Either he was thinking what to say, or his anger was about to explode. "I could've misunderstood, though."

He wagged his finger. "No. No, you're right, I confess, though I am truly ashamed. You see, I tied one on the night before. That's the real reason I slept in the shack. I told Benny—that's my cousin—to keep the car overnight and come around sometime the next afternoon before his shift at the Blue Whale. Anyways, I woke with a painful hangover, so I got a bucketful of water and poured it over my head. I set the bucket down near the deck's edge and was about to order breakfast from Spill the Beans—my usual, scrambled eggs, bacon, toast, and a large glass of juice—and that's when I found her. Not a pretty sight for a man with a hangover." He rubbed his jaw. "Probably would've missed her, if it hadn't been for that darn log keeping her afloat. Almost wish it hadn't, you know?" He stared at us. His eyes filled with pain.

I eyed a sailboat skimming across the lake. Its bright yellow and green colors reflected in the blue water. One of its passengers waved as the vessel passed by. I turned to Dewey, who went on with his job pushing the mop across the deck floor, like it was the only thing he could do to keep from falling apart. Shifting my attention to Izzie, I shrugged, palms up. I wasn't sure if there was anything left to ask.

Izzie moved to stand in the path of Dewey's mop. "You know, if I'd found someone floating facedown in the lake like that, my instinct would be to jump in and check if she was still alive. Why didn't you?"

I groaned and sent her a glaring look of disapproval. What part of my warning had she missed about not pressuring him too hard with those kinds of questions? My heart sank as Dewey lifted his head. He tucked the mop handle under one arm and exercised his jaw, working it side to side while his tongue pressed against his teeth to make a sucking sound.

"I'd say unless you two ladies need a ride across the lake, I got a job to do and no more time to gab." Giving us his attention another few seconds, he then resumed swabbing his mop across the deck floor.

I leaned toward Izzie. "We should cut our losses and move along," I whispered.

With a disappointed frown, Izzie led the way to the car. She yanked open the door and threw her bag in the back seat before climbing in. "Well, that was a waste of time."

I took my place in the passenger seat. "It could've gone better."

"We should've kept trying." She started the engine and steered out of the lot. "I thought we decided to view Dewey the way Hunter would, as a suspect."

I shifted my rear end and quickly buckled up. "I told you not to press too hard."

"What do you mean? How did I press too hard?" She blinked, then slouched in the seat. "Great. I did, didn't I?"

"You practically accused him of not trying to save Viola. Not the question to ask a man who'd just found a dead body, especially a man with anxiety problems. No wonder he clammed up."

"How else were we supposed to get an answer if we didn't ask the question?" Izzie swerved around the intersection to avoid a red light.

My shoulder slammed against the door. "Hey! Take it easy." I waited for my heart to stop racing. "I'm sorry. Let's not get into an argument. I want this to work as much as you do. So, how about we start over? What do you say, Watson?" I shifted into a British accent.

Izzie smiled. "Maybe I want to be Sherlock."

"Fine. You do make a perfect Sherlock. With that nose and pinched look you get when you're concentrating." I tickled her face, and she slapped my hand away. I laughed. "We're good then?"

"Yeah, we're good." She parked the car. "Now, we can get back to what we do best."

"Paint party planning, here we come." I struck out across the alley. The sun dipped toward the horizon. The afternoon was almost over. I looked forward to a quiet evening at home, sharing dinner with our parents and snuggling with Max before bedtime, to relax. If only I could forget, for just one night, about Viola's tragic death, the ghost of Abigail Bellows, and poor Aunt Constance, who only wanted to save her chapter and job as president. I sighed. *If only.*

*   *   *

The high-pitched trill of a nightingale perched in the tree next to the bedroom window filled the silence as I stepped onto the front porch ahead of Izzie.

"Great. Another bird to keep me awake tonight," she muttered.

"Cheer up. He has to sleep sometime," I teased with a grin, and held open the door for her to go ahead of me. The sound of voices echoed across the hall. I cocked my head to one side to listen.

"Well, I'm not waiting for Dad to do something about the noise, this time. I'll call—"

"Shh!" I clutched her arm. "Listen." A tiny moan escaped my lips, and I froze. "It can't be. No way would he come here—not until I call for help."

"Who? What are you talking about?" Izzie slipped her arm from my grasp.

A bellow of laughter interrupted and panicked me into action. First, I pivoted on one heel and turned to the stairs. Hesitating, I winced, then shifted back around to face the kitchen doorway.

"Oh, I see," Izzie said. "What a surprise. Do you think Mom invited him to spend the night?" She winked. "You two could have a late-night rendezvous."

"Stop." I shrugged off my jacket and hung it on the coatrack. With one hand, I smoothed my hair and adjusted the hem of my shirt before striding down the hall, resisting the urge to rush.

Izzie caught up and whispered over my shoulder, "Take a deep breath and don't say anything we'll both regret. Remember, we need him to represent Aunt Constance."

"She hasn't been charged with anything yet," I hissed under my breath, and a second later, I entered the kitchen. "We're home," I announced, pasting on a smile that couldn't possibly reach my eyes because the irritation in me had to show. I leveled my gaze at Ross, who took the glass of tea Mom offered.

He walked to the table and set the glass next to his place setting before walking toward me, the moves deliberate and slow. His eyes sparkled, and he grabbed me in a hug. Without missing the opportunity, he planted a kiss on my cheek. "Hi, Chloe. You look as beautiful as ever."

"Why are you here?" I wiggled out of his arms and stepped back to stare at his face.

"Chloe," Mom reprimanded me with that tone of hers that meant serious business. "Ross is our guest."

"Guest. Uh-huh." I geared up to say more, but Izzie laid her hand on my shoulder.

"Easy," she whispered.

I waited until my heartbeat slowed. "I thought we agreed you would wait until I called you to come. Not that you'd arrive the next day."

He adjusted his glasses. "I don't understand. She didn't let you know?"

"Who? I have no idea what you're talking about, and since when did you start wearing glasses?" I had to admit he looked good in them, like someone I could almost take more seriously. On second thought, they could be fake. I wouldn't be surprised if he only wore them to convince the jury to take his side in a case. My face grew warm as everyone stared at me.

"I think he's talking about Aunt Constance." Izzie leaned around me and waved. "Hi, Ross. It's great to see you."

I jabbed her in the side, then quickly tucked my arm behind my back.

"Ouch! Well, it *is* great," Izzie argued while massaging her side.

"Hi, Izzie. You're right. Constance called me this morning at the office, pleading with me to come. She rambled on about how the authorities were coming to arrest her for—and I quote—'the murder of my dearest friend, Viola Finnwinkle.'"

"I don't understand. Why would you drop everything at home and drive for hours to get here without checking to see if she was right?" I looked away from him and tried not to sound petty. "Unbelievable." The word slipped out and I bit my tongue. Maybe I was a little bit jealous. I couldn't recall him dropping everything for me. Of course, I reminded myself this was work related, not personal.

"I'm not a fool, Chloe. I contacted Hunter as soon as I finished the call with Constance. It's true. Well, mostly true."

"He's going to arrest her? Why? On what evidence?" My voice cracked.

"That's ridiculous." Izzie chimed in, nodding her head firmly. "Her neighbor, Mr. Bennington, swears he saw her pull into her driveway that evening before he went to bed."

Ross cast a glance at Mom and Dad. He rubbed his fingers along the stubble on his chin. "Hunter claims an early report came back from the lab. The forensic tech estimates from the lividity and the texture of her skin that the victim died at approximately eight thirty."

"But—" I started.

"There's more. Hunter spoke with Constance's neighbor. Like Mr. Bennington told you, he saw Constance come home before he went to bed. He remembers turning off the TV after his favorite show ended, and then going to the window to pull the shades. That's when he noticed the headlights of her car as she drove into the garage. Afterward, he took off his watch and noted the time. Nine thirty."

"Oh no." Izzie hiccupped.

"Both your aunt and Viola left the party at around eight." Ross grew stern. "She can't account for the time between leaving the lodge and arriving home. She has no alibi."

"So? That doesn't mean she went to the dock and murdered Viola," I argued. "They need hard evidence. Physical evidence. Don't they?"

"What about the hat?" Izzie groaned.

"You're right. Physical evidence is important. Right now, Hunter says he has no plans to arrest your aunt, which tells me he doesn't have enough evidence. Not yet, anyway." Ross walked around the table and reached for his glass.

"Why don't we sit down to dinner and put this conversation on hold?" Mom said.

"Good idea, Kate. I'm starving." Dad rubbed his stomach and groaned. "The manicotti smells wonderful."

"Healthy too. I bought pasta shells made out of chick peas, not flour."

I had no chance of arguing that the conversation was far from finished and that I'd prefer to finish it now. Mom and Dad were already dishing out portions on our plates. Maybe some pleasant talk about anything but murder would calm my nerves.

"How is life in New York? Busy with cases, I'm sure." Mom heaped Ross's plate with pasta and a salad made mostly of spinach.

"A lot more hectic and crowded than here in Whisper Cove. I think about how nice it would be to hang out my shingle and start a small law practice." He winked at me.

I choked on a piece of spinach and gulped water to wash it down.

"What about the social life? Broadway, the clubs, the art museums. Wouldn't you miss all that? Chloe, you know what I mean." Izzie gave me a reassuring smile.

I nodded without comment, afraid that whatever I'd say would lead somewhere I didn't want to go—that is, reminiscing about my past with Ross.

"When I have the time, I like to take in a show." He dabbed his lips with a napkin. "In fact, I've seen several in the past two months. Went with a friend of mine who loves theater."

My fork slipped from my hand and clinked as it hit the plate. Quickly, I dropped my head and forked up a bit of manicotti. I squashed the urge to ask. I had no interest in whom he took to the theater. There was no reason for me to care. I'd moved on.

"I think he loves the theater too much. That's all he talks about at work." Ross chuckled. "Maybe in another life he was a stage actor. Who knows, right?"

"I remember going to see *Cats* with your dad. That must've been twenty years ago. Wasn't it, Joe?" Mom hummed a few bars of "Memory" while she dished more salad onto her plate.

"You wore that leopard print blazer." He laughed. "I remember that part best."

* * *

After nearly an hour of eating pasta, salad, and blueberry tarts for dessert, and having an endless conversation about musicals, the meal was over. I suggested we finish talking about Aunt Constance in Dad's study, which was actually the family den, but he had claimed the room and situated his desk there to prove it. Mom and Dad passed on the invitation. They wanted to catch tomorrow's sunrise. Mom was working on a painting commissioned by a customer from Charleston, and Dad planned to fish off the dock.

Izzie walked over to the hearth. Picking up the poker, she stoked the fire. Soon, the crackle and pop of flames filled the silence in the room. After a few seconds, she stood and stretched her arms. Her mouth widened in a yawn. "I'm dead-dog tired. No offense, Max." She ruffled the fur on his head. "You can catch Ross up to speed on everything that's happened, can't you, Chloe?"

My head shot up. As she passed by me and winked, I ignored her and stroked Max, who'd jumped up in my lap to cuddle. "Sleep tight." The words escaped through gritted teeth. Adding to my irritated mood, now I would have to deal with Ross alone. Hopefully, he'd leave any personal remarks out of the conversation. "How about we wrap this up? I'd like to head off to bed too."

"Sure thing. Why don't you tell me who you think is responsible for Viola's death?" Ross sat on the sofa across from me.

"Well, our first thought was Dewey Sawyer." I explained how we'd found him at the ferry that morning, and covered the conversation we'd had that afternoon. "I'm trying to look at his behavior from both angles. What if how he acted wasn't a reaction to finding a body?" I held up a finger. "What if he was shaken up *because* he murdered Viola? Unless, of course, Viola's death was an unfortunate accident, which would make Dewey's behavior irrelevant."

"But it could be murder. We can't rule it out until the coroner finishes his report. It's best to build a defense before it's needed."

"Good point." I sipped my wine. "I'll admit, I'm having trouble seeing Dewey as a suspect. He didn't know Viola. What motive would he have to harm her?"

"You said he admitted he was drunk. Maybe they argued. With his emotions fueled by liquor, maybe Dewey got so angry, he pushed her into the lake."

"I guess." Shifting in my chair, I put Max on the floor. He trotted over to Ross and hopped up in his lap. "You always were one of Max's favorite people," I said.

"Max has good taste." He smiled and scratched him under the chin. "Don't you, boy?"

"Well, Max is easy to please." I smirked. Releasing a somewhat exaggerated yawn, I stood and walked over to the fireplace and shut the glass doors.

"Who else would have reason to harm the victim? Constance believes any of the Sisterhood members who overheard Viola say their chapter was finished had to be angry, possibly angry enough to take revenge."

My shoulders dropped. How much of a hint did he need to leave? "I can't think about this anymore. Like Izzie, I'm exhausted and ready for bed. Besides, you'd probably like to be on your way to the hotel." My brow squirreled up. "You are staying at the hotel, right?"

He sat on the sofa with his arms draped across the back. "Actually, your parents invited me to spend the night here."

My knees wobbled, and I sank into the chair once more. I opened my mouth to speak but couldn't manage the words. Instead, I squeezed my stomach to relieve the uneasy feeling.

"You should see your face." He laughed. "As for the invitation, I wouldn't think of imposing on you."

"Wise decision." My voice steadied. As I dared to put weight on my legs again, I led the way out into the hall. As we reached the front, I flipped the lock and opened the door. A soft breeze filtered inside. I took a deep breath and slowly released it.

Ross stepped into the open doorway. "Besides, the temptation of being right down the hall from me would be too much for you to resist, wouldn't it?"

I gawked at him and felt my face burn.

"Night, Chloe." He winked and sauntered outside, whistling a tune as he crossed the lawn and hopped inside his car.

"Men." I slammed the door. A soft whimper came from behind me. I scooped Max in my arms and walked upstairs. "Promise me you'll never act that way around any of your lady friends, okay?" I was rewarded with a lick on my nose. "Good boy. I knew I could count on you."

Chapter Six

I stacked plates on the counter, and Dad set them in the cupboard. This was a once- or twice-a-week ritual that Izzie and I shared with him. Our daughter-and-dad time gave us a chance for conversation without interruption and promised a few laughs. Joe Abbington and his jokes could easily be a hit on *Comedy Central*. Today, though, wasn't so humorous.

"I might say some unkind things about your aunt, but as for her having what it takes to kill someone . . ." He scratched his chin and after a few seconds shook his head. "I very much doubt she's capable. In fact, I'm sure of it. She's a bit emotionally unstable, at times, but definitely not a murderer."

"I'm sure she'd love to hear you say so." I stood on tiptoes and pecked him on the cheek.

"Nope. I wouldn't give her the satisfaction." He turned and smacked the counter. "Do you know how much she spent this past summer remodeling her house? The things she buys. It's insane. Real marble from Italy. Two Greek statues—from Greece, of course. And how about that tapestry she has hanging on the den wall? Twenty thousand dollars because it's one of a kind. Handwoven by Tibetan monks, I'd imagine."

"Dad. Dad. *Dad.*" I tugged hard on his shirt sleeve. "Stop. You're turning purple. I don't want to do CPR if you go into cardiac arrest." I breathed in and out, over and over, rolling my hand for him to follow me. "Calm yourself. Aunt Constance is still mourning Uncle David. Maybe buying more than usual is her way of coping with grief. I have an idea. Why not put those yoga exercises you and Mom do to some practical use?"

"They're practical in every way, sweetheart." Mom stepped into the kitchen. "Are you about ready? The lake is calling to us." She hugged Dad's arm.

"It's a beautiful day to sail. Where are you going?" I closed the dishwasher door.

"Mayville to visit Constance. We figured she could use some cheering up and moral support from family," Mom said.

"Speaking of family support, why isn't Spencer here? You'd think a daughter would want to comfort her mother." Dad pulled me close and tousled my hair. "I can count on you when I'm in a fix, can't I?"

"What about Mom? Shouldn't I be there for her too?" I smiled.

"Not necessary. Your mom would never get into trouble." He winked.

"While you two decide who deserves comfort and support, I'm heading to the boat dock. Don't forget your coat, Joe," she called out while walking down the hall.

"You and your sister have a great day. Stay out of trouble, and you know what I mean." Dad lifted his brows.

"Tell Aunt Constance. She's the one who thinks we're snoops for hire," I quipped.

"Just be careful." He waved and disappeared through the kitchen doorway.

I refilled Max's water bowl while he munched on his breakfast, and then I hurried upstairs to change. Izzie had left earlier to catch up on emails and go over our inventory list for tomorrow's event. The weather forecast looked promising, with no chance of rain, snow, or plummeting temperatures. We'd posted a list of dos and don'ts on our website—do bring along a coat or jacket being the most important advice.

Charging out the front door, I rummaged around in my bag to find my phone. Once inside my car, I searched through my recent calls to find the rental company we'd hired to deliver chairs for the event. We ourselves could handle carrying outside the easels and trays to hold the paints and brushes. Later, we'd set up our projector and a makeshift screen to display the artwork instruction.

Hovering my finger over the call button, I startled as the phone rang. Aunt Constance's face appeared on the screen. I shoved my sunglasses farther up my nose, powered on the engine, and answered. "Hi, Aunt Constance. How are you doing?"

"How am I doing?" Her voice pitched higher. "That's a loaded question, which I'll pass on answering for obvious reasons. Anyway, I'm calling to see if you've made any headway in your investigation into Viola's death, meaning whatever can help clear my name from Detective Barrett's list of whodunnits."

I put the phone on speaker, set the device in the dashboard holder, and pulled out of the driveway. Exasperation filled me and I gritted my teeth. "We only started looking yesterday afternoon. Not much to tell." I recapped the conversation with Dewey. "He claims it's the same story he told the detective. Nothing new." I stopped for the traffic light at the Whisper Cove Boulevard intersection. The stray cat who often sat on the corner bench was licking its fur. I'd nicknamed the feline Picasso, one of my favorite artists and a total free spirit in his painting. "Of course, I'm sure Ross filled you in on those details, since you've been in touch." I clicked my tongue. "Not a cool thing to do, Aunt Constance. Why didn't you tell me that's what you were planning? He showed up at our house, totally unannounced."

"Oh, Chloe, I'm so sorry," she sobbed. "After Detective Barrett called yesterday, badgering me with his questions, wanting to know where I'd gone after I left the painting event—because he knew I didn't get home until nine thirty, thanks to my nosy neighbor and his snooping—I panicked. I told him I drove around, trying to work through what Viola had told me." The sobs turned into caterwauling. "He . . . he accused me of lying. I know he thinks I killed her. That's why I called your Ross and asked him to come here immediately. They'll be knocking on my door any minute now, ready to cuff me and drag me to jail." The last word dragged out in a screeching howl.

"He's not my—forget it. Ross assured me you won't be arrested. Hunter doesn't have the physical evidence he needs to charge you. So, stop stressing, okay?" I maneuvered my car into a parking spot next to Izzie's vehicle. "Now, Ross told me what you said about your chapter members. Do you really think any of them is capable of murder?"

"I don't know." Her voice steadied. "My phone has been ringing nonstop. The sisters are angry and miserable. A few even admitted thinking Viola got what she deserved. I shuddered hearing that. I know people say things they don't really mean when they're upset, but still, I can't help suspecting people who say those sorts of things. That's why I suggested the sisters should be questioned. You can do that, can't you? Call them, get them to open up. You'd have a much better chance to get answers than the authorities would."

I drummed my fingers on the steering wheel, giving her suggestion and reasoning some serious thought. "You might have something there. I'll talk to Izzie, and we'll work out a schedule to call those who attended the event."

"Thank you, Chloe. You can't know how much this means to me. Support from family is everything," she sniffed.

I recalled Dad's comment. "Speaking of family, how is Spencer doing these days? Have you heard from her?" A car horn honked, and I glanced in my rearview mirror. The driver steered his car to go around a vehicle stopped on the alley road. As if by reflex, I frowned, and not because of the blaring horn. Thoughts about my cousin got that reaction. She and I butted heads more often than not over just about everything. Her views were the opposite of what I would call kind and compassionate. She was selfish, entitled, and so whiny when life didn't go her way. It took all my strength to be civil and considerate when I was around her. But I did it for Aunt Constance's sake, and Mom and Dad's. They all wanted peace in the family.

Aunt Constance cleared her throat. "Oh, Spencer is busy conquering the world. We spoke yesterday. Of course, you know she's still living in Los Angeles, working on important business deals selling software to big companies, even internationally. Such a go-getter. You have to admire that kind of drive."

I stamped out the urge to criticize the go-getter for not putting her mom's welfare first in this situation. "Well, I have to do some go-getting of my own. Talk to you after we have some news."

"I hope to hear back soon."

"Have a nice visit with Mom and Dad. It's a beautiful day for sailing. You should persuade them to take you out on the lake."

With that comment, I hung up and slipped out of the car. Calling all forty-some members who'd attended the event would be a time suck, but as a bonus we'd have the opportunity to ask them if they'd noticed anyone adding the figure of a dead body to their painting, or caught someone hiding a canvas in the hall. Possibly one of them had ventured outside and witnessed Viola and Aunt Constance leaving the lodge, maybe to continue their argument or, worse yet, heard Aunt Constance threatening the director. With luck, we'd get some new information.

I picked up my pace and skirted around the side of the building. Voices filtered through the window, and one of them was the deep tone of a man. Opening the door, I faced none other than Wink Lawrence, the editor-in-chief of the *Whisper Cove Gazette* and our landlord. His crooked teeth showed through the smile on his face. Stubble on his chin was dark brown to match his eyes. He was bald as a billiard ball because he shaved off whatever strands of hair he had left. I'd nicknamed him Kojak, after the character in the old crime drama Mom and Dad loved to watch. which he didn't seem to mind one bit. I figured his age was somewhere between forty and sixty, though he acted more like a guy in his twenties. He drove a sleek red sports convertible, one telltale sign of a man going through male menopause. The music blaring from his car stereo would fit the seventies top-forty list of europop and disco tunes that made me gag. Bottom line, he was both loveable and annoying.

"Hey, Kojak. How's the newspaper business?" I grinned and poked him playfully in the arm.

"Pretty darn slow until that body turned up the other day. I'm hoping you'll do a guy a solid by sharing whatever news about the case comes your way. You know"—he winked—"since you and the detective are cozy."

My head reared back. "Me and Hunter? Not a chance." I slipped by him to set my bag and jacket on the counter. I stared at Izzie. "Have you been feeding him lies?"

"Who, me?" Izzie blinked with wide eyes and shrugged.

"Uh-huh. What brings you here, Wink?" I straddled the stool closest to me and propped my feet on the spindles.

"Besides fishing for information about the body in the lake? Well, the rent is due, and if I recall correctly, the payment for the last ad you bought is a little behind." He stretched his neck to peek at a box of bakery goods labeled "For Sweet's Sake" in pink swirly letters, which was sitting at the far end of the counter. "Of course, I might be persuaded to give you some wiggle room and wait to come by and collect next week if you'd satisfy my sweet tooth with one of those chocolate croissants."

"Oh, here." Izzie slid the box his way. "I don't need a thousand calories added to my diet. Not sure what was going through my head when I bought them."

I chuckled and picked up the cup of coffee Izzie passed to me. "My guess is Claire had something to do with it." Claire ran For Sweet's Sake. Its selection of bagels was well known in and around Whisper Cove, but customers were offered a wide variety of sweets. When it came to baking, Claire loved to add new items to her selection, like chocolate croissants. Her enthusiasm was contagious. In fact, she could charm most anyone into eating one of her delicious baked goods.

Wink moaned as he finished the croissant in seconds. "Well, since you're not having any, I'll take seconds."

He stuck his hand in the box, and I smacked it. "Not so fast. I'll take the rest home to share after dinner." His lips pouted in dramatic fashion as he rubbed his hand and mouthed the word *ouch*. I rolled my eyes. "Fine, one more, if you give us a discount on that ad. Say, twenty percent?"

"I'll save this goody for later." He wrapped a napkin around the pastry, then held up one finger. "You can have fifteen percent off, and I'll give you until next Tuesday to pay for the ad and the rent if you give me some information. Why is Detective Barrett looking at your aunt as a murder suspect?"

I choked and sputtered coffee out of my mouth and onto the counter, nearly spraying Wink's napkin-covered croissant. "Wherever did you hear that crazy story?" Might as well try for a bluff, I figured.

He straightened and puffed out his chest. "Don't play dumb. I'm the editor-in-chief of this paper, and it's my job to know what goes on around here." He grinned slyly. "I'm right, aren't I? Your aunt is a suspect, maybe even the number-one suspect, eh?"

"You don't know what you're talking about." Izzie scooted next to me.

"I don't, huh?" Wink sat on a stool and, leaning to the side, rested one arm on the counter. He looked relaxed and not ready to go anytime soon. "How about there was an argument between your aunt and Viola Finnwinkle—yes, I know those details too—and a purple knit hat was found at the crime scene. A little gossip here and there goes a long way to inform this guy. All I had to do was listen to the talk at Millie's Diner last evening and those tongues wagging at Spill the Beans this morning. Yep, I learned plenty. Like how that hat fits the description of the one your aunt has been seen wearing. Now, you want to tell me again how I don't know what I'm talking about?"

I crossed my arms. "For one thing, nobody has said it was murder. Viola could've slipped and hit her head before falling into the lake."

"Don't you wonder why Finnwinkle was on the ferry deck in the first place? Why didn't she get in her car right away and leave, after being dropped off? And where was your aunt? Did she follow her to the dock?" Wink's eyes gleamed with excitement. "I can see them now. In a fit of uncontrolled anger, your aunt hits Finnwinkle and shoves her into the water, all because she lost her job as president of some silly, snooty women's club. Not her finest moment, I imagine." He got off the stool, and stuffing the croissant in his jacket pocket, headed to the door. "I'll come around next Tuesday to collect rent and payment for the ad. You ladies have a fine day, and tell your aunt I said good luck." He stepped onto the porch. A cacophony of laugher followed in his wake, as if he saw something really humorous in the situation. The noise was enough to scare a flock of geese eating nearby. They squawked and flew away in a frenzy.

"And the Chautauqua Sisterhood is not snooty! They raise money for charities. So there." I tilted my chin and huffed, but I doubted he heard me. Wink was already powering down the alley and nearly out of sight.

"He could stand to lose some of that mean, snarky attitude," Izzie whispered.

My brow squirreled up. "Why are you whispering? He can't hear you."

She shrugged. "He's intimidating."

"Not as much as *we* can be if pushed." I stabbed a finger at the doorway. "At this point, Wink Lawrence *is* pushing.'" My drive to speed up our sleuthing kicked in, though I wasn't sure if the motivation came more from wanting to help Aunt Constance or to prove Wink was wrong. I hoped it was the former because my better angel was telling me that acting out of spite was petty and childish.

Izzie sat next to one of the easels. Her shoulders drooped, and she twisted her hands in her lap. "I don't blame you, but let's admit it. Other people in town might be thinking the same way as Wink. They're already bringing out the handcuffs, ready to haul Aunt Constance to jail. Figuratively speaking, of course."

"Don't say that, Izzie." I hitched my breath.

"You know it's true. Those rumors Wink heard at dinner and breakfast will be spreading like wildfire, and I don't see how we can stop them."

"We keep searching for answers." I hopped off the stool and paced the room. "First, we divide up the list of the people who attended the party event. We'll call each one—we have the contact info on their registrations, don't we? Oh, and we should cover up the real reason we're calling. With something . . ." I snapped my fingers. "We can say we want to display some of their paintings at the Hallows Eve celebration at the end of the month."

"Perfect." Izzie straightened in her chair. "Maybe stroking their egos by commenting on how special their paintings are will make them relax. Then we work what happened that evening into the conversation."

"What they thought about the argument between Aunt Constance and Viola," I added.

"And how they feel about the chapter being dissolved." Izzie tapped her finger on the table.

"Don't forget about the painting left behind. We need to ask if anyone noticed who left it."

"Hold on a sec." Izzie tapped a few keys on the laptop. Soon, the printer hummed and spit out paper. She handed me a copy of the list from the lodge party event. "There are forty-six names, not including Aunt Constance. How about you take the top half of the list?"

"Sounds good. At least things aren't too busy at the shop. We should be able to talk on the phone without much interruption," I reasoned out loud.

The chimes tinkled as the door opened. "Morning." Willow smiled and stepped inside. "I know—you weren't expecting me until later, but I woke up, had breakfast in my apartment, staring at the TV that hasn't been connected to Wi-Fi, yet. Sooo, yeah." She sighed. "I think I miss the constant noise my brother and his partner made because they had the brainiac idea to start a band. I wouldn't call what they play music—more like screeching and banging sounds that have no melody. Anyway, I couldn't take sitting around, alone in my apartment, with nothing to do but stare at a blank screen, so here I am." She threw up her arms.

"It's like you read our minds." Izzie tugged at Willow's arm and pushed her to sit in a chair. "We need you to cover the shop because the snoop team extraordinaire—that's Chloe and me—have some investigating to do, ASAP."

I snorted. "Hardly extraordinary. We're going to spend the next several hours making phone calls."

"Which will give us important information to help solve this case." Izzie pointed at me.

"Look at you two." Willow laughed. "Like Cagney and Lacey, or Rizzoli and Isles, or Beckett and Castle."

Izzie screwed up her face. "Just how much TV do you watch? Never mind." She shifted to me. "We should go. Who knows how long these phone calls will take or how many people won't answer, which is a real probability, right?" She rambled on. "We may never get done."

"Hey, Rizzoli, Cagney, Beckett, or whoever, calm down. We'll get the job done. If not today, then tomorrow." I aimed for a look of confidence and gave her a thumbs-up. "Okay?"

"Right. We can and we will." She nodded.

I opened the box of pastries and looked at Willow. "Would you like a chocolate croissant?"

"No thanks. Chocolate makes me break out. I'll finish up the canvases for the Autumn Sizzle and add the notes for instructions while you're gone. Anything else you need me to do?" She picked up the canvas she'd only started to sketch.

"Double-check the list of names for the event and get online to see if any answered my email reminder or whether any canceled and need a refund. We really need to change our policy. No refunds within three days of the event. That way there's time for others to take the open spots. Oh, and call me if you get busy and need one of us to come back to the shop." Izzie picked up her coffee cup, took a sip, then tossed it in the trash. "Probably don't need any more caffeine."

"Yeah, probably not," I echoed, and opened the door.

* * *

"This is exhausting. Respect to all the telemarketers and what their days must be like." Izzie sighed.

I grumbled a response to agree. "I've talked to a dozen women so far and have nothing to show for it except the occasional thank-you for us wanting to display their paintings." I poured more coffee into my mug and sat to rest for a moment before I picked up the phone again.

"Even if your idea was meant as a ruse, I think displaying some of those paintings at the festival will work. Great promotion, you know?" Izzie said.

"Not a single one of them noticed anyone leaving the building or stashing that painting in the hall. Unbelievable. How could that happen?" I shook my head.

"Oh, I don't know. Did you notice any empty seats at any point?"

"I did. One seat near the back. But with everything going on, I can't say who or when." I moaned. "You're right. Not so unbelievable."

Izzie stretched her arms. "Okay, I'm going back to my room to make more calls. Let me know if you hear anything useful."

Max hopped up in my lap. "Yeah, I'd rather be playing fetch with you, buddy." I scratched his head. "Maybe later this evening."

I picked up my phone and stared at the list. "Unlucky number thirteen. Good thing I'm not superstitious." On the second ring, someone picked up.

"Hello?"

The deep voice sounded grouchy and short. "Hi, is this Sarah Gilley?" I asked. Maybe I'd caught her at a bad time.

"Yes. Who is this?"

I cleared my throat, determined to push on, no matter if it was a waste of time. "I'm Chloe Abbington, one of the hosts at the paint party event at Bellows Lodge earlier this week. You were at the event, right?"

"Certainly was. I participate in all the Sisterhood activities." The voice grew bold, almost defensive.

"That's so supportive of you. It must've been hard learning the chapter will be dissolved," I said.

"Well, it certainly wasn't good news. Of course, it didn't surprise me in the least how your aunt reacted. She is your aunt, right?"

"Yes, she is." I squirmed in my seat and gripped my phone tighter. "By 'surprised' do you mean because she's president of your chapter and was disappointed by the news?"

"Hardly," she sniffed. "In my opinion, Constance didn't have the temperament to run the chapter."

"Oh?" The direction the conversation was taking worried me.

"The job was like an addiction to power for her. She was quite unprofessional at times, playing favorites and punishing some members by assigning them the tasks nobody wanted." She lowered her voice. "Just between you and me, I suspect she's even dipped her hand into the chapter coffers once or twice."

"Oh! That's . . . not good." I winced, feeling blindsided. I didn't know how to respond.

"Trust me. It's not. I emailed Viola about my concerns, more than once, but all she gave me is a 'we'll check into it' kind of response. That's not very professional either. So frustrating."

By now, her tone had turned surly. Something told me to end the call before I snapped out a response I'd regret. As I saw it, her opinion of Aunt Constance was fueled by hatred and more than a little bias. None of the others I'd spoken to had talked that way. They'd only had nice things to say.

"Well, thank you, Sarah. I hope I didn't take up too much of your time."

"I'm surprised you haven't asked me what I think about Viola's death. I'd love to discuss my theories with you some-time soon, but right now I've got to get ready for my date this evening. He's a hottie. Can't let this one get away."

Before I could respond, she hung up. *Theories?* As in more than one. I shook my head. She certainly had me curious. However, what I was focused on at the moment were her comments about Viola. I imagined Sarah might've had a grudge against the director, who had brushed off her complaints. I didn't know Sarah Gilley, but she definitely was someone to keep an eye on.

I jogged up the stairs to Izzie's room and shared the conversation. "What if Sarah murdered Viola, and all this trash talk is to help Hunter build a case against Aunt Constance?"

Izzie braced her arms on the bed and leaned back. "Kind of a weak motive for murder, but like you said, we don't know the woman. Maybe Sarah snapped after Viola ignored her emails." Izzie sat up straight and widened her eyes. "Ooh. Maybe she's done this before. A woman with a criminal past, hiding out in Mayville where no one would think to look for her."

I picked up a pillow and tossed it at her. "Seriously, we should check and ask other members about her."

"Or we tell Hunter, and he can ask the questions." Izzie fell back on the bed. "I finished my half of the list. Three didn't answer, so I'll try them again tomorrow."

"I still have nine to go." I held up the list and waved it in her face.

"Nope. I did my share." She wagged a finger.

I snuggled next to her on the bed and rested my head on her shoulder. "Remember the time when you were twelve and broke Mom's favorite porcelain figurine? I spent two hours helping you glue the pieces together before she could find out. *Two hours.*" I punctuated and dragged out the last words.

"Fine. I'll take four and you take the other five. With any luck, we'll have this finished by dinnertime." Izzie ripped the list in half.

"Thank you!" I sped out of the bedroom and down the stairs before she could have second thoughts. "You're the best sister."

"Yeah, yeah. You better know it," she called out.

I finished making my calls in less than twenty minutes. Not too much chitchat, but also no useful info to add to our search. I was discouraged. My investigative mind had hit a brick wall. The idea to question people in town would probably give us nothing more than the gossipy banter that Wink had talked about. We needed evidence or a witness or an alibi for Aunt Constance, other than her neighbor's account which had turned out to be more damaging than helpful.

At least dinner was a pleasant distraction, for the most part. I shoveled down the baked chicken with linguini and a huge portion of avocado salad Dad had prepared. However, conversation ventured into a discussion about Aunt Constance when Izzie asked how their trip to Mayville had gone.

"Oh, your aunt gave us the usual dramatic act she does when things aren't going her way," Dad said.

"Which in this case is justified." Mom tempered the mood with a cheerful smile. "Wouldn't you say, Joe?"

He forked some chicken and linguini and stuffed the bite into his mouth without comment.

"I hope you three took a sail on the lake together. The weather was perfect this morning." I broke the awkward silence and steered the conversation far away from Viola's death and whether Aunt Constance would be fitted for an orange jumpsuit anytime soon.

"We sat out by the lake and had brunch. The beautiful view from the shore was just as nice." Mom folded her hands underneath her chin.

Dad washed down his dinner with the rest of his wine. "We'll support her through this, no matter what happens. I promised David I'd watch out for her. I owe him." He picked up his dishes and carried them to the sink.

Izzie and I glanced at one another, then at Mom, who heaved a sigh. The mood in the room became more somber as Dad and the rest of us remained quiet in our own thoughts. For all his bluster, he was loyal to family, and that included Aunt Constance.

I rolled the handle of my fork between my fingers. "I asked Aunt Constance if she'd talked to Spencer. She rambled on and boasted about Spencer's job and how successful and busy she is, but never said she planned on returning home."

"That would hurt any parent. I can't imagine how awful I'd feel if I didn't hear from either of you or see you for months at a time," Mom said. "Of course, I don't believe Spencer is acting intentionally. That would be spiteful."

Dad returned to the table with a cup of coffee. "Constance accepts Spencer for who she is. Parents love their children unconditionally."

"Well, I can't think of anything worse than not getting to see or talk to you guys." Izzie stacked dirty plates and utensils in the dishwasher.

"Absolutely." I poured both of us coffee and held up the carafe to Mom, who shook her head. "I think I'll head upstairs and do a bit of reading. It was a scrumptious dinner, Dad. Thank you." I patted my thigh. "Come on, Max." He trotted after me and up the steps.

I snuggled in bed with Max and opened the Agatha Christie novel I was reading. After an hour, I'd nearly dozed off, when my phone rang. Startled, I dropped the book. I waited a few beats, rubbed my eyes until the drowsy feeling lifted, then answered. "Hello?"

"Good evening. I hope I didn't wake you. It's late, but I just now got home and listened to your voicemail, which got me to thinking, and—maybe I should start over." The nervous sound of laughter interrupted. "My name is Marilyn Pervis. I'm one of your aunt's closest friends."

"Oh." I squirmed to a seated position and rubbed Max's fur. I'd never heard Aunt Constance talk about anyone named Marilyn, but then again, she had plenty of people in her life, and I couldn't possibly have heard about all of them. Even close ones, like a member of the Sisterhood. "No worries. I was just reading when you called." I pulled the covers up and over my chest, as if Marilyn had physically come into my bedroom rather than interrupting by phone.

"That's a relief. I probably should've waited until morning, but this is too important."

"I see. You want your painting to be included in the display at the Hallows Eve celebration? Not a problem. We have plenty of space," I said, making a stab at what she meant by "too important."

"Oh no. I don't care about the painting. In truth, I'm surprised you offered. Mine's not very good. What I have to tell you shouldn't be said over the phone. Someone might be listening to our conversation." Her voice lowered. "Wiretapping, you know."

I frowned and pulled the phone away from my ear, to stare at the screen. I was beginning to have my doubts about Marilyn Pervis and this conversation. The term *conspiracy theorist* came to mind, along with thoughts about the paranoid people who tended to fit that category. "It's late. Maybe we can talk again tomorrow? I'll call you." I was ready to hang up.

"No! Wait. I'm sorry." The nervous tittering came again. "My late husband warned me people wouldn't understand my worries about things like wiretapping phones, computers, even your television, and—listen to me. I'm rambling again."

"Marilyn," I began, "what is this about?" I grew concerned. Whatever she had called about seemed less important in my mind than her odd behavior.

"Yes. Again, I'm sorry. I have something to say about Viola's death. I know—well, that is, I *believe* I know how she ended up in the lake, which was no accident, I tell you." She dragged out a rattled breath. "And I have a pretty good idea who pushed her in."

Chapter Seven

For Sweet's Sake sat on Main Street, near the *Gazette* and the courthouse. Across the street, boutique shops like Casually Done and La Chic lured visitors to Whisper Cove to find a unique outfit, since the shops carried clothing made by local designers. The bakery building's retro fifties design carried from the exterior to the inside. Scalloped canopies shaded the windows and accented the white siding with a bright coral shade. Inside, the walls, tables, and countertop were painted a matching color. Checkered tablecloths and napkins completed the theme.

I sat at a table across from Claire, my arms folded and resting on the tabletop. I blushed as Claire's warm brown eyes sparkled and a wide grin spread across her face.

"You're wrong. I'm not romantically involved with anyone. This is just my natural look. Rosy cheeks and all." I lifted my chin and straightened my posture to emphasize my point.

"You don't fool me. And I have a pretty good idea who has your heart racing. Just mentioning his name makes you blush. I've seen it. Now, the next time he's in town, you call me. I'll see for myself if his reaction matches yours." She laughed and waved her arm. "I swear, I can tell. Call it a curse or call it a blessing, but when it comes to matchmaking, the women in my family always get it right."

"Then let me be the one to ruin your perfect record because I don't have feelings for Hunter Barrett," I argued.

Her brow arched up. "Who said I was talking about him?" She tapped her lip. "Now, I might have to rethink this. Two men complicate matters, don't they?"

"Oh, for—please stop. I don't have time to discuss or listen to your wild predictions about my personal life." I checked my watch. "Marilyn will be here any minute." I poured more coffee from the pot Claire had brought to the table.

Claire raised a palm and stood. "No need to tell me twice. I'll let it be . . . for now." She winked and laughed, then walked back to her kitchen. "Holler when you need to order."

I slumped in my chair and moaned. I'd rather be like Izzie and put men out of the picture. However, I wasn't like Izzie, not when it came to men. In the past, I'd enjoyed having a guy in my life. Just not one who brought all the problems I'd had with Ross. His all-work-and-no-play attitude had pushed me to leave that relationship. Otherwise, he'd been a great guy. Attractive, funny, considerate, but too often not around when I was lonely or needed a shoulder to cry on or simply someone to share a quiet evening with. Work was number one with him, and I came in as a distant second place—and maybe third when it was time for a guys' night to play poker or watch a Giants game. Perhaps that's why I was skittish about diving into another relationship, even if I wanted one.

The tinkling of the door chimes broke my train of thought. I glanced around to see a tall woman dressed in a wool sweater and knit pants, with a matching scarf draped around her neck and shoulders. Her hair was silver and cut in a neat bob. I waved. "Mrs. Pervis. Over here."

She returned the gesture and hurried to take a seat across from me. "It's *Miss* Pervis, but call me Marilyn. After my husband passed away, I took back my maiden name. Much simpler to say and spell than Koppalopski, don't you think? Thank you for meeting so early this morning. I have a lot of business to do for the Sisterhood. The interim director asked me personally to help, as I'm the secretary of our group, you know." Marilyn jutted her chin, punctuating her words with self-importance.

"So, I take it the plan to dissolve your chapter is still on schedule." I turned her cup over and poured coffee into it.

"Well, I really can't say." She pulled a towelette out of her bag and wiped her hands and the spoon, then added a generous amount of creamer to her coffee and stirred. "That's up to whoever is elected to replace Viola as director. Agnes is pleasant but doesn't have what it takes to manage a whole district."

"Seems to be a common opinion about directors." I folded my hands around my cup.

"What was that?" Marilyn leaned forward. "My hearing isn't as sharp as it used to be."

"Nothing. Why don't you tell me what you think you know about Viola's death?"

"Would you ladies care to order breakfast? I have blueberry scones, bagels, and doughnuts, hot out of the oven. Made with blueberries from our local vendor." Claire stood close, her height towering over us.

I caught the slight tilt of her chin and sideways shift in her eyes. "Would you like something, Marilyn? I'll buy." I asked the question but followed Claire's gaze to the other side of the room. A tiny gasp escaped my lips, then quickly I covered my mouth and chin with a napkin. Hunter stood by the door, talking to someone waiting in line. He hadn't looked my way, but I doubted that would last.

Claire must've read my startled expression because she moved sideways to block Hunter's view, though she couldn't stand here and handle customers at the same time.

"No thank you. I'm watching my weight nowadays. Is everything okay, Chloe? You look paler than Abigail Bellows's ghost." After a second, she giggled, like she had suddenly caught on to the humor in her comment.

Claire shrugged and mouthed the words that she had to go back to work. As she stepped away, I was left squarely in Hunter's line of sight.

I squeezed my eyes shut for an instant, then leaned forward and spoke fast. "Marilyn, I don't have much time. Tell me who you think pushed Viola into the lake, and please be brief." I prayed she wasn't offended. Making a last-second recovery, I added, "If we get the unpleasant part of our conversation over, then we can relax and have a nice visit. Right?"

"Oh, of course." She shifted in her seat, cupped one hand around her mouth, and leaned in. "I think Sarah Gilley did it. She never liked Constance or Viola. In fact, she told me all about writing to the head of the Sisterhood to say she had proof that would get the director fired. She wouldn't say what that proof was, but my guess is her claim was a whole lot of nonsense because nothing happened to Viola's position. To make matters worse for herself, she wrote letters and emails to Viola about Constance. None of what she said was taken seriously."

She pursed her lips. "Sarah is the gossipy sort and has a sour disposition, likes to boss everyone around. No one in our chapter really likes her. She even told several of our members, including me, that she'd do everything she could to replace Constance as president. Chloe, I'd bet my last nickel she had a fight with Viola and pushed her in the lake. Viola stood in the way of her plans. What frightens me is that she'll try to frame Constance for the murder."

Her spoon clanked against the table as she fiddled with it. "Of course, I don't know if Sarah meant for Viola to die, but she's the person the authorities should take a look at. Sarah should be the prime suspect, not Constance, who I've found to be the sweetest, dearest lady. She'd never hurt anyone." Marilyn sniffed and dabbed her eyes with a napkin.

Sarah had certainly been keeping busy writing letters to get people fired. I wondered if Marilyn was right. Maybe Sarah had reason to harm Viola, but was it any more of a motive than Aunt Constance had? Or strong enough to convince Hunter to take a look? I wasn't so sure.

From the corner of my eye, I watched Hunter approach. The steady gaze and set jawline hinted to me that he suspected something. Of course, he had a right, since I tended to take matters into my own hands, like snooping in this past summer's murder investigation without letting him know. I slouched in my chair, wishing for the encounter to be over before it even started.

"Mind if I join you?" Hunter waited a few seconds, and when neither Marilyn nor I objected, he pulled a chair next to our table and sat down. "Good morning, ladies. I didn't know you two were friends. What brings you here together?"

He glanced only for a second at Marilyn before settling his attention on me.

I licked my bottom lip and worked my brain to think of some excuse that he'd believe. Nothing came to mind because I knew he'd suspect anything I said when he wore his "detective hat." Desperate, I had to at least try. "Hunter. What a surprise. Marilyn is a friend of my aunt. She and I were having a friendly visit, just us ladies." Brief, vague, and with a hint to say he was crashing our party of two, though I doubted it would make him leave.

"Detective, why don't you join us for coffee? Chloe and I were discussing our favorite artists. We agree that Claude Monet was a pioneer of the Impressionist movement, but disagree as to who was the most popular. I believe it was Renoir, though Cezanne was quite talented. Chloe insists it was Monet. What's your opinion, Detective?" Marilyn raised her chin and offered a questioning gaze that demanded an answer.

I grinned while Hunter scratched the back of his neck, clearly thrown off guard. Whether he was stumped by the topic of art or discouraged that his suspicion as to why we were meeting could be wrong, I wasn't sure. "Maybe we should let him off the hook, Marilyn. I don't think Hunter's into art history."

Hunter's tongue poked the inside of one cheek. He nodded. "No, actually I do have an opinion. I'd say you're both wrong. Vincent Van Gogh has my vote. He might've been a Postimpressionist, but you gotta admit, *Starry Night* is really something. Anyone who can work through insanity by painting the way he did has to be admired."

I blinked. *Where did that come from?* In all the visits to our shop, even when attending one of the paint parties, he'd never talked about art.

He winked as his lips spread into a grin. "Surprised? My mom teaches art history at a local college. For as long as I can remember, conversations around our dinner table were usually about art. In fact, when I was a kid, Mom had to take me to some of her classes if there was no one to babysit. Not the idea of fun entertainment for a four-year-old."

"You are a mysterious and complicated man, Hunter Barrett." I shook my head. In one brief conversation, he'd become much more interesting to me. A man who knew so much about art history didn't come along very often, if at all. Maybe in New York or Paris, but not in Whisper Cove.

He shrugged. "I guess you could say that, but I didn't come over to discuss art."

I couldn't read the meaning of the gleam in his eyes or guess why he wanted to talk. I'd already made up my mind to tell him about the conversations I'd had with Sarah and Marilyn, but later, after I had a chance to mull over the information, and not before I talked to Aunt Constance about the two sister members. With any luck, I'd manage to figure out something in those details that could help her instead of hurting her case even more. Sarah's opinion of her was too damaging, and Marilyn's was too flattering. If I was a member of a jury, I wouldn't put much faith in what either one of them said. I was sure Ross would agree. Bias in either direction didn't help any defense. I imagined a detective gathering data for this case would feel the same.

He cleared his throat. "Do you think I could speak to you in private?"

I scowled. "Private? In the middle of a crowded bagel shop?"

He blushed. "Yes, well, . . . maybe outside? Away from the crowded bagel shop."

Marilyn's eyes lit up, as if she suddenly understood. She tucked her bag underneath one arm and scooted out of her chair to stand. "I can't believe it's already nine. Time for me to go if I want to make any headway in my workload. Nice visiting with you, Chloe. I'll be in touch." She primmed her mouth. "About that art exhibit, you know."

"Ah, yes, the art exhibit. You have a productive day, Marilyn." I shook her hand.

"Same to you. Good day, Detective. It's been an enlightening experience. Tell your mother I'd love to meet sometime and talk about the Impressionists." She waved and headed to the door.

Hunter took her chair. "Interesting lady."

"She's not what I expected." I admired her quick wit and clever response to cover up our conversation. I had a hunch there were several layers to Marilyn's personality. Dismissing her theory about Viola and Sarah so quickly and labeling it as the rant of a paranoid woman might not be such a wise move.

"Listen." He cleared his throat again and tugged at his shirt collar. "I was thinking—that is, I was *hoping*—maybe you'd want to go to dinner with me this evening. It's short notice, so I understand if the answer's no, but I just thought . . ." His mouth lifted in a sheepish grin.

I took a sip of my coffee and motioned to Claire. My heart raced into a panicked state, and I scrambled to think of a response. "You mean we could talk about my aunt and Viola's case, exchange theories and information? Yeah, sounds like a good idea."

He tugged harder at his collar. "That's not—"

"What can I get you?" Claire broke into the conversation as she stood at an angle with her face turned in my direction. Her mouth opened to form the word *wow* in silence.

"I'll take two blueberry bagels to go." Since Willow hadn't been available, Izzie had generously offered to cover the shop while I met with Marilyn, though I knew from her look with those sad eyes and downturned mouth that she desperately would've liked to come along. A blueberry bagel should cheer her up—that and my account of Marilyn's theory.

I took a quick glance at Hunter. He gave Claire his take-out order for a dozen muffins. It was obvious his invitation had been intended as something more personal. Nothing like being a coward who avoided uncomfortable moments, but that had been my reaction. I'd put romance on hold. Even if this man pulled me and my heart in his direction, I reminded myself that Aunt Constance's dire circumstances took priority. Maybe after that, I'd take a chance on Hunter. I groaned and mumbled. Who was I fooling?

"What was that?" Hunter said after Claire walked away. He seemed to have recovered from our earlier conversation since his voice held steady, and his coloring had lost that red blush.

"Nothing. I was stressing about all I need to do at work today." I stood. "Which means I should go. What time do you want to meet for dinner? Is the Blue Whale okay with you? They have a special on their grilled fish."

"How about seven thirty? I have some footwork to finish on a case before I leave work today."

I paid for my order and waited at the counter for him to get his. "Sounds fine. I have lots to tell you. About the case, I mean."

"Great." He opened the door for me to step outside. "Do you need a lift to work?"

"No. I parked behind the courthouse." After an awkward handshake, I hurried to my car, anxious to leave Hunter and all the talk about dinner. This was my first real date with a guy other than Ross since I'd left New York. I hated firsts of any kind. First day of high school, first day on a job, first time on a plane, and now a first date with Hunter Barrett. Firsts made my stomach churn and head ache.

I munched on my blueberry bagel while walking around the corner to the front of Paint with a View. Firsts also made me stress eat. I slid the strap of my bag over one shoulder to free my hand. Opening the door, I was confronted by Izzie and the ladder she'd climbed. "Why are you up on a ladder?" I mumbled around a mouthful of bagel. Quickly swallowing the bite, I tried again. "Are you hanging those new chimes?" I peered up at the ceiling. The blue and white shells tinkled and clinked while Izzie adjusted the cord. I heard the choice expletives while she made a second and then a third attempt to balance the chimes.

"There. What do you think?" She gripped the ladder and stepped down.

"Oh, I don't know. I'm kind of partial to the other one." I tapped a finger on my chin and kept a serious face long enough to see her scowl. A snicker escaped my mouth, and I pointed. "Gotcha."

"You're such a pain." She laughed and tossed a rag at me. "How did things go with Marilyn?"

"You wouldn't believe her theory of whodunnit. Or maybe you would." I explained our exchange, ending with Hunter's interruption.

"Well, I'd say she has a point about Sarah's sour attitude, but I'm more interested in hearing about Hunter." She elbowed me and winked.

I helped carry the ladder to the storage room. "We're going to dinner to discuss the case. I'll tell him about Sarah and Marilyn then." I fixed a blank expression on my face when she glanced back.

"Mm-hmm. Well, as for Marilyn and Sarah having anything useful to defend Aunt Constance, I have my doubts. My guess is Hunter will think the same way."

"That's what I thought." I smacked the side of the ladder. "What if we've overlooked some tiny detail, though—something that could help Aunt Constance? I think we should keep track of those two. Dig a little deeper into their backgrounds." After leaning the ladder against the back wall, I paced the room. "Who knows? If we do this, we might find other members who look suspicious." I snapped my fingers. "We can go to the Sisterhood's memorial for Viola this Friday. People get emotional at those gatherings, and emotional people tend to talk. They share stories about the deceased. Those stories could reveal how people felt about Viola."

"Kind of a morbid idea, attending a memorial to collect information for the case, but detectives do it. So why not go? Besides, we should pay our respects, for Aunt Constance's sake." Izzie wiped dust off her shirt.

The door chimes sounded and Izzie smiled. "Much better than that irritating clatter of the other one. You gotta admit."

"I'm here." Willow plopped in a chair and took several breaths. "Finally. The trip to Buffalo was brutal."

"Remind me again why you had to go there instead of him coming here?" Izzie handed her a bottled water from the mini fridge.

"Because my dad is too busy, or so he claims." She took a swig of water. "And also, if I gave him time, he would change his mind and refuse to sign."

Willow had a contract drawn up to sever all ties to the family fortune. When she'd told us that was her plan, we'd both tried to talk her out of it. Proving her independence by living on her own and holding a job was one thing, but there were no guarantees in life as to how things would go in the future.

"Now, I don't have to worry about inheriting all their problems."

"Or their money," Izzie added. "Let's hope you never regret it."

"I won't. You should know, money doesn't make you happy." Willow set the empty bottle on the floor. "How did your meeting with Marilyn go? Any juicy, gory details to add to the story?" She rubbed her hands together and let out a *muahaha* with a ghoulish grin.

"Stop. This is serious. Our aunt could go to jail," Izzie scolded.

"Sorry. You're right. She's not my relative, but from your description, she seems too sweet to survive behind bars."

"What she had to tell me was more gossip than anything else." I quickly recapped the conversation.

"What I do find juicy is the date Chloe is having with the handsome Hunter Barrett." Izzie wiggled her brows.

"How romantic." Willow tipped her head to rest on folded hands and batted her lashes. "Will true love be in Chloe Abbington's future? Stay tuned for the next episode of 'Romance Comes to Whisper Cove.'"

I glared at the two of them, but then we all burst out laughing. "Just see how funny you think this is when I'm the one going on a date this evening, while you single ladies end up joining 'Sergeant Pepper's Lonely Hearts Club.'"

"It's the Lonely Hearts Club *Band*, which doesn't make it an actual club."

I gasped, then locked my lips as Ross stepped into the shop. The rustling of paper came from behind me, and Izzie hurried to the counter where Willow now stood.

"Willow, would you take half of these flyers and distribute them to the shops along Whisper Cove Boulevard? I can cover handing out the rest to the businesses on Artisan Alley and Main Street."

I cleared my throat and caught Izzie's eye, then gave a slight head shake. Left alone with Ross, I would most likely spill what we'd been talking about, and that would make me sound like I was bragging, which is how I'd take it if our roles were reversed.

"Later. I'll take care of these later. Much later because my feet are sore from going up and down the ladder and bringing in supplies from my car." She rubbed the back of her neck and puckered her lips to whistle as she gazed at me.

"Good grief. Enough." I mumbled the words while smiling at Ross. "What brings you here? Good news about Aunt Constance, I hope."

Ross gave Izzie a brief, quizzical stare then turned to me. "I wanted to let you know I was able to get information from the coroner's office. With a little help from Hunter, of course."

My shoulders stiffened. Picturing the two of them in the same room talking to one another made me nervous. The last time it happened, Ross ended up telling Hunter all sorts of stories about our past relationship, blabbing like a teenage girl at a slumber party. Even Hunter admitted he was uncomfortable hearing all those personal details. "Please tell me you only talked about the case." I held my breath.

His brow creased. "What else would we talk about?"

"Like before when you—never mind. What did you learn?" I crossed my arms.

"Well, for one thing, the coroner discovered a gash on the back of the victim's head. From the shape of the wound, he suggested she was hit with an object that had a long, narrow edge to it. Either that, or she hit the side of the deck before landing in the water. The coroner's thoughts are steering away from this being an accident, though. At least, that's the feeling Hunter got after visiting the coroner's office." He rubbed the stubble on his chin. "Blunt force trauma would be a game changer."

I groaned with exasperation and threw up my arms. "Still, nothing so far proves her death was murder."

"No, and neither do the wood fibers found embedded in the wound. The lab in Buffalo is testing those to see if they match the wood on the deck. That's taking a while." He sucked on his tongue, then rolled it around in his mouth. "I don't have to tell you what it'll mean for your aunt if the test doesn't match the fibers of the deck wood."

"Why do you always look on the negative side?" I scowled. "Even if the coroner finally decides her death was murder, that doesn't mean Aunt Constance did it."

Ross rolled back on his heels. "Doesn't mean that she didn't either. Look, I'm sorry, but as a defense attorney, I have to consider all angles, and that includes the worst-case scenario. What about Dewey Sawyer? He had opportunity. The town drunk who fought with the victim, or maybe he got fresh with her. She fought off his advances, lost her balance, hit her head on the deck, and fell into the lake."

"I wouldn't call him the town drunk. He's really pretty well liked around here. Dependable at running the ferry, always generous with his help, and he never drinks on the job," Izzie said. "But you're right. He admitted to drinking that day and can't remember a lot of that evening. So I guess it's possible he caused Viola's death. Maybe not intentionally, though."

Willow walked out of the storage room, carrying the flyers and her jacket. "He helped me when I first came to town. I got a flat tire and was stuck near the ferry dock. Of course, I didn't know anybody yet. Dewey came over, changed my tire, then gave me directions to the shop. Really nice guy."

"Even nice guys do horrible things sometimes," Ross argued. "If your aunt is charged and this goes to trial, I can still argue my theory about Dewey. Puts doubt in the jury's minds."

"Well, I'm out of here. Shouldn't take more than an hour to deliver these." Willow waved and disappeared outside.

Ross stepped closer to me. "Chloe, could I have a moment alone with you?" His gaze wandered to Izzie, who quickly excused herself.

"Hey, I was thinking maybe we could go out this evening? Make reservations at that place we met for lunch that time. We can catch up, like I mentioned over the phone. You know, we had such a great time together this past summer." He shifted his weight, leaning against the table next to him. "What do you say?"

I fidgeted with my hands, then dropped them to my sides. That awkward moment I'd hoped to avoid, the one where I sounded boastful and made him feel like crud, was about to happen. "I can't. I already have plans with a friend this evening at the Blue Whale." I blurted out the words, then stepped away to put more distance between us. "In fact, I'm seeing someone now. So you and I going out wouldn't be a good idea. Because we aren't a couple any longer, and it's time for both of us to move on." I cursed under my breath. I didn't need to go that far, but I did.

"Ah, okay. Yeah, I get it." He nodded and backed away until he reached the door.

The dejected, sad look in his eyes nearly broke me. I didn't want to hurt him, but I didn't want to be the one who got hurt either. And I would if I raised my hopes and tried to rekindle what we'd had. I lifted my chin and clenched my fists, determined to stick to my guns. "Bye, Ross. Thank you for helping Aunt Constance." I spun on my heel and headed toward the storage room, not able to look at the disappointment on his face for a second longer because I was afraid I'd crumble and change my mind.

I heard the door shut. Bracing my hand against the wall, I let go of the breath I had been holding.

Izzie peeked around the stack of boxes, with a box cutter in one hand and an inventory list in the other. "A little harsh, but then who am I to judge?" She set the tool and list on the shelf and walked toward me, arms outstretched, fingers wiggling. "Come on. Let's hug before you start bawling."

"I'm not going to cry, you goof." The sound of my words was muffled against her chest.

"Sure, he loves you. We know he's a great guy and has a successful career, but none of that matters. Right? Someone who drops whatever he's doing when you ask for help and drives over seven hours to get here, no questions asked. Why should you owe him anything?" Izzie stroked my head.

I pulled out of her grasp and wagged a finger at her while I shook my head. "He dropped everything and came because Aunt Constance asked him to, not *me*. And why are you getting all judgmental?"

"I'm not." She blinked.

"Yes, you are, and you know it." I smoothed my hair. "How I handle Ross is my business. I don't tell you how to handle the men in your life."

She frowned. "I don't have any men in my life."

"Well . . . if you did, I wouldn't tell you what to do." I huffed, then stormed to the front of the shop and grabbed my jacket and bag.

"I'm not telling you what to do. I'm just giving you my opinion." She hurried to keep up.

"Same thing. I'm leaving to visit Aunt Constance so I can ask her about Marilyn and Sarah." I turned on my heel and glared. "The subject of Ross is closed for discussion."

I headed to my car and sped north toward Mayville, putting all thoughts of Ross out of my head.

Chapter Eight

Doing ten miles over the speed limit, I arrived at Aunt Constance's in record time. I sat still in the car for a moment to calm myself. There was no point taking my agitated mood with me into the house and upsetting Aunt Constance. Once I had my emotions under control, I walked to the front door.

"Chloe! What a surprise. Come in. I was fixing lunch. Would you care to join me?" She waved the towel in her hand. A smudge of dirt covered her cheek, and as if she was aware of her appearance, she cleaned the sweat and soil from her face. She was dressed in jeans and a Henley shirt with long sleeves. Not something she'd ever wear in public.

"Maybe a glass of something. Cider or tea, whatever you have on hand." I followed her to the kitchen. "I won't stay long."

"Nonsense. Stay as long as you like. This big old house makes me feel too alone somedays when I'm missing your uncle. Besides, I'll get to put off cleaning the attic for a while longer." She sighed while putting her sandwich on a plate. She poured two glasses of tea and handed me one.

I walked with her to the back deck. With its view of the lake, I could see sails dotting the water with a rainbow of colors and fishermen casting reels from their boats. Gulls cried as they flew across the sky while others dove into the water to catch a meal. I stared into the distance, taking in the peaceful scene, and sipped my tea.

"I suppose you came for something besides a visit with me." Aunt Constance nibbled at her sandwich. She chewed quickly and swallowed as her gaze flitted from side to side. "Not bringing me bad news, are you? Wouldn't be right to spoil such a beautiful day."

"Not at all. I wanted to ask for your opinion of Marilyn Pervis and Sarah Gilley, two of your chapter members. I spoke with them earlier." Looking over the rim of my glass, I kept a watchful eye on her, not wanting to miss the slightest reaction—a tiny twitch, raised brows, darting eyes, tense jaw—anything that might hint at her discomfort. Surprisingly, I noticed none of those.

She nibbled another bite in silence. Then, washing it down with tea, she opened her mouth to speak. "Two of our most productive members, but they each have their quirks. I'm sure Sarah spouted off her complaints about me. I'm not alone. She criticizes most everyone she meets." Placing the rest of her sandwich on the plate, she gave me a half-hearted smile. "No one's perfect. I make mistakes and learn from them, like anyone else. Sarah is insecure and constantly seeks attention. If there's a way to get it, she'll find it. I understand she lives alone and has no family to speak of. That's why I try to include her in as many of our activities as possible. Keeping busy helps one forget the loneliness. I know that very well." She wiped the corner of her eye.

I traced a line through the cloud of sweat covering my glass. "She also told me about taking her complaints to Viola, insisting that you were unprofessional and treated some of the members unfairly."

"I know. Viola confronted me. I convinced her that Sarah wanted my job. You see, I'd overheard her tell someone in our group that she'd make a much better president if she had the chance. I guess the emails she sent to Viola were her way of making that happen."

"Do you think Sarah was angry that Viola dismissed her complaints?"

"You mean angry enough to harm her?" Aunt Constance shook her head. "I'm not sure. I mean, how well do we really know people or what pushes them over the edge to do something horrible?"

I shivered as a cold chill ran through me. My hand trembled when I took another swig of my tea. "Marilyn Pervis seems to think Sarah wanted Viola out of the picture, and even suggested she's the one responsible for her death." I skirted around the word *murder* because I worried how Aunt Constance would react.

"Marilyn is a sweetheart, but she tries my patience at times." Aunt Constance sighed. "That woman will do anything I ask of her, which under normal circumstances would be fine. Remember Uncle Seymour, the one your granddad used to tell stories about?"

I snapped my fingers. "Right. He worked for Granddad on one of his fishing trawlers."

"And he followed your granddad around like he was his shadow, complimenting him, defending him, even getting into a fistfight on occasion. He was loyal to a fault." Her eyes narrowed. "You see where I'm going with this?"

"Oh." I leaned back. "Oh wow. You're saying Marilyn is like Uncle Seymour. She's your shadow." I let the rest of my thoughts go unstated. If Marilyn was loyal to a fault and willing to defend Aunt Constance, she might be someone Hunter should look at as a suspect. Or even Sarah who might have been so angry that Viola ignored her complaints that she took her revenge too far. The question was, had either one left the event at any point and been gone long enough to hurt Viola? "I don't suppose you noticed anyone in the parking lot, leaving when you and Viola did?"

"No. I was too upset to pay attention. I don't even remember seeing who gave Viola a lift, or whether she left before or after I did, though I will say I couldn't get away from the lodge quickly enough." She shuddered. "Probably broke the speed limit leaving town."

I shifted uncomfortably in my chair, hesitating to contradict her. "If you were in such a big hurry to get home, why did you tell Hunter you drove around awhile to sort out your thoughts?"

"I meant I was in a hurry to get away from the lodge, not to get home," she snapped, then at once reared back and widened her eyes. "I'm so sorry. I don't mean to be defensive."

"It's okay."

"No. No, it isn't." She reached for my hand and squeezed. "I appreciate everything you and Izzie are doing to help me. If only this nightmare was over, and things could go back to the way they were."

"I'm sure Hunter and the coroner will have Viola's death figured out soon. Please, try not to stress too much." I left the suggestion at that. The doctor had already warned her that being overweight could cause health problems. My adding that she might have a heart attack or stroke wouldn't be taken well.

I excused myself after finishing my tea, anxious to share Aunt Constance's comments with Izzie. In my opinion there were three possible suspects—Dewey, Marilyn, and Sarah—who could've had reasons and opportunity to harm Viola. I hadn't thought about it until Aunt Constance mentioned it, that the person who had the ideal opportunity was whoever had given Viola a lift to the ferry dock to pick up her car. Maybe there were more suspects out there. We'd only started our search. Anyone we found to take Hunter's eyes off Aunt Constance, no matter how flimsy the evidence, was a victory. We couldn't give up.

* * *

The Blue Whale opened in the early forties, after the country was slowly picking itself up and out of that hole in the ground that had been the Depression. Seafood was pricey, but the owner offered specials to please customers on a budget, which covered most of the residents from Whisper Cove. However, the restaurant's success also depended on tourists, who came to spend their vacation money on food, souvenirs, and entertainment.

Today's special was grilled haddock, fresh caught and delivered every morning, served with scalloped potatoes or lemon rice, and stir-fried vegetables. I closed my eyes and breathed in all the smells wafting from the kitchen while clutching my stomach as it churned.

"So, how did your day go?" Hunter broke through the silence.

I opened my eyes. Hunger wasn't the only reason my stomach was making such a fuss, and that other reason was sitting across the table from me. Not the guy I might have feelings for, but definitely the detective on the job caused my nerves to react. I doubted Hunter Barrett and his brain ever clocked out. Even if he had blushed when inviting me to dinner, which told me there was a chance he felt something for me too, the detective wasn't about to give up a perfect opportunity to interrogate me. My guess was he had a list of questions already prepared to ask me concerning Viola's murder, and a second list of ways to persuade me to spill everything I'd learned while moonlighting as a snoop. Well, the joke was on him. I'd already planned to tell him everything. No persuasive tactics needed.

"Wine?"

"Hmm?" I tore myself away from those thoughts to stare.

"Wine? Would you like some?" He held up the bottle and smiled.

"Oh! Yes, please." I steadied my grip on the glass as he poured. "I suppose you'd like to hear more about my conversation with Marilyn." Taking a sip, and then another, I set the glass to the side.

"No. Not really." He leaned back in his chair. "Unless you want to tell me."

"Huh. Okay, then what do you want to talk about?" Playing indifferent could work both ways. "How about art? Besides Van Gogh, whose work do you like? I'm a fan of the more modern artists, like Picasso. His Blue Period works are my favorite." Elbows on the table, I steepled my fingers underneath my chin.

"Fine. What did Marilyn Pervis tell you? Wait—let me guess." He stroked his chin. "She thinks Sarah Gilley killed Viola because she wouldn't remove your aunt as president."

I had to admit, he was pretty great at his job. "Yes, but did you also know Sarah told some of the members that she would make a much better president and would do anything to get the position?"

Hunter's brow arched. "Which members?"

"Aunt Constance, Marilyn, and others I can't name." I fingered the side of my glass. "Maybe you should talk to some of the members. See what they think of Sarah Gilley."

"Even though I don't need to share every detail about this investigation, I know how worried you are about your aunt. My team is already gathering info on each of the sister members, including Marilyn and Sarah. As for today, I visited a few of the local businesses and asked if they'd seen or heard any commotion that night at the dock. So far, I have zero leads." He pressed his knuckles to his chin. "Even the Uber service is a dead end. None of the places my deputy called has a record of anyone giving Viola a ride that night."

"Which means someone from the event must have. I wish I could remember who left early, but I can't. Neither can Izzie." I sank down in my seat, discouraged more than ever. Even if we figured out who had given Viola a ride, it didn't mean that person was the one who had hurt her.

"I guess it was too much to hope that there'd be security cameras at the lodge." He pressed his lips together.

"A building over a century old? Nope. At least not this one." I blew out a puff of air. "You know, I was thinking: Marilyn has an unusual attachment to my aunt. She was going on about how wonderful, kind, and generous Aunt Constance is."

"Have you asked your aunt about her?"

"Aunt Constance told me Marilyn was like her shadow. She follows her around at meetings and events, always offering to help, and she always defends her when anyone says something critical about the way Aunt Constance runs the chapter. Kind of like a groupie who doesn't understand personal boundaries. Creepy, right?" I shuddered.

"A little odd, but I've seen worse."

"She had to have overheard the argument between Aunt Constance and Viola. Everyone at the event must have, because they were practically shouting—at least Aunt Constance was." I stopped as I recalled how angry she'd been. That tiny voice of suspicion niggled at me. At once, I shoved it out of my head. "Maybe Marilyn snuck out and saw an opportunity to help Aunt Constance."

"By killing Viola?" Hunter's eyes widened.

"By her crazy way of reasoning, yes. Aunt Constance says Marilyn is like my Uncle Seymour."

"You lost me." He shook his head. "But, go on. I'm curious about Uncle Seymour."

I explained Uncle Seymour's adoration for Granddad. "Every so often, he'd get into fights to defend Granddad's honor."

"You're saying Marilyn gets physical to defend your aunt? I'm having a tough time picturing that. She seems so prim and proper to me." He lifted the wineglass and raised his pinky finger to illustrate what he meant. "Putting on boxing gloves or swinging a bat at someone's head doesn't match."

"Fine, but shoving someone into the lake while in a fit of anger isn't such a stretch. At least consider it." I hoped my voice didn't sound whiny, like I was begging, since I definitely was.

"I consider every possible scenario and suspect. I'm thorough. You should know that by now."

The server approached with our dinners, and the conversation lulled while we ate. My mind worked out what I'd been dying to ask him, especially since Izzie's mouth shut tighter than a clam when I tried to talk about it. Besides, it would be nice to talk about something other than his case. As soon as I cleared most everything off my plate, I took a dive into the past. "So, what exactly did you do to upset my sister? I know whatever it was must've happened years ago, but she won't tell me a thing." I pointed my fork.

He dabbed his lips with his napkin, then laid it on his empty plate. "If she doesn't want to talk about it, maybe I shouldn't either."

"Come on. I want to understand. Think of it as an important step in our sister relationship, like bonding. It will bring us closer." I could tell he wasn't buying any part of my pitch. "Okay, I'll confess. I'm asking because it's killing me. I mean, how bad could it have been? Some schoolboy prank? Ooh!" I leaned forward and whispered. "Did you have a crush on Izzie, and when she gave you the brush-off, you got your revenge? That's it, isn't it?" I smacked the table.

He rolled his eyes. "No crush. This was a moment of stereotypical high school drama. Geeks versus the popular kids. Real lame, but so was high school for me and my friends."

He licked his bottom lip. "Not my proudest moment, but there was this football game, and I came up with an idea. You have to understand, we were constantly made fun of. Name-calling, lockers trashed, bullying, and lots more. Getting a little revenge seemed justified."

My eyes widened. "What did you do? I was a geek in high school but way too scared to act out. Revenge would've been suicidal."

"Guess we were too desperate and humiliated to care." He shrugged. "The prank went without a hitch. When the cheer squad led the student body in our fight song, several of us raced across the field and dumped chocolate syrup on all the girls. And someone took a picture—I don't know who—maybe the photographer for the school newspaper who came to take shots of the game."

I snapped my fingers. "The picture that went viral on social media! That was you?" I leaned back. "Izzie cried for weeks. Kids at school were relentless, calling her and the other girls the chocolate squad and asking them whether they needed any sprinkles or whipped cream."

"A few weeks? She got a little taste of what we were subjected to for years. Hard to feel sorry for her." He sighed. "But yeah, it was wrong. I apologized in front of the whole student body during a pep assembly. None of my other friends would. Of course, the bullying and name-calling got worse, so we'd pranked them for nothing. You were right. It was suicidal."

"Aw, I feel for you." I spoke with a touch of sarcasm and patted his hand. "But I don't buy your story. There has to be something more because Izzie wouldn't hold a grudge for this long over a chocolate syrup prank."

He shrugged and pulled out a stick of gum. "Nothing more to tell. I swear."

"Okay. I won't push, but I know there's more to the story." With my stomach full and my body pleasantly calm, thanks to the wine, I sat back and gazed around the dining room. People were laughing and enjoying their conversations and meals. Turning to the far right, I could see into the bar lounge. It was filled with customers sitting at the bar while several sat at the tables for two, including Ross and Aunt Constance. My eyes popped wide, and my mouth gaped. "What in the world?" I kept my voice low, but Hunter heard anyway.

"What in the world what?" he asked.

"Oh." I fluttered my eyes and snapped my head away from the scene that took me by surprise. Resistance was pointless. Without turning, I shifted my gaze sideways for a glimpse just as Ross smiled and waved at me. I stiffened but made a point to focus my attention on Hunter. "My eyes are playing tricks. Don't laugh, but I thought I saw Bono seated at one of the tables." *Bono?* I gave myself a mental slap.

"Bono, the singer from U2?" He bellowed out a laugh. "Sorry. Though I wouldn't mind seeing Camila Cabello or Carrie Underwood sitting at a table."

"Funny guy." I pressed the pad of my thumb against my teeth and willed myself not to look at Ross again. The odds he'd walk over to our table, just to make me uncomfortable, were without a doubt favorable. I slid my chair back. "Well, I enjoyed the dinner and the company. Thank you for inviting me."

"What? No dessert? I'm thinking cherries jubilee or maybe a slice of their key lime pie. I hear they have the best in New York."

He covered his mouth, but the crinkles around his eyes as his cheeks lifted gave away the smile. I sucked on my tongue. "You already noticed him, didn't you?"

"About the time we were ordering dinner."

I sent him a pointed stare, flip-flopping between feeling angry and grateful. "And you didn't say anything?" Knowing Ross was here would've spoiled the grilled haddock and potatoes for me. So yeah, I'd go with grateful but wouldn't admit it.

"Why does it bother you?" His creased brow vanished in an instant, and his lips turned up at the corners to smile once again. "I don't suppose Ross being here is a coincidence, is it?"

"Could be . . . but probably not." I gave an instant replay of Ross's visit to the shop but left out my comment about seeing someone, which would be totally embarrassing to admit since I wasn't. "That's how he knew I'd be here." I smoothed the rumpled tablecloth, looking away.

"But you didn't tell him who'd be with you." He chuckled.

"Well, he knows now," I muttered while clutching my bag in my lap. "It's getting late."

"It's only a quarter after nine, but we can go now if it will make you more comfortable."

I gave my answer by standing. My mind raced with a more acceptable explanation. Aunt Constance must've called Ross to pick his brain about a defense strategy in case she was charged with murder. She'd suggested having dinner at the Blue Whale because it was her favorite seafood restaurant. Of course, he couldn't say no to her. No one did. I eased the breath out of me and relaxed. That had to be the story. Ross wouldn't be so insane with jealousy as to come and spy on me, would he? Absolutely not.

127

"You're mumbling again. Like to share your thoughts?" Hunter rested his hand on the small of my back as we walked to the door.

I shivered. "Nothing important. Just griping to myself again." I tapped my head. "We working ladies can't afford to waste a second's thought when we have so much to do."

"I'm sure that's what it was." Standing alongside me, he held the door open and grinned.

I ignored the comment and the grin. Instead, I moved on to my car. We'd driven separately since he'd been working a case in Jamestown that afternoon. I was desperate to avoid any awkward goodbye, like the kind where two people move close together, and one expects a kiss while the other only wants a hug. I stuck out my hand to shake his. "Goodnight, Hunter. I had fun. Except for the part about seeing Ross. That I could've done without."

His hold on my hand lingered as he gazed at me. "Please be careful. If you and Izzie insist on trying to help your aunt by snooping around, I might have to deputize the both of you, and there's not enough money in the budget to pay for two more employees." All at once, his face sobered, and he cleared his throat. "I enjoyed the evening too. Let's do it again sometime. Soon." Without waiting for my response, he turned and jogged down the block to his car.

"Well, that wasn't such a disaster." I shrugged and hopped inside my car. While warming up the engine, I turned my phone back on. Five missed calls lit up the screen, but no voicemails. "Izzie." I read the name attached to the number and sighed. If her call was an emergency, she'd have left a message. Still, five calls was somewhat urgent. I stabbed the callback button and waited, leaving my car in park.

"Thank goodness. Why didn't you answer?" Izzie sounded out of breath.

"Is everything okay? Why are you winded?" I clicked on my turn signal. Seeing I had a clear path, I pulled onto the road.

"Everything is not okay. Do you know what I'm holding in my hand?" Her voice squeaked and paper rustled.

"How could I know what—just tell me, Izzie." I made a left onto our road. The soft patter of raindrops hit the windshield.

"It's from a lawyer representing the northern region of the Chautauqua Sisterhood. We are being sued for hosting an unsafe event that resulted in Viola's death."

Chapter Nine

"Stop worrying. Trust me when I tell you they haven't a chance taking this to court." Ross sat on the far end of the sofa, near the fireplace. "The owners of the lodge are responsible for security and lighting the parking lot. They should take the heat, not you. Besides that, the Sisterhood's theory that she was accosted outside because the area wasn't safe is pure supposition, and even if true, it's not your fault."

I'd waited to call Ross until the morning to ask for his advice. He'd come by the house around eleven, even though I insisted that wasn't necessary. I kept telling myself that we wouldn't talk about last evening at the Blue Whale. I wasn't too worried about him bringing it up because switching topics of conversation was my specialty.

Sitting at the other end of the sofa, Izzie clutched the pillow that lay in her lap, her chin resting on top. "What if they do? That means we need to hire a lawyer and dodge all the bad publicity." She shifted her chin to stare at me. "You know Wink won't pass up an opportunity to sensationalize the news. I can see it now, on the front page of the *Whisper Cove Gazette*. With our luck even the neighboring towns will carry the story, maybe as far away as Buffalo." She groaned and smashed the pillow in her face.

I blinked and shrugged at Ross, who was trying not to laugh. "That's way beyond reasonable, Izzie. Nobody in Buffalo cares about some silly lawsuit and our little shop."

She flattened the pillow and glared. "Well, maybe some would care."

"No one's going to read about this because—I repeat—the lawsuit doesn't have a chance in hell." Ross sounded and looked exasperated.

"I agree. We need to focus on Aunt Constance and her situation. This will only take away our time and energy, if we let it." I stroked Max's fur while he slept next to me.

"I wouldn't be surprised if that's what they hoped would happen," Izzie said.

"You mean stopping you from helping Aunt Constance? Oh, come on. Now that *is* crazy." Ross smacked the sofa arm with the flat of his hand.

"See what I mean? We should be discussing our plan to find out who might've killed Viola, not talking about this stupid lawsuit." I scowled and crumpled the letter from the attorney, then tossed it in the fireplace.

"Hey! We might need that." Izzie stood, but Ross reached across the sofa to stop her.

"We won't, but I can get in touch with the attorney and have a nice chat with him." He rose and stood next to the sofa, stretching his arms as he yawned. "Okay, I'm leaving. I have a video conference with a client in twenty minutes."

"Thanks, Ross. You've made me feel better. Mostly, anyway," Izzie said.

"I'll walk you to the door." I got up from my chair, and Max hopped down to follow me across the room.

As he reached the front, Ross opened the door and turned to face me. "Are you and Izzie still going to the memorial for Viola?"

I nodded. "No one will suspect anything. Aunt Constance is telling everyone we're coming to give her emotional support."

"I was going to say, if you find out anything useful, call me."

He tapped the frame of the door and grew silent, as if waiting for me to carry on the conversation. Either that or he was thinking of a way to bring up the thing I didn't want to discuss.

"You're letting in the cold air," I said pointedly.

"Oh, sorry. I guess I am." He stepped out onto the porch. "Good luck with your painting event this afternoon. Lucky for you the weather is cooperating."

"Thanks. I'll call you." I gave a slight wave and quickly shut the door. With a huge sigh, I walked back into the den. Any conversation about the Blue Whale, my date with Hunter, and how I'd stretched the truth about dating him had been avoided.

Izzie stood facing the fireplace, her arms folded over her chest. "Do you really think Ross is right about this?" Turning on her heel, she faced me. The troubled frown creasing her forehead hadn't disappeared.

"I do. He's good at his job and at reading people. I trust his gut instinct. Anyhow, we don't have time to stress about it." I tapped my watch. "It's almost noon, and the memorial is in an hour. We should get changed."

"You're right." Her chest heaved. "I signed up for yoga classes yesterday and start tomorrow." She pressed fingers on her wrist, taking her pulse. "I don't know what's wrong with me, but I've got to stop stressing over everything. Otherwise, I'll end up in a psych ward."

"Stop. I'm proud that you're taking steps to help yourself. So, no psych ward talk. Besides, if you go there, I'm coming with you. I couldn't handle life without you." I squeezed her hand.

"Aw. You do love me, after all." She grinned and pulled me in for a hug.

"Izzie, I can't breathe." My voice was muffled against her chest.

"Sorry." She held me at arm's length. "I'm just so glad to have my big sister back. All that time you were living in New York was the worst. Don't you ever leave me again."

"I'll see what I can do." I linked my arm through hers and led the way toward the stairs. "What about marriage? Can I leave you then? Or do you want to come live with me and my husband? I draw the line when it comes to the honeymoon, though. Oh! What if *you* get married first? Do I get to live with you?"

She patted my arm. "We'll see. I have to think about it."

"You are such a goof, you know that?" I swung my hip against her thigh.

"Forever and always."

After a quick shower, I slipped into the only black dress I owned, one I'd bought at a thrift shop in Soho two years ago, and met Izzie downstairs. We drove north along the lake to Mayville. The venue for Viola's memorial was the reception hall of Saint Anne's Church. Aunt Constance attended services there and had offered to speak with Pastor Josephine who graciously agreed to midday Friday since the hall was booked for a wedding reception that evening. Members from every chapter of the Chautauqua Sisterhood planned to attend. It seemed that, contrary to Sarah's and Aunt Constance's opinions, Viola had been well liked. Her memorial page on the legacy website was filled with hundreds of condolences, including mine and Izzie's. That gesture, along with attending the memorial, seemed appropriate, even though we had an ulterior motive for joining the function.

Soothing music piped through the speakers and filled the hall with Debussy's "Clair de Lune." According to her sister, this song had been Viola's favorite. I scanned the crowd, searching for Marilyn. I had no idea what Sarah looked like. In the far corner, a middle-aged woman with bright red hair closed her eyes and swayed back and forth, as if enjoying the music. A pleasant smile softened the features of her face. Maybe she was Sarah.

"Are we going to mingle?" Izzie nudged my shoulder as she whispered.

I leaned her way. "How about we split up? You take the right side of the room, and I'll cover the other." I set a slow pace across the floor, weaving around some guests while stopping to exchange words of sympathy with a few. I kept one ear on any conversation that raised suspicion, meaning one with negative comments about Viola, but I only overheard remarks like "She didn't deserve to go that way" or "How will the Sisterhood ever replace her?" Frustrated, I ended up near the back wall, where tables were lined with refreshments and food dishes ranging from lasagna to fried chicken, plus plenty of sides and desserts such as pumpkin roll and pumpkin pie. There had been a bumper crop of pumpkins this year.

I loaded a plate with my choices, munched on a cheese puff, and moved on to the punch bowl. Looking up, I spotted Aunt Constance dabbing her eyes while standing next to Pastor Josephine. My gaze shifted to the right. I choked and quickly washed the bite of food down with punch.

Glaring at me from across the room was a tall, large-framed, white-haired woman. This felt like déjà vu. I recognized her from the night of the lodge party. She was the one who'd bullied her way to take a front-row seat. She still had the same steely-eyed stare and scowl. Scary to think the expression might be permanently frozen on her face.

"Are you all right, Chloe?" Aunt Constance patted my back. "Should I get you another glass of punch?"

I turned. "Oh, no thanks. I'm fine." I heaved a breath and smiled. "See?" I tipped my chin. "Who's the woman with the white hair standing next to Viola's photo display?"

"Huh. She looks pretty upset. Can't imagine why. She didn't like Viola very much. Come to think of it, she doesn't care for *anyone* very much. That's Sarah Gilley. You asked me about her yesterday. Remember?"

I chewed the inside of my cheek, contemplating my next move. I stared for a long moment at my plate, sighed, then shoved it at Aunt Constance. "Here. Save this for me. I think I'll go have a chat." Before she could respond, I grabbed a napkin to wipe my lips, then marched across the room. My gaze locked on Sarah, who hadn't stopped staring at me. One thing was for certain: if looks like hers were any indication of being a killer, Sarah would be a perfect candidate.

Her shoulders pulled back and chin lifted as I neared. "Hi. You're Sarah, right? I believe we spoke on the phone the other evening." I extended my hand. "Chloe Abbington. My sister and I run Paint with a View. You were at the painting event at the lodge, weren't you?"

"Yes to all of that." She gripped my hand and shook it hard. "Nice turnout for someone like her." Sarah's voice matched the scowl on her face, gravelly and grumpy.

I skipped over the "someone like her" description, already guessing what she meant. "Lots of folks wanted to pay their respects, I suppose."

"Probably hearing about the huge spread got them to come." She ended the reply with a throaty harrumph.

I rolled my tongue across my teeth. This conversation wouldn't be easy. "Have you eaten yet? I hear they catered with Delmonico's, one of the best in New York, in my opinion." Shifting the conversation to neutral topics seemed wise. I'd let her be the one to bring up murder or death.

"Not hungry yet." She hitched her thumb back over her shoulder. "I don't think that detective knows how to do his job."

Or she could bring up how the investigation was going and skip right over the pleasantries. I screwed up my mouth as I glimpsed Hunter standing at the entrance, talking with one of the guests. "Oh? How's that?"

"For starters, shouldn't he and the coroner be checking into Viola's background? Her medical records? Her family?" She snorted. "Anybody with a lick of sense would want to find out if there was a reason her death could've been due to some medical condition, or maybe an enemy no one knew about.

There could be any number of possibilities instead of going with the obvious."

Now, my curiosity was piqued. Natural cause of death for a woman only in her forties or early fifties who looked and acted healthy wasn't a conclusion I'd jump to. "I'm sure the coroner checked her medical records."

"You'd have to dig deeper and elsewhere. Can't find everything in medical records, you know. And families have all kinds of secrets." She wiggled her brows.

I blinked. "Do you know something that the police don't? Something you're keeping a secret? It would be your civic duty to tell them, wouldn't it?" The questions fired out of my mouth in quick succession, which didn't seem to rattle Sarah.

She counted on her fingers. "One, I'm not implying I know anything. Two, I would absolutely do my civic duty if I found any information that was relevant. Three, if she did have a medical condition, how could I have access to information about that? I'm not a doctor. And four, what I do know is that I keep a very close eye on what goes on around me, which is something that detective should be doing."

I took a moment to digest everything she'd told me and consider any possibilities that would explain Viola's death. "So, this is all speculation on your part? You don't have any evidence."

Sarah shook her head and laughed. "You're missing the point. As long as the detective doesn't have concrete evidence, he's the one speculating. Anyone can do that. For instance, I could say she walked onto the ferry deck, maybe to get a breath of air and calm herself after that ugly incident with Constance, then she stepped near the edge, had a fainting spell, and before she could stop herself, fell into the lake, hit her head, and *kaboom*"—she snapped her fingers—"just like that she was dead. See what I mean?"

Kaboom? My mouth gaped as she turned on her heel and walked away. "Holy wow. She's good." I spoke aloud to no one but myself, though I did get a few puzzled stares.

"Who's good?" Izzie leaned over my shoulder.

I startled, and my hand flew to cover my chest. "Good grief. Don't sneak up on me like that."

"Sorry. Aunt Constance sent me over to give you this." She held my plate. "She's been summoned to the kitchen. Some sort of food crisis. Now, who's this person you say is good?"

I took the plate and motioned to a free table in the far corner. "Sarah Gilley. She threw out all these suggestions about how Viola could've died. Like maybe having some sort of medical condition that killed her. Or a secret enemy who wanted her dead." I took a huge bite of lasagna and mumbled my words. "She's only guessing, which is something Hunter wouldn't approve of."

"But if she's right, Aunt Constance will be free from facing a murder charge." Izzie picked a piece of rotini off my plate and popped it in her mouth.

"A long shot at best. She was evasive answering my questions. She didn't admit to knowing relevant information about Viola, but if she found any, she'd tell the authorities. How do we know what she considers relevant and important?" I chewed slowly. "You know, there's another explanation."

"What's that?"

"It's something so obvious. If she killed Viola, it would make sense to throw off the authorities by suggesting other suspects. A textbook diversion."

Izzie snorted. "Come on. She's a busybody who wants to look important, so she noses into people's business and spouts off murder theories."

I sucked my tongue. "Hey, we're busy bodies of a sort. Snooping around to find out who could've killed Viola."

"That's different." She tapped the table with one nail, painted tangerine orange to match the Halloween season.

"How is it different?" I frowned.

"Well, we do it to help others, like Aunt Constance. She's doing it because she wants to dig up dirt on people."

I dropped my fork, and it landed on the plate with a clatter. "*We're* trying to get dirt on—never mind. I'm telling Hunter about this. Sarah Gilley should be on his suspect radar. He might agree she's hiding something. If it takes his mind off of Aunt Constance for a while, then it's worth mentioning." I'd take any amount of time we could get to keep looking for who or what was responsible for Viola's death, whether it was Sarah or Dewey or some person we didn't know—or simply an accident.

"Your call." Izzie glanced at a pumpkin cream cookie, then picked up a piece of chocolate walnut fudge instead.

"I'm sure there's plenty of food left, if you want to go make your own plate." I slid mine a few inches closer to me.

"No, that's okay. I'm not really hungry." She licked her lips. "Why didn't you get any sugar cookies? I hear Delmonico's are the best."

I rolled my eyes. "Maybe we should get going. We only have two hours before the event. Why don't you grab our coats while I finish my meal?"

"Sure." She picked up the slice of pumpkin roll and walked away.

"Sisters," I mumbled, then shoveled pasta salad in my mouth.

* * *

The weather was perfect for our paint party along the shore. Cool, but not too cool to be uncomfortable; clear skies without the threat of rain; and only a slight breeze off the lake, so our canvases and paint materials wouldn't scatter across the lawn. Though the unseasonably warm October had delayed the autumn peak of color, trees in the distance were dotted sparsely with golden-yellow, bright red, and burnt-orange leaves.

One row of twenty chairs and easels skirted the lawn a few yards from the shore. At four thirty, the sun hovered slightly above the tree tops. We had a little over an hour to paint before dusk would take away our light. Willow and I placed canvases on the easels while Izzie filled cups with water and set three different brushes on top of each of the placemats. Thanks to Dad, who had recruited our neighbor, Tod Bixby, the projector and screen had been set up, along with two sets of Willow's step-by-step, illustrated painting instructions. Izzie was pleased that everything was in its proper place and we were as ready as we could be.

After getting home from the memorial, I'd called Hunter to give him a brief account of my conversation with Sarah. His reaction surprised me. Instead of dismissing my suggestion, he complimented me and said it was worth keeping an eye on Sarah. He also told me that the coroner had checked with Viola's doctor about her medical history to see if anything in her records could explain what had happened. That's where our phone conversation had taken a turn for the worse, when he refused to tell me what exactly he'd learned from the coroner. I ended with "I can find out on my own" before stabbing the end call button. What happened to quid pro quo between friends?

"Hey, Izzie, Chloe. Everything looks great. I finally got away from the shop. We got slammed at around four, but as soon as the place cleared, Mom scooted me out the door. She's such a big help. I couldn't do this without her support—and Dad's." Megan flopped down in a chair and straddled the seat. She smacked her thighs. "I almost forgot to tell you the news."

"I think our guests are arriving." Willow popped up next to Megan, interrupting whatever she planned to say. "I turned on the projector to warm it up and set flyers for our upcoming events on each of the chairs."

"Can your news wait, Megs?" Izzie squeezed Megan's arm. "If we don't stay on schedule, the paintings won't be finished before we lose daylight. Thanks."

Megan opened her mouth to speak, but Izzie had hurried off to the front and now stood next to the projector.

Seeing Megan's expression, I shrugged. "That's Izzie. Like one of those windup toys, she's this never-ending whirlwind of energy."

"Got that right." Megan sprang out of her seat. "I see Bob coming with his drink cooler and boxes of goodies. I'll go help him."

I laughed. "You mean to get first dibs on his barbecue puffs."

She waved to dismiss the comment and jogged over to meet him.

"Good afternoon, everyone. It's a beautiful day to paint, isn't it? So, please claim your seat, and we'll get started soon.

Chloe and Willow will come around to fill your plates with paints. If you have any questions along the way, ask one of us for help. Or you can check out the step-by-step illustrated instructions at either end of your row. Notes are attached at the bottom, along with tips. Remember, we're here to have fun." She grinned.

I leaned close to the mic. "I'm Chloe, Izzie's sister and partner. Just wanted to add that, if you're like me, painting will work up your appetite. Bob's Barbecue has got you covered. There's plenty of food and drinks over there, so help yourselves."

We stood back while every guest swarmed the table set up for Bob's food items. A huge cooler filled with bottles of Fizzy Pumpkin and Fizzy Orange sat at one end. Bob recruited Megan to help hand out boxes of puffs, sandwiches, and fries. Bottles of the two Fizzy flavors went fast, though the pumpkin seemed to be the favored choice.

As a couple of guests passed by me, I got a whiff of Bob's special extra-spicy sauce. My eyes stung, but the mouthwatering smell also made my stomach growl. "I'm gonna grab a quick bite. You want some?"

"Yes, please. A box of those puffs, but with mild sauce, and a bottle of Fizzy Pumpkin," Izzie said.

"Coming up." I hurried to take my place in the line, which had dwindled down to three or four people.

Megan was keeping up her conversation with Bob while managing to pass out food. "I tell you, the sight of her standing in front of Sammy's shop, Quaint Décor—or what used to be her shop, sadly to say—was strange. I mean, what could she be up to? I recognized the two men with her. They run Buell Brothers Construction." Megan nodded.

I stepped out of the line and closer to the table since Rita Morgan, a Whisper Cove resident, was laughing and talking in a high-pitched, loud tone, making it difficult to hear Megan. Rumors had been circulating for several years that Rita had lost her hearing in a factory accident, but refused to believe anything was wrong with her.

I gasped and gripped the table as the word *Spencer* popped out of Megan's mouth. "Spencer?" Maybe she'd had a change of heart and came home to help her mother, but it wasn't easy wrapping my head around that possibility.

"Oh! Hi, Chloe." Megan smiled. "That's what I was trying to tell you earlier. Your cousin Spencer is in town. I spotted her in front of Sammy's shop this morning, or what was her shop until it burned down and she moved away to live with her cousin, to partner up in a new business. Anyway, I thought I'd mention it in case you and Izzie didn't know." She shrugged with both palms up.

I filtered through all the backstory of Sammy, which I already knew, to what was important. "Spencer is *here*? In Whisper Cove?" I blinked. "Did you speak to her?"

My brain caught up and fired off more questions. Why come home now? Did Aunt Constance know? Most always, Spencer did what benefited Spencer. Did Sammy's shop have something to do with all this? A queasy feeling rippled through my stomach, ruining my appetite.

"I didn't have time to stop and talk, but I saw her and those construction guys. What do you think it means?" Megan sipped on her bottle of Fizzy Pumpkin, then bit into a barbecue puff. We were the only ones left at the table. Even Bob, after taking my order, had loaded boxes and was carrying them to his vehicle.

"I have no idea, but I plan to find out. Thanks, Megan." I hurried back to Izzie with our food. "You will not believe what Megan told me."

My chest heaved, and I forced myself to calm down while I told Izzie the news. The very thought of our cousin irritated me. I found her to be annoying, selfish, and manipulative. Even though I knew it was petty to hang on to them, those childhood memories flooded back. Whenever we'd spent time together as kids, Spencer had used just about every trick in the book to get her way—crying, cheating, tattling, bullying—you name it, she'd try it.

"Why are you so upset? That's good news. Aunt Constance needs all the support she can get," Izzie argued.

"Support? Since when has Spencer ever been supportive?" I scoffed and took a huge gulp of my drink. "I tell you, she's up to something."

"Like what?"

"Like, well, maybe she's planning to build and open a business right where Sammy had her shop. That's what." I scowled. The thought of Spencer as one of our neighbors on Artisan Alley made me shudder.

"Don't be silly. She has a great job, making lots of money in her business deals." Izzie poked my arm. "I think you've never gotten over that time she locked you in the closet and told Mom you'd left the house."

"I was eight, and I spent over an hour in that dark closet until Mom found me." I sulked and planted my butt on a stool while Izzie moved on to get everyone's attention.

"Okay, everyone. Let's check your supplies. You should each have three kinds of brushes—a flat one that has wide bristles like this, a liner brush—that's the pointy one, and a round brush." Izzie listed all the other supplies, then started to draw on her canvas, the results projecting on the screen.

I shoved my worries about Spencer to the back of my mind and circulated to help the guests. The time went by quickly, and six o'clock approached. The paintings were impressive, and guests complimented each other on the results as they dumped their trash in the bag Willow passed around.

Dusk soon turned to dark, with the stars and moon casting a yellow glow. A few guests lingered to talk with friends. One or two helped Izzie and Willow carry chairs and easels back to the shop while I stayed behind to clean up. A burst of laughter echoed and filled the air but was cut short when a piercing scream interrupted.

"Look! Out on the lake." With her arm trembling, Rita Morgan pointed toward the water.

Everyone's gaze, including mine, turned to face that way. I squinted to see in the dim light. A small fishing boat floated by, and sitting inside was a figure in white.

"What the . . .?" I gave my head a firm shake, blinked, and studied the image again.

"It must be the ghost of Abigail Bellows," Rita screeched. "She's come to warn us."

"Warn us of what?" Izzie ran up behind me, out of breath. "I heard the scream. What's going on?"

I pointed out at the lake. "That."

"It's her ghost, I tell you. The Lady of Chautauqua Lake is coming for one of us." Rita covered her face and turned away. "I'm going home and locking my doors. You all should do the same." With that, she ran across the lawn to the parking area, leaving her painting behind.

"Oh wow." Izzie wrapped her arm around my shoulders. "Who would be mean enough to play such a prank?"

"Yeah, I wonder." I hugged her close and forced my imagination to shut down. Pranks and superstitious beliefs like Rita's would only add to the already creepy mood of the Halloween season and make it worse.

Chapter Ten

Overnight, word had spread across town about the white figure in a boat floating along the lake at our painting event, and about Rita's hysterical breakdown that followed. Most people who knew her figured she was not only deaf but a bit on the crazy side, which meant only a handful of people believed her hocus-pocus nonsense about a ghost coming to take another victim. Before last night, no one had claimed Viola Finnwinkle's death had anything to do with ghosts. Sadly, now that Rita had planted the suggestion, plenty of people were thinking just that.

"Hey, look on the bright side. This takes the heat off of Aunt Constance." Izzie popped a vitamin in her mouth and washed it down with juice.

"This whole idea is ridiculous." Mom swiped a stray curl from her face and walked to stand next to me. "Chloe is right. Detective Barrett won't let up. In fact, after hearing about Rita and her ghost story, he'll most likely double down on his efforts to solve the case and at the same time squash those ghost rumors from spreading any further."

I nodded. "He will. Hunter would think superstitions are for gullible people, and he'll work hard to prove those folks are full of crazy nonsense. I just hope solving the case leads him anywhere but to Aunt Constance." I picked up Max's empty food dish and rinsed it out.

"Shortcake, your aunt can handle herself. Now that Spencer is in town, that will cheer her up." Dad kissed my forehead, then walked to the coffee maker to pour another cup.

Spencer. My stomach soured at the mention of her name. "Yeah, let's hope so." I kept any surly comments locked inside my head. Mom and Dad shouldn't have to deal with family drama. Besides, any gripe I had with Spencer should be between us and no one else. "Well, Max and I are heading out for our morning walk. I'll be at the shop in an hour or less." I glanced at Izzie.

"An hour's fine. I should get to the shop around then. First, I'm helping Mom and Dad decorate their boat for Halloween. Willow promised to start on our window display. Later this morning we can carve our pumpkin for the contest." She pulled her shoulders straight and smiled. "With our talent, we're sure to win."

I clipped on Max's leash. "I don't know. I hear Joanna Bixby has a secret weapon to decorate hers." I winked at Mom.

"There are rules about that." Izzie huffed. "No bedazzling or beading or painting. Only the carving can be judged."

"Your sister is joking. I'm sure Joanna will follow the rules," Mom said.

"Come on, Max. This is a tough crowd to please." I tugged on the leash. "See you in an hour or two, or maybe three." I waved.

"Chloe," Izzie started.

"Kidding! Sheesh, humor has really gone out of style in this family." I laughed and jogged down the hall. Grabbing my jacket, I skipped outside to the front walk, with Max trotting alongside me. The air was cool and crisp, with only tiny wisps of clouds in an otherwise blue sky. Sunlight sparkled on the water. I waved to one of our neighbors who was at his dock, tacking orange plastic streamers to the sides of his boat. A strand of orange lights lay close by his feet.

Halloween festivities in Whisper Cove rivaled our Christmas ones. Kids loved both holidays equally, but I suspected some adults favored Halloween fun more. It was a chance to tell scary ghost stories, dress up in frightening costumes, and hand out tons of candy to kids without feeling any guilt because, after all, it was Halloween. What I loved most was the Hallows Eve celebration. Merchants decorated their shops with all sorts of ghoulish items, and some played soundtracks of ghosts howling and witches cackling or songs like "Monster Mash" to please the children. We'd hand out candy, apple cider, caramel apples, apple dumplings, apple fritters, and any other treat you could make with apples, since Frank Dunlap's orchard always donated bushels of them to whoever needed some for their holiday recipes. Families, as well as out-of-towners, came with their chairs and blankets to Artisan Alley and camped out in front of the lake. Some even set up night vision cameras in hopes of catching the ghost of Abigail on film. One of those ghost tales I knew Hunter would make fun of had been passed down through the years and carried on as part of our Halloween tradition. Why people had decided that the Lady of Chautauqua Lake should come to haunt us only on Hallows Eve, no one could explain. Abigail didn't die on that day. She'd drowned during the summer. I guessed since the holiday was meant partly for hauntings and other scary stuff, Abigail was a perfect fit.

We took the walking path that skirted the lake and ran past the area where benches sat underneath several oak trees. I tugged at the leash as Max sniffed the sandy patch of ground near the shoreline, his paws sinking into the soft, wet surface. "Let's not get too dirty, buddy. I don't have time to give you a bath this morning."

Up ahead, I spotted the ferry. A sudden thought stirred me into action, and I picked up speed. "Come on, Max. Let's visit the ferry."

With any luck, Dewey would be getting ready to open for business. I hoped to ask him a couple more questions; because a few days had passed, there was a chance he might recall more details about the night Viola died. Rather than getting closer to figuring out what had happened to her, it seemed like everything was becoming more complicated. First, Marilyn implied Sarah might be guilty of murder, then Sarah suggested Viola's death may have been merely an accident. Meanwhile, Hunter had built his case against Aunt Constance, who had no alibi, plus her hat found at the scene was considered evidence. Hunter loved physical evidence. Of course, the painting left at the lodge that portrayed Viola's body in the lake muddied the waters. On top of all that, the Sisterhood had shoved some frivolous lawsuit at us. I was desperate to learn anything that might help clear Aunt Constance's name and uncover who killed Viola. No doubt, when the coroner finished his report, her death would be confirmed a homicide. My gut told me as much.

Stepping onto the deck, I scanned the area side to side, back to front. No sign of Dewey. My shoulders drooped, and I let out a sigh. "Well, maybe tomorrow. Right, Max?" Within seconds, he gave a hard tug at the leash, and I lost my grip. "Hey! Where do you think you're going?" I hurried across the deck to follow him. He scurried toward Dewey's shack enclosure.

"Why didn't I think of that?" Dewey admitted he sometimes spent the night and slept inside his shack where he kept a cot. Plus, his car wasn't parked in the lot. I gave my head a mental slap. My brain was obviously not keeping up to speed. Maybe that extra cup of coffee would've helped.

I came within inches of the doorway when Max came trotting out, holding the strap of a large object in his mouth. My eyes widened as, all at once, I recognized the oversized crimson red bag Viola had been carrying the night of our painting event. I lowered my head when Max dropped the bag at my feet and wagged his tail. My mind raced toward the implication of what this meant. Not exactly the evidence I had expected to uncover, but selfishly, I was glad to find anything that put Aunt Constance in the clear. I liked Dewey. He was a kind man with a big heart, always helping others. Maybe he tipped the bottle too much on occasion, but I'd never heard a story about him getting into fights or acting out because of it.

I stared at the bag without picking it up. Sure, he could've found it after Viola's death, the next morning. But if that was true, why hadn't he told Hunter when questioned? Omission of the facts was still deceit, and some of the time, people lied to cover up a guilty act.

I glanced down once more and shooed Max away before he could pick up the bag and carry it off. Pulling my phone out of my jacket pocket, I punched in Hunter's number. I listened to his voicemail pick up and cursed under my breath. I tugged Max along and reentered the tiny structure to see if anything else belonging to Viola was hidden inside. "Hi, it's Chloe. You need to come to the ferry dock right away. I found evidence that could help Viola's case." I hung up and dug underneath a pile of papers, where I found a half-empty bag of Cheetos. "So, this is what you were after. Huh, Max?"

The sound of a car engine drew near. I peered out the window to see Hunter's vehicle pull into the lot. "That was quick." I snatched Max off the floor and carried him outside. We stepped next to Viola's bag and waited while Hunter walked to meet us. A tiny rumble came from Max's throat, but he stopped short of a growl or bark.

Hunter hitched his thumb over his shoulder. "I was at Spill the Beans having a cup of coffee and chatting with the owner when you called. What's the evidence?" He reached out to scratch the top of Max's head. "Hey, little guy. How's it going?"

I blinked. Max didn't flinch or snap or bite. This was a first. Max usually took his time before letting anyone get close. What was it they said about a dog's instinct? Maybe Hunter had passed the test and gained Max's approval, which told me Hunter was one of the good guys. Regaining my composure, I pointed at my feet. "Viola's bag."

"How do you know it's hers?" His brows knitted in an angry line. "You didn't look inside, did you? Or touch it. That would be tampering with evidence."

I huffed and shifted Max in my arms as he wiggled to escape. "No. Of course not. I have better sense than that." Indignation burned through me. "She had that bag with her the evening of our painting event at the lodge. Crimson-red, oversized, designer bag. See?" I pointed. "The designer's name is etched in gold letters at the top. I mean, is there really a chance someone else carried one just like this to the ferry and left it?"

He shrugged. "Maybe." He returned to his car and brought back a large evidence bag.

"*Maybe?* Seriously?" My voice cracked.

He enclosed Viola's bag safely, then stood. A grin spread across his face, and he winked. "Sorry. Couldn't resist. I'll get this back to the lab and have it tested. Was it lying on the deck when you found it?"

I opened my mouth to explain, when a car pulled up alongside Hunter's. Dewey popped out of the driver's side. I gulped to swallow the lump lodged in my throat. He was walking right into a Detective Barrett ambush and hadn't a clue. I quickly recovered and, speaking out the side of mouth, I mumbled, "Max found the bag hidden inside Dewey's shack, er, I mean that tiny building behind us."

Hunter shifted his weight and held up one arm. "Hey, Dewey. Just in time."

"Time?" Dewey's attention turned from Hunter to me and back again. "For what?" His gaze now fixed on the evidence bag Hunter lifted.

I was surprised. Not a flicker, not even a flinch. Just a frown on his face as his forehead wrinkled. He looked genuinely puzzled.

"Do you know anything about this?" Hunter waved the bag.

With a wide-eyed stare Dewey slowly gave his head a shake. "No. Can't say I do. Where'd you find it?"

I figured either Dewey must make a killing at playing card games with that poker face, or he was telling the truth. Before Hunter could say a word, I blurted out, "Max found it in there." I pointed to Dewey's shack.

Hunter scratched the back of his neck. "Are you saying you don't know anything about this red bag or how it came to be in what you call your shack?"

"That's what I'm saying. Yes, sir. I never seen that before, and somebody musta put it in my place, which they ought not to do because it's private. Nobody but me goes in there. Nobody, no, sir." He backed away, holding both palms out in front of him.

"Now, Mr. Sawyer—Dewey—I'm not accusing you of anything. What I'm trying to do is figure this out. Asking questions is how I get answers. Understand?" Hunter inched forward.

Thank goodness, Dewey dropped his arms and paused his steps because I felt sure Hunter would've run after him if he'd tried to flee.

"Well, then, are we finished? 'Cause I got a ferry to run. Been trying to get the back part of the deck floor cleaned in the morning before folks start rolling in, but now it'll have to wait another day, thanks to all this jibber-jabber. Passengers dropping food without so much as a care is shameful. That's what it is. Shameful. Leaving all sorts of things behind so's I had to start a lost and found, you know." He grumbled as he marched onto the deck and past us, with his chin down and eyes averted.

"Guess we can continue the conversation later, if need be." Hunter held up the evidence bag once more. "I'll send this to the lab and see what comes up." He stared at Dewey, who went about his business.

"Chloe, can I speak with you privately?" Hunter nodded his head to one side.

"Sure." I set Max down and secured the leash. We followed Hunter out to the parking lot. Turning, I watched one, then two more vehicles get in line as Dewey waved them onto the deck. My guess was Dewey would plan to leave town, if he was the one who had hidden the bag. He wasn't the sort to survive a police interrogation or jail. Dewey was a solitary soul and too sensitive, which puzzled me. How could such a person kill another human being, then act as if nothing had happened? Of course there was another possible explanation. He had seen or witnessed the whole incident—Viola struggling with some-one before ending up facedown in the lake. At least, that's how I pictured the scene since the idea she'd had an accident seemed less and less conceivable to me. If only I could be absolutely certain Dewey was innocent. I worried my friendship with him kept me from being objective.

"I thought maybe I'd finish that coffee with you at Spill the Beans? I mean, if you want to and aren't busy?" He cleared his throat and suddenly stooped down to pet Max. "Cute. He's yours, right?"

I hid the grin by reaching up to scratch my nose. "Yeah, he's my buddy. We go back several years." I giggled as Max sat up on his hind legs and licked Hunter's face. "I think he likes you."

Hunter gave Max a final pat on the head and stood once more. "I get that a lot. I'm a likeable sort of guy."

"Do you have a pet?" I sidetracked the conversation.

"No. I work long hours. It wouldn't be fair to leave one alone all day or night." He raked his fingers through his hair. "About that coffee, I should go. I forgot to pay, and I don't want to get a reputation for being the sort of cop who expects free stuff."

I anchored my fist on my hip. "Seriously, do cops expect that kind of thing? Seems pretty shady to me." A grin wiggled its way onto my lips. "I'd join you, but I promised Izzie I'd be at the shop in . . ." I glanced at my watch. "And I'm late." I tugged on Max's leash and led him across the drive toward Whisper Cove Lane. "Bye, Hunter! Enjoy your coffee." I waved.

"I could give you a lift," he called out.

"We're fine. Thanks." I didn't need Izzie or Willow peering out the shop window to see Hunter dropping us off. The more I avoided their teasing jabs, the better.

We rounded the corner and jogged toward Paint with a View. "Sorry, Max. You're spending the morning at the shop. I'll take you home at lunchtime." Looking down at him, I wasn't watching as I collided with someone coming from the opposite direction. "Good grief! I'm so sorry." I clutched a hand to my throat and stared straight at Spencer's irritated scowl, deepening the creases along her forehead. "Spencer." I stepped backward. "How great is this? A cousin reunion." My voice fizzled at the end, and I shrugged to dismiss the awkward moment.

Spencer flipped her long curls over her shoulder. "Cousin reunion. That's so clever. You always did have a way with words, Chloe." She leaned in to air-kiss each of my cheeks. "Are you on your way inside? I wanted to have a talk with both you and Izzie."

"Um, yeah, sure. I mean, we are kind of busy." I hurried along behind her as she marched her lanky, mile-long legs up the steps and pushed open the door with unnecessary force.

"Wow, you ladies are impressive. Just look at this place." She twirled around on her spiked heels with both arms held high.

"Spencer." Izzie squealed and tackled her with a tight hug. "You look amazing." She stroked Spencer's face with the back of one hand. "How *do* you keep your skin so soft? Are you staying at Aunt Constance's house? It's so good to see you."

I turned away, too embarrassed to watch. Izzie had always gotten along well with Spencer, but she did all the work. I wasn't sure Spencer appreciated the effort. They were alike in many ways, except Izzie didn't have that same self-serving, manipulative personality. Thank goodness. I heaved a sigh. What was it they said? *Forgive and forget. The past is the past. Let bygones be bygones. Turn the other cheek.* Maybe I was acting too petty or feeling insecure, but some memories were etched in my brain like an ugly tattoo, a permanent reminder of the past.

"Actually, I just got a room at the hotel in Laurel Bay. Not as close as I'd like to be to Whisper Cove, but closer than Mom's house in Mayville. I have to oversee the construction of my shop, right? You know, this will be such fun. You're right, Chloe. It's a cousin reunion. We'll be the coziest business neighbors too. We can help each other out. I'll suggest to my customers if they enjoy painting and drinking, they should check out Paint with a View for an event. And you can return the favor by letting your customers know about my shop, A Stitch in Time. Isn't that the cutest name ever?" Spencer clasped her hands together.

My brain stalled on the words *neighbors* and *my shop* since that meant Megan was right. Spencer was building her shop on Sammy's lot, which she had almost certainly purchased. Her scheme had already been set in motion. I opened and shut my mouth several times, trying to wrap my mind around the idea while looking for the holes in her plan.

"Hey! That's great. Isn't that great, Chloe?" Izzie gave me an encouraging smile.

"Yeah, really great. Congrats, Spencer. That's a huge step. I mean, running a craft shop without experience—and what about investment? Takes lots of cash." I stepped over to one of the stools and hitched my rear on the seat.

Izzie cleared her throat and gave a slight shake of her head, along with a reproachful glare.

"I'm just complimenting Spencer on her courage to leave a successful career in Los Angeles and jump into a risky and costly venture." I smiled.

Spencer blushed and fingered the strap of her bag. Her chin lifted. "I'm not so sure you meant that as a compliment. Risky business ventures aren't unfamiliar to me, you know. I deal with them all the time. Besides, I love a new challenge, and living closer to family is a plus. I think we should be celebrating this moment." She let go of a rattled breath. "Now, enough talk about business. What I really came to talk about is my mother."

I had to admire the swift segue, taking the focus off herself, especially to talk about Aunt Constance.

"Have you spoken with her since you got back?" Izzie's lips pressed in a tight line.

"I have." Spencer dropped her bag on the table as she sat in a chair. "She was very upset and repeated over and over how she was going to jail." She threw up her arms. "How could you two let that happen?"

I threw Izzie a puzzled glance and shrugged. I had no clue where Spencer was going with that question, other than some place not good.

"Let what happen?" Izzie finally spoke.

"You knew she was upset at your paint party after the argument with that director. Still, you allowed her to leave without taking even a few seconds to make sure she was okay. How could you?" A headshake followed along with a tsk-tsk.

Was she serious? Resentment surged through me as if a spark of anger had suddenly lit. Saying it was our fault she was a suspect was totally out of line. "Did you ask her about that night, like where she went after leaving the lodge? There's an hour missing from her account of that evening, Spencer. She can't or won't explain it, only that she drove around to clear her head. It's no wonder Hunter is highly suspicious." My voice tinged with irritation as it pitched higher.

Izzie stepped in front of me. "What Chloe means is we're frustrated too. We're trying really hard to help your mom, but she needs to do her part and give Hunter a solid alibi." She touched Spencer's arm. "Hey, we're worried right along with you, but it'll be okay. She's innocent. We know that too."

Spencer sniffed. "Is she? How do you know for sure?"

I blinked. If this had happened to one of our parents, I'd have total confidence in their innocence.

"Well." Spencer sprang out of her seat and grabbed her bag. "I should go. I have a meeting with the construction company to go over plans for my shop." She leveled her gaze at me with that last comment.

"Good luck," Izzie called out as Spencer disappeared through the doorway.

"Can you believe her? That took some serious nerve, blaming us like that." I struggled for my kinder self to take control.

"Yeah, she's not being fair, but she's upset." Izzie picked at a hangnail on her thumb.

"Of course, when Aunt Constance is unhappy, then Spencer can't get whatever she wants," I quipped.

"I'll admit Spencer has a history of asking for, sometimes demanding, a lot. Especially since Uncle David died." Izzie grabbed her phone. "I'm calling Aunt Constance to make sure she's okay."

"Good idea. While you're talking to her, I'll call to see if I can warn Ross. Chances are, Spencer will pay him a visit too, and who knows what accusations she might throw at him?"

This visit triggered my memory of the wake we'd had for Uncle David. The blowout between Aunt Constance and Spencer was both uncomfortable and embarrassing. Even though they'd talked privately in the next room, everyone who'd attended could hear their shouts. Spencer had refused to accept the terms of the will. She had demanded her share of the inheritance immediately, but Aunt Constance held firm on her husband's wishes. Spencer wouldn't receive any money left to her until she turned thirty. It didn't take much of a guess as to why Uncle David had set those terms. Spencer hadn't exactly been careful with her money or lifestyle during her late teens and early twenties. Most likely, he hoped that, with time and living independently, Spencer would become more responsible. I wasn't so optimistic. In two years, she'd turn thirty, and I hadn't noticed much improvement. However, maybe I was wrong. She'd only been back to visit a few times in the past couple of years. She could have saved enough to take on this business venture without any handouts from her mother. I groaned and walked back to the storage room to take inventory of our supplies. Two things I was sure of: First, Aunt Constance didn't need any extra stress or distractions. Not when she had a murder rap hanging over her head. Second, Spencer living in the area, with a shop close to ours, where we'd see each other almost every day, would be a challenge.

Before I had the chance to call Ross, my phone buzzed. I recognized the number and picked up. "Hi, Hunter. Did you find out any more about Viola's bag?"

"No, but I did get a call from the lab about something else." The crackling sound of paper filled my ear.

I pulled bottles of paint from a box and shoved them on the shelf as I tensed. I'd have felt more confident if he'd started with, *"I've got great news."*

"One of the items inside your aunt's car causes concern. I'm sorry to say, analysis of all that evidence the team collected took time, and the lab's been slammed with cases. Chloe, there was a glove found underneath the back seat."

"Aunt Constance leaves things in her car all the time. I know. I've ridden with her." I rushed my words, hoping that what my gut told me wasn't true. He wouldn't call about anything belonging to her. My breath hitched. Unless there were traces of blood on it.

"I'm afraid that's not the case. Chloe, the glove is embroidered with the initials *VMF*."

Chapter Eleven

Izzie and I sat like bookends on either side of Aunt Constance. The clock located on the mantel in her living room chimed nine times. I stifled a yawn. Worrying about Hunter's discovery of Viola's glove had caused me to toss and turn all night.

Spencer hadn't answered her phone when I'd called earlier this morning. Frustrated after trying her number three times, I had given up. Aunt Constance would miss her daughter's support at a time like this. I reminded myself Spencer had no idea what was going on with Hunter's latest find and how it implicated Aunt Constance. Still, irritation colored my mood.

This morning had been the first opportunity that Hunter had to talk to the person who'd become his prime suspect. Poor Aunt Constance. After several failed attempts to contact her yesterday, Hunter was not a happy man. I could tell by the edgy tone of his voice when we had spoken last night.

Unfortunately for Hunter, Aunt Constance had been without her phone for several hours. In her absentmindedness, probably as a result of how unsettled her life was right now, she'd left the phone at the grocery store yesterday afternoon, then spent the entire evening searching for it. By the time she'd remembered where she'd last had it, the store had closed.

As it was, I had finally gotten a hold of Aunt Constance early this morning, to pass along the news about Viola's glove. At once, she broke down and cried. The incessant sobs made her end of the conversation confusing, with lots of incoherent babble. I gave up and told her Izzie and I would be right over. No surprise, Hunter showed up at the house minutes later.

The tea kettle whistled, and I jumped out of my seat. "I'll make tea. Chamomile to calm us, or at least me. I really need calming. Anyone else?" I shifted my gaze around the room.

Aunt Constance wiggled her hand. "I'll take mine with a shot of brandy."

"But it's only nine in the morning," I said, which earned me a deathlike stare. I gave her a thumbs-up. "One spiked tea, coming up."

"Grab me a water from the fridge, please," Izzie said. "How about you, Hunter?"

He shook his head. "If we could, I'd like to get started with a few questions."

"Wait until I get back, okay?" I jogged to the kitchen, poured two cups of tea, added a teaspoon of brandy to one, and placed both on a tray. Stuffing a bottle of water in my back pocket, I hurried back to the room. "Here you go," I said as I handed each of them their beverage.

Hunter held up his notepad and pen. "Now, I was about to ask—" He was interrupted when the doorbell rang, and he fell back against the chair and groaned.

Before any of us could answer, Ross stepped inside. "Don't worry, Constance. I'll take it from here." He swiveled to face Hunter. "Have you read Mrs. Abbington her rights?"

"Have I . . .?" Hunter threw up his arms and grunted. "No, I haven't read the Miranda warning to *Mrs. Abbington* because I'm not here to arrest her. Just to ask a few questions, if you don't mind."

With curled lips, Ross folded his arms over his chest. "That depends on the questions. I'll stop this interrogation at any hint of impropriety and if my client's rights are being violated."

Hunter scratched his jaw. "Just a couple of questions, Attorney. Nothing to break a sweat over. Okay?"

"I'm simply looking after my client, Detective. You understand." Ross relaxed his shoulders and smiled while taking a seat next to me.

I released my breath, and the tension eased out. The surly behavior between them seemed to be over. Why it had even started, I didn't know.

Aunt Constance gripped my hand. "Here goes. True confession time."

As she slid a quick glance my way, I shot her a puzzled look. Whatever she meant by that remark, I could only guess it must involve the glove, which might also explain where she'd been during that missing hour.

"As you probably already learned"—Hunter's eyes sparked without casting his look of annoyance at me or Izzie—"my guys found this underneath the back seat of your car." He held up the evidence bag with the glove inside. "The initials *VMF* are embroidered on the glove. I don't suppose you can explain how it got in your vehicle?"

Several heart-pounding seconds passed before Aunt Constance cleared her throat and shrugged. "Not a clue, though I imagine Viola could've dropped it when I gave her a ride to Bellows Lodge for the paint event."

Hunter's eyebrow inched up. "In the back seat?"

Aunt Constance squirmed and shifted her rear end and sipped her tea without a word.

"I think that's enough. If my client says she doesn't have a clue, then she doesn't know," Ross interjected.

Hunter leaned back in his chair. He ran his tongue across his lower lip. "I think your client could explain more. For instance, did Viola ride in the back seat to the event? I mean, that would make sense since the glove was found there. I'm simply trying to clarify."

"Or maybe Viola put her bag in the back seat. You know it was pretty big, almost the size of an overnight case," Izzie said. "Maybe her glove dropped when she reached in to grab her bag."

"Excellent theory, Izzie," Ross added. "What about that, Detective?"

"According to my team's report, the glove was underneath the seat. If she dropped it, the glove would've landed on the floor mat."

"Oh dear." Aunt Constance pressed both hands to her cheeks. "I'm feeling flushed and a bit faint. Maybe the brandy wasn't such a good idea."

"It was only a teaspoonful." I touched her forehead. "You don't seem hot, but maybe you should go lie down."

"Chloe's right. Besides, my client has answered your question to the best of her knowledge. I think we're done here," Ross said.

Hunter's jaw grew taut. He gripped his thighs and stood.

I kept a wary eye on him while he struggled to keep his cool. "We don't want another fainting spell. That's for sure." That appeared to calm him, and he gave me a slight nod of the chin. "Great. Aunt Constance, let's get you upstairs."

"But—" Ross started.

"You can speak with her later." I gave him my don't-mess-with-me look. "I'm not sure what's going on between you two, but figure it out, and manage a little patience while you're at it. Okay?"

Without waiting for either of them to respond, Izzie took Aunt Constance's arm and led her up the stairs while I went to the kitchen to rummage in the fridge for something warm and comforting that she would eat. I worried this was far from over. Viola's glove being in the back seat of Aunt Constance's car meant something. One more piece of the puzzle to figure out, and right now, Aunt Constance's refusing to talk wasn't helping.

I grabbed a container with what looked like soup and pulled off the lid. I gave the contents a sniff and wrinkled my nose. "Yuck. How old is this anyway?" I peeked underneath and on the sides, but no date label was attached. Dumping the contents down the drain, I tossed the empty container in the trash. In the cupboard was a microwavable packet of chicken noodle soup. I poured the contents and water in a bowl, then set the microwave. While looking for a paper towel or napkin, my eye caught sight of a folded piece of paper tucked in a corner. Curious, I unfolded it and read the message scribbled inside. I chewed on my lip, then stuffed the note in my pocket, puzzling over the contents. I carried the bowl of soup upstairs.

"Hot soup is here." I set the bowl on the table next to my aunt's bed. "You know, you really should check your fridge. I found a container of something spoiled." I shuddered.

Aunt Constance's brow knitted. "I can't imagine why, though I haven't been checking all the containers that have been delivered in the past couple of days. Doesn't make sense why anyone would give me spoiled food." She sat in the rocking chair next to the table. "My neighbors have been so nice. A few ladies from the Sisterhood have even stopped in to offer their help, which I don't need, obviously. Lots of casseroles and desserts. Anyway, I won't be cooking for a week."

I fingered the note in my pocket. "Has Marilyn been stopping by?" I handed her a napkin and the bowl of soup.

Aunt Constance sniffed. "Every day, sometimes more than once. The woman is generous with her time, but maybe a little less would be better." She took a sip. "Trying to feed me, tucking me into bed, drawing me a bath, and—well, I shouldn't complain. She's only trying to help, but I'm not a child."

"All the help in the world won't be good enough if Hunter doesn't find the killer. I'm worried for you, Aunt Constance." Izzie turned down the bedcovers.

I stared at our aunt, who set the bowl back on the table, then slid into bed. Tucking the blanket underneath her chin, she ignored the soup.

"Aren't you worried? As I see it, Hunter is building a strong case against you with each piece of evidence that pops up. Not a good sign." I leaned down to plant a kiss on her cheek. "We love you and only want to keep you safe."

"Everything will work out. You'll see. I'm not worried at all. Now, I'd like to be alone to rest for a bit. You understand."

She closed her eyes. After a few seconds, one lid slid open. "Well?"

"Oh sure. We're leaving. You feel better and forget about all that talk. Hunter's just looking for answers." I backed up a few steps and straight into the vanity table. Turning, I noticed a small paper bag with Halloween stickers pasted on it. "What's this?" I laughed. "Someone delivering treats for Halloween a week early?" I peeked inside. A dozen or so peppermint candies filled the bag, and an orange sticky note shaped like a pumpkin was tucked inside.

"It's nothing. I found it outside my front door after getting home from my shopping trip last evening. Some neighbor kids playing a prank, no doubt." Aunt Constance closed her eyes once again. "Nothing more than that."

"What's the sticky note for?" Curious, I plucked it out of the bag and read a typed message. *Trick or treat, which shall it be? If you don't tell the truth, you'll soon see.* I shivered. "Aunt Constance, this doesn't seem like nothing to me. Izzie, take a look." I handed her the note.

She gasped. "Oh wow. 'If you don't tell the truth?' What does that mean? This reads like a threat, Aunt Constance. You should show it to Hunter."

"I agree. Whoever wrote this isn't playing around, what with words like that." I patted the top of the blanket where I figured her arm was resting. "You have to tell Hunter."

"I'm telling you it's a child's prank. You know how they act around Halloween. All fun and games." Aunt Constance snapped open her eyes and moved beyond my reach. "Now, you both need to go and get on with your day. Don't you have a party to plan? What about the Hallows Eve celebration coming up? Plenty to do to prepare for that. I'll be supervising from my bedside and on my phone until I'm through convalescing."

"Fine, but I'm taking this and giving it to Hunter." I clutched the bag and note in my hands. "My guess is this isn't a coincidence. Someone either thinks you know something about Viola's death that you're not telling or believes you killed her."

Constance sputtered and gasped. "That's ridiculous. I'm not, and I don't know anything."

"Of course you don't." I tapped the note. "But whoever wrote this thinks you do. That's the problem."

"Aunt Constance, the person who left this on your doorstep sounds angry, maybe angry enough to do something rash." Izzie twisted the tissue she held.

Aunt Constance widened her eyes. She pulled the blanket up to her chin. "Maybe you're right. Give your detective friend the bag and note. Chloe, tell your Ross he needs to call me."

I rolled my eyes without reminding her, again, that Ross and I were no longer a thing. "We'll let you rest. Keep the door locked and your phone on, in case one of us calls. We love you." I closed the bedroom door and followed Izzie downstairs.

"That's so creepy." Izzie rubbed her arms. "Gives me chills."

"Yes. I doubt it's a harmless trick-or-treat prank." I scowled, and giving the matter a second thought, I pulled a tissue out of my back pocket and wrapped it around the threatening note. "Should've thought of that before. They'll have to check all of our prints to find the sender's."

"*If* that person left prints. I certainly wouldn't if I meant to threaten somebody." Izzie opened the front door and stepped aside for me to pass through. She turned the key to lock the door, then followed me to the driveway.

"Good point. If there are prints, either our trick-or-treater isn't too bright, or this really was meant to be an innocent prank, which, like I said, is highly doubtful." Getting into the car, I stuffed the candy bag and the note wrapped in tissue inside the glove compartment.

"Let's think positive. The lab will find someone's prints other than ours or Aunt Constance's, and Hunter will track down the trick-or-treat prankster." She turned up the car heater and snuggled deeper into her seat. "Do you really think the person who wrote the note knows something?"

"About Viola's death? Oh yeah. I really do. And take a look at this." I handed her the note from Marilyn that I'd found in the kitchen, then backed out of the drive and nearly into a car passing by. I gasped as the driver blasted the horn once and then again, as if to make his point clear. In my rearview mirror, I spotted a powder-blue convertible with a white leather top as it continued down the street.

"That was rather rude." Izzie scowled.

"Yeah, sure was." Inching out of the drive, I made a slow turn into the street. At the end of the block, I let the car idle and stared at the rearview mirror. The convertible had turned around and pulled into Aunt Constance's driveway.

"Why aren't we moving?" Izzie asked.

"Look in your side mirror." I nodded. By now, the driver had exited the convertible. Tall, smartly dressed, and with a short bob of silver hair. "Marilyn Pervis," I whispered.

"That's her? Guess she didn't want to miss her daily visit. Do you think we should go back and tell her Aunt Constance is resting?"

"Maybe we've done enough for one morning." Not giving the matter more thought, I headed for the highway, traveling south. One of my gut feelings rippled through me. I couldn't pin down exactly what or why, but something more than the candygram was bugging me.

"Wow. Marilyn really is the clingy type. 'Let me know if you need anything, day or night. Call me, and I'll be at your door in five minutes. I care about you, Constance, and would never let anyone hurt you.' No wonder Aunt Constance thinks Marilyn comes on too strong. Now, I wish we'd gone back to the house and shared a few words with her about personal boundaries."

"Oh, I bet Aunt Constance wouldn't hesitate giving Marilyn the heave-ho if she felt like it." I chuckled. "Did I tell you she compared Marilyn to Uncle Seymour?"

"Seriously? Ha. Great-uncle Seymour. Those stories about him are entertaining, but in a scary way." Izzie grinned.

The car speaker rang out with a phone call. I eyed the name lighting the display screen. "Hunter. I should answer, right?" I dreaded talking to him for several reasons. I'd had my fill of both him and Ross sniping at each other. Plus, I needed to relax a bit and take a break from all things about murder. The last words I wanted to hear were more complaints about Aunt Constance being uncooperative. Did he think I didn't know that?

"Yeah, you probably should." Before I could react, Izzie reached across me and punched the button to answer the call, nearly making me steer off the road.

"Geesh. Be careful, will you?" I steadied my hands on the wheel and kept the car in my lane. "Hi, Hunter. What's up?"

"Have you left your aunt's house yet?" His voice crackled.

"Your connection is breaking up. Where are you?" I glanced at Izzie, who shrugged.

"At the ferry dock. Chloe, the lab came back with findings on the wood fibers. They don't match the wood from the deck. The coroner is classifying this as a homicide. Right now, we're searching the area again to look for anything we might've missed."

"Like a weapon." My heart raced. Even though I'd expected Viola had been murdered, I had hoped Sarah Gilley was right.

And now the idea of Viola dying from an unfortunate accident had, figuratively speaking, taken a nosedive into the water.

Chapter Twelve

The wind gusted and scattered leaves across the ground. An autumn chill from earlier that morning had turned almost frigid. I hugged Max to my chest and hurried inside the house. After getting home from Aunt Constance's, I'd promised Izzie I'd meet her at the shop as soon as I finished my conversation with Hunter. We had pumpkin carving to finish and decorations to hang in the window. The festival was on Saturday, less than a week away. Plus, we had the Trick Your Pumpkin painting event on Friday. As Aunt Constance reminded us, we had plenty to do.

"You be a good boy and keep warm." I ruffled Max's fur and kissed the top of his head. He let go with a *woof*, then licked my hand. "I love you too."

Grabbing my bag off the hall table, I hollered, "I'm leaving. Don't wait up." Mom and Dad were cozied up on the family-room sofa, watching a documentary on how art culture influences society's behavior. Or something like that. I replayed my conversation with Hunter when he had stopped by earlier to pick up the treat bag and note. I had asked what the wood-fiber results could mean for Aunt Constance, but he'd refused to comment. Instead, the conversation had stayed in the lane of pleasant, everyday topics and ended with an agreement to meet for coffee sometime. So much for being open and honest with each other.

I hopped in my car and sped across town toward the shop. As I stopped for a red light at the boulevard intersection, something caught my eye, or I should say some*one*—no, *two* some-ones. Sarah Gilley stood arm in arm with a man outside Spill the Beans. They smiled and chatted. Then, as if her companion had said something funny, Sarah threw back her head to laugh. I shuddered. The grouch could manage to turn on some charm and wear a smile. Go figure. As the light turned green, and I waited for the car in front of me to move forward, I took one last look, and my mouth dropped open. The man had his arms wrapped tightly around Sarah while he locked lips with her in a way that could only be described as passionate.

The car behind me beeped, and I pressed my foot on the gas pedal. My brain reeled with all sorts of thoughts as I struggled to make sense of what was going on in front of the coffee shop for all to see. I drove onto Whisper Cove Lane and steered into a parking spot. Hurrying to the front door of the shop, I pulled up the collar of my coat to shelter against the wind that stung my cheeks like shards of ice. I glanced up at the sky. Huge dark clouds drifted across and cast a gloominess that fit the Halloween season. Shivering, I entered the shop.

"I'm here. Finally." Shedding my gloves, I warmed my cheeks with the palms of my hands. "It's positively nasty out there. What's the forecast? Please don't say snow."

Izzie twisted her head around to stare at me while her hands were busy stapling a string of orange and yellow lights to the wall. "No snow, but a storm is coming off the lake. Everyone is panicking about the decorations set up outside."

"Maybe we should go help? I noticed a half a dozen or so people scrambling to anchor down items, especially those blow-up figures." I hadn't yet removed my coat.

"Willow left a few minutes ago to check. She should be back soon." Izzie hopped off the step stool and laid the staple gun on the counter.

"You will never guess who I saw on the way over here." I unzipped my coat, not wanting to sweat while waiting for Willow. "Sarah Gilley getting cozy with a man outside Spill the Beans." I pulled off my gloves.

Izzie shrugged. "So? She has a man friend. Kind of surprising, considering her gruff personality, but there's nothing groundbreaking about it."

I wiggled my eyebrows. "Ah, but it's *who* the man is that's groundbreaking, or at least raises my curiosity. Wink Lawrence."

Izzie gasped. "Wow. Isn't she older than him? I mean, lots older?"

"Maybe a little, but that's not where my mind went. Think about it, Izzie. First, Wink comes here spouting off about Aunt Constance being guilty of Viola's murder. Then at the memorial, Sarah tries to convince me Viola's death was an accident. What if Sarah killed her, and Wink is trying to cover for his lover by pointing a finger at Aunt Constance?" The idea that I could be close to an answer in this case sent a rush of adrenaline through my insides.

"I don't know." Izzie's head bobbed back and forth.

"Even Marilyn Pervis thinks Sarah could be the killer. I should call Hunter."

"Marilyn?" Izzie scoffed. "She's guessing and has no proof, kind of like you. Sorry, but Hunter wants evidence. That's all he'll take seriously. You know it's true."

"Yeah." My shoulders slumped. "Still, I'm keeping a close eye on the two lovebirds in case there is something going on besides them playing kissy-face."

A gust of wind blew a stack of paper towels across the floor as Willow pushed open the door. "The storm's coming," she gasped. "Everyone is running around trying to catch their decorations before they end up in the lake."

"Then we should get out there." Izzie pulled on her jacket and gloves as the lights flickered.

"Oh boy. That's not good." As soon as I finished speaking, the flickering lights popped, and we were left in the dark. I inched my way forward with my hand on the counter to guide me. "Izzie, are the flashlights in the drawer behind you?"

"Got them." She turned one to shine on me.

I tented a hand over my eyes. "Aim that lower, would you?"

"Sorry. Here's one for you. Willow, you take the other," Izzie said.

"Who keeps three flashlights?" Willow smacked the casing to coax hers to light.

"Wait awhile. You'll get to experience all her extreme behaviors. Overprepared doesn't even begin to cover it," I quipped with a grin, bumping my hip against my sister's. "Right, Izzie?"

"Just remember. We share the same genes. Now, let's go rescue some runaway goblins and ghosts." She held the beam of her flashlight on the door and led the way.

My hair whipped in my eyes. I brushed it back and pulled up the hood of my jacket. The entire area along the lake was bathed in light. Someone had placed LED lanterns in trees and on tables and benches. Dozens of people scattered across the lawn, from one end of Artisan Alley to the other. They snatched up all the flyaway decorations they could carry and stuffed them into garbage bags and huge trash containers dragged outside from shops. My heart fell. In a matter of minutes, all the work everyone had done to prepare for the festival and decorate for Halloween was almost a total wash.

Izzie ran to catch up with Megan near the lakeshore while Willow joined a group of teens who had rescued the scattered pumpkins that once lined the dock. I peered across the area near the path leading up to the ferry. A few of the inflatable figures had blown in that direction. I snatched a garbage bag from the stack, pinned down by a rock, and jogged across the lawn. As I grew closer, a familiar figure came into view. Near the storage shed, situated yards from the ferry dock, Ross leaned over to pick up paper lanterns that the wind had torn off the trees.

"Hey. What a nice guy you are, helping out like this," I greeted him.

"Oh! Chloe." He chuckled and wiped his forehead. "Glitter. Seems to be all over the place."

"That would be our fault. Izzie and I used glitter at our last paint event. It sticks like glue to whatever comes near." I folded my bottom lip underneath my tongue while I thought about this morning. "Things okay between you and Hunter?"

He glanced up, and a confused look knitted his brow. "Sure. Why?"

"You two kind of snapped at each other. About the case, I mean." Was that what I meant? I picked up an orange streamer and stuffed it into the garbage bag. "So, what was it? Why were you acting like that?"

Ross stood straight and brushed off the glitter clinging to his jacket. "Chloe, I don't know what you're talking about. You know me. I stand up for my clients. That has nothing to do with my feelings toward Hunter."

I scratched behind one ear. "Uh-huh. I saw the look. Just now."

"What look?" He scowled.

"Don't deny it. First your nose twitches, and then you blink your eyes at least five times, really fast, before your face goes blank. You can't hide when you're lying. Not to me." I wagged a finger.

"Attorneys don't have a tell. We can't afford that risk in the courtroom." He moved closer to the storage shed, picking up any debris he found and stuffing it in the bag.

"Maybe you're right. In other news, what do you think about that candygram Aunt Constance received? Innocent prankster or dangerous stalker?" I stepped next to him.

"Here." He handed me a mostly deflated ghost. "It's leaking air. Probably got pricked by a branch."

"Ross." I tipped my head and sighed. However, my thoughts were sidetracked by the strained, high-pitched whimper coming from the direction of the shed. "Is that a dog?" I ran toward the building, with Ross following right behind me. The sky opened up, and tiny pebbles of hail fell. I flipped my hood back up again and tightened the drawstrings.

Ross skirted around me. Gripping the handle, he gave it a hard yank. The door swung open, and the whimpering grew louder.

I stooped down and at once felt a wet tongue on my face. I chuckled and cuddled the dog in my arms. "Hey, little one. How'd you end up in here?" I stepped outside. "Ross, could you shine this flashlight on us so we can get a better look?"

"Sure. Hold on a sec."

I stared at a curly-haired brown and white face with a pug nose and long ears. "You are so lucky we found you. Must've been scary inside that shed, huh?" I peeked underneath. "A boy. Well, little guy, we need to get you warmed up. You're shivering."

"The door must've been left open, and then it slammed closed in the storm and trapped him. I'm going to take a quick peek. Maybe there's a leash or something that might tell us who he belongs to," Ross said.

"Hear that? We're going to find out where you live and get you back home." I tucked his head under my chin and held tight while waiting for Ross.

"Well, nothing inside to tell us more about the dog, but I did find this hidden behind a pile of firewood." He held up a wooden boat paddle. "I haven't seen one like this in ages. Looks old."

My eyes grew wider. "Yeah, Mom and Dad kept a pair that belonged to Granddad Abbington." I stepped closer and squinted at the flat end of the paddle. "Is that . . .?"

"Looks like blood, doesn't it?" He turned the paddle and examined it without touching. "Along the one edge." His gaze lifted to stare at me. "Are you thinking what I'm thinking?"

The dog squirmed in my arms, as if he was frightened by the sight of the paddle. I felt the same way as a cold chill ran through me, and one thought entered my mind. "We may have found the weapon used to murder Viola."

* * *

I sat with the dog I'd secretly named Milo, my arms wrapped around him as he cuddled on my lap. He'd stopped shivering but kept his head tucked under my arm.

Next to me, Ross tapped his foot, then checked his watch. "Don't you think he should be here by now? It's been almost an hour."

We were in the shop alone. Izzie had called to check in and explained that she and Willow were going to continue helping the others clean up the storm mess.

"I told you. He had to finish his business in Silver Creek, and the trip to Whisper Cove takes over forty minutes without any traffic." I studied the nervous tapping and poked my finger in his side. "Why are you being impatient? Is there someplace you need to be?"

"I do. I mean, yeah. I have to be someplace and meet someone later. Not much later. More like soon." He scraped a hand along his jaw.

"Huh. Okay, well, then go. I can handle this." A soft breath tickled my arm as Milo snored. At the moment, all I could think of was getting this guy home. His owner had to be frantic.

"No. I'm staying. I need to hear if Hunter has any update on the victim's bag or the glove."

"I hardly think the lab will know anything yet. Look how long it took them to get the report on the wood fibers. Besides, I already asked about the bag yesterday. Hunter told me the lab has been slammed with case evidence." I glanced with a wary eye at the paddle propped up in the corner and thought of Dewey. He kept all his supplies inside the shed. Did he know about the paddle? If that was the weapon used on Viola, and Dewey had murdered her, why would he hide it in the shed where someone could easily find it? After all, he didn't lock the door. Maybe he'd panicked. Maybe he had hidden the bloodied paddle in there and planned to return later and ditch it somewhere else, in a place where no one would find it. *Too late for that now,* I thought.

"Let me just make a quick call." Ross stood and walked to the rear of the shop and through the doorway leading to our storage room.

All I could make out was a murmuring of words. I stretched my neck to hear, trying to keep still and not disturb the bundle of fur sleeping in my lap.

"Are you eavesdropping?" Hunter walked inside.

I jumped in my seat, which woke up Milo, who immediately whimpered. "Sorry, buddy." I stroked his back. "I didn't hear you come in." My face heated.

"That's because you were too busy snooping." Hunter chuckled as he nodded toward the back of the room.

Ross approached. "Did I miss something?" He stuffed the phone in his pocket. "Hey, Barrett. Any updates? Good news to clear my client would be nice."

Hunter took the seat next to me, where Ross had been sitting. "No. The lab techs promise something by tomorrow, but don't hold them to it."

Ross rubbed his fingers along his jaw, staring at Hunter. He opened his mouth for an instant as if to speak, and then, without a word, sat on one of the stools and leaned against the counter.

"Who's this guy?" Hunter smiled and scratched Milo's chin.

"He was in the storage shed, keeping company with the paddle. Poor thing cried. That's how we found him. No ID." I looked sideways. "I don't suppose anyone's reported a missing dog?"

Hunter shrugged. "We get plenty of reports about runaway or missing pets, but none recently. We could take him to the local vet and see if he's microchipped. That might help."

"Maybe you should focus on that paddle?" Ross interrupted. "Asking Dewey Sawyer some questions would be my next move. After all, Chloe tells me he's the one who uses the storage shed. You can see the paddle has blood on the end of it. We're guessing it might be Viola's."

"Is that so?" Hunter shifted his gaze from Ross to me.

"Just a hunch," I said.

"Guesses and hunches won't help solve a case. I'll have one of my guys take it over to the lab. We'll put a rush on it, for all the good it'll do. Meantime, I'll pay Dewey a visit first thing tomorrow morning." Hunter stood and stretched his arms with a yawn. "Been a long day."

"Of course." I handed Milo to Ross. He had fallen back to sleep and didn't stir. "Thanks for coming over, Hunter. We figured you'd want to have the paddle right away."

"Wise decision." Hunter nodded and pulled on a pair of lab gloves before picking up the paddle.

"I'll walk you out."

I heard Ross talking to Milo in a soft tone and smiled. He'd always wanted a pet, but his apartment complex in New York didn't allow them. Zipping up my jacket, I stepped onto the porch. "I don't think Aunt Constance has the strength to swing that paddle. It's really heavy. I mean, if it does turn out to be the weapon, but as you said, the lab has to determine that." My words trailed off and ended with a breathy whistle. "Sorry. Too much going on. And I'm worried about finding Milo's family."

"Milo?" He shifted the paddle from one hand to the other.

"Oh yeah." I laughed. "I named the dog Milo. Sounds better than calling him 'dog' all the time. Right?"

A grin stretched his lips. "Right." Pausing a few seconds, he then hitched a thumb over his shoulder. "I really need to go."

"Sure! Sorry, again, for making you drive down here."

"Not a problem. Talk later. Maybe get that coffee together some morning soon," he hollered while jogging down Artisan Alley toward the parking area. "I'll let you know right away if someone reports a missing dog."

A high-pitched whine came from behind me. I turned to see Milo yawning while Ross snuggled him in his arms. "Thanks." I took Milo and received a lick or two of appreciation.

"What are you going to do?" He tipped his chin at the bundle of fur.

"Keep him until we find out more. Let's hope we do soon." I nuzzled the top of Milo's head. Max might get jealous, but that would pass. Milo was too nice not to like.

"Max will be jealous," Ross said.

"Yeah, I know. He'll adjust. Plenty of love to go around." I skirted past him to step back inside, then pivoted on my heel to face him. "I know you have to get to your meeting. Hope it goes well, and thanks for helping out this evening."

Ross stuffed his hands in his pockets and glanced down at the porch for a second. "Not a problem. I'm glad this guy has a warm place to sleep tonight." He lifted his head and tapped Milo's nose. "Count yourself lucky, pooch. This lady is special and will take great care of you."

"Yes, I will." I rested my chin on Milo's head. "Again, thanks. I was freaking out a little back at the shed, especially after seeing that bloody paddle."

"If you're trying to say that having a man around helps ease your 'freaking out,' as you call it, glad to be your knight in armor." He winked.

"No. That wasn't—can't you just accept the thank-you and not make it about a macho male thing?" My cheeks grew warmer.

"Absolutely. I was only kidding. Look, I need to say something." He shuffled his feet.

"Go ahead. I'm listening." I puzzled over why he was acting nervous. Talking came easily to him, which was a must for trial lawyers.

He tapped his watch and stepped off the porch. "But it'll have to wait. I'm ten minutes overdue for my appointment. I'll call you tomorrow." Waving goodbye, he hurried over to his car.

"That was strange, wasn't it, Milo?" I set him on the floor and walked around the shop to grab what needed to be put away. Pulling out my phone, I sent off a quick text to let Izzie know I was heading home. I didn't bother explaining about Milo and the paddle. She'd find out soon enough this evening.

"Let's get you home for a big bowl of kibble and to meet your new brother." I hefted him in one arm while locking the door. "At least for now, you're one of the family."

Traveling across the boulevard toward Sail Shore Drive, I sorted through all that had happened in the past two days. Finding Viola's bag in Dewey's shack and Viola's glove in Aunt Constance's car, the rather threatening trick-or-treat message left on the doorstep, and then this evening's discovery of a bloody paddle in the storage shed. Was Dewey behind all of it? Could he have planted the glove in Aunt Constance's car? He'd need to have had access to the car, but when? I found it hard to imagine he'd have dared to leave the trick-or-treat message on her doorstep. The risk of being caught in the act would have given him a nervous breakdown. And what about the candy? When we were kids, Izzie had offered Dewey some of her peppermints as a thank-you for fixing her bike chain. He had declined, saying he hated anything with peppermint flavor and how even the smell made him nauseous. If he had delivered the candy, he would've chosen a different kind. The paddle was the most incriminating evidence. No one but Dewey used that storage shed. At least as far as I knew. However, Hunter would say the killer could easily have hidden the paddle in there, since Dewey never locked the door. Same thing with Viola's bag. Slipping it inside the shack would have been easy. Dewey never locked that either. Just like Aunt Constance, Dewey was an easy target to frame as the killer. Or he could be trying to make it look like he was being framed, but he really *was* guilty of the crime. I groaned. Now, I was overthinking it. I turned into the driveway and killed the engine.

Then there was my theory about Wink and Sarah, which further complicated the case. What if she was the suspect Hunter should keep an eye on? Too bad this was all pure conjecture and more like fodder for a soap opera than solid evidence. All of this back-and-forth reasoning was giving me a migraine. I kneaded my temples while staring down at my passenger who sat quietly in his seat.

"I figure this much, Milo. We're dealing with a dangerous and clever killer, which means we have to be very careful." I shuddered at the thought of putting myself in another deadly situation. This past summer's incident had been frightening enough. I came around to the passenger side, swung open the door, and scooped up Milo in my arms. The sooner this case was solved, the safer it would be for all of us.

As we approached the front door, I heard the pounding of footsteps. I turned to see Izzie as she sprinted up the drive. Out on the road, a car horn beeped as the vehicle drove off.

"Wait." She cupped her hands together and blew on them. "Should've worn warmer gloves. It's brutal out here."

"What's going on? Is everything okay? And where is your car?" I peered at her face with a frown of concern. "Maybe you should come inside and sit down. You don't look so good."

"Sorry." Her lips quivered in an attempt to smile. "My car wouldn't start, and everyone else by the lake was busy cleaning up. I started walking home, but then Gwen passed by and offered me a lift. Did Hunter call you?" Her brows knitted.

"Uh, no. What's this about? Your conversation is all over the place." Milo squirmed, and I shifted his weight in my arms.

"Hey, who's this guy?" She ruffled Milo's fur. "What a cutie you are."

"Izzie. Izzie. Please tell me why you asked about Hunter calling. Is he okay?" My heart was beating in double time.

"No. He's fine. It's Dewey. Hunter says he's missing."

Chapter Thirteen

I passed the basket to my left and reached for the tub of butter. Breakfast was an assortment of pumpkin bran muffins, egg and veggie omelets, and fruit salad. Everything had been prepared by Dad. We all took turns in the kitchen and kept our menu of breakfast items as original as we could. Around any holiday or season, Dad threw in something to celebrate. Pumpkin was obviously the perfect choice for autumn and Halloween.

"I wonder how many on Hunter's team are out searching for Dewey," Izzie said.

"As many as the department can afford to tie up." I smiled as Max and Milo growled and barked. They romped and chased each other down the hall. Never had I imagined they'd get along this quickly. Max had ignored the new guest for about ten minutes, but Milo had used his charm and never once went near Max's bowl of food. Total dog respect must've gained him some points. For whatever reason, Max had a play buddy, and he didn't growl in protest once when I had snuggled both pets in bed last night.

"I say he's guilty. No one runs if they have nothing to hide." Izzie added a firm nod to cement her opinion.

"Or he could be innocent and too afraid he'll be accused anyway. You know how flighty he can be," Mom said.

"Your mom's right. Dewey has gone into hiding before. Remember when a few people accused him of stealing personal items during a ferry run? Dewey couldn't stand the rumors and accusing stares, which were baseless and uncalled for, in my opinion. He hid in his cousin's hunting cabin for a week because of it," Dad said. "Of course, the whole incident turned out fine in the end. The thief was a total stranger who was arrested days later and found with those stolen items in his house."

Izzie chewed a bite of omelet. "I wonder if that's where he is now? His cousin's hunting cabin?"

"Most likely." Dad pointed his fork. "The thing is, I hear that cabin is deep in the woods, somewhere in the Allegheny Forest. His best friend, Marvin Timms, swears no one could find the place because Dewey refuses to tell anyone exactly where it is, not even Marvin."

I dabbed my lips with a napkin and pushed away my empty plate. "Good grief. This story sounds like an episode from one of those crime shows."

"Or a scene from a Halloween horror movie." Izzie's mouth formed a circle, and her eyes widened while she slapped both cheeks with her hands. "Eek!"

I tossed my napkin at her and laughed. "Stop. I'm sure the authorities will find him soon."

Or at least I hoped so. Even if he was innocent, the idea of a frightened and terrified Dewey running loose, maybe even hiding close by, wasn't comforting. Desperation might trigger him to do something crazy. Not safe for him or for anyone else.

The doorbell rang, and Izzie bounced out of her seat. "I'll get it." She jogged to the front door, zigzagging to keep from colliding with Max or Milo.

I had a clear view of the hall and front entrance. After Izzie opened the door, I made out the figure of Aunt Constance, waiting on the porch. She stepped inside and stood next to Izzie. Today's ensemble was casual denim. Her jacket had orange and red embroidered flowers sewn along the sides, and she wore skinny jeans that weren't as flattering as she probably imagined them to be. Wrapped around her neck was a red scarf with green and brown sequins. No one could deny she was a walking fashion statement—maybe not to everyone's taste, but fashionable all the same.

"Good morning, family. I see you've added a new member." She batted away Milo as he tried to lick her hand. Finally, giving up, he trotted away to play with Max again.

"He's a stray we found trapped in the storage shed close to the ferry dock," I explained.

"Yes. The shed Dewey uses." She sighed and plopped down in the chair next to Dad. "How are you, Joe? I don't suppose you've had a chance to look at this month's stock report."

"No, Constance. I haven't." Dad pushed away from the table. "I'd imagine all the investments are doing well, as usual."

Constance fussed with her scarf. "Yes, but some of them took a hit. Maybe it's time to do some adjusting and invest in others."

I blinked and held my breath as my attention held on Dad, who by now had turned red and clenched his jaw.

"I'll have a talk with the financial advisor and see what he has to say. I trust his opinion."

190

The implication wasn't lost on Aunt Constance. Without comment, her gaze flittered, touching each of us for a brief instant before settling on me. "I heard about the paddle. Your Ross called to tell me. I don't mean to sound callous, but if Dewey Sawyer turns out to be the one who killed Viola, I'd be relieved."

A sharp intake of breath burned my throat. Callous and lots more. Poor Dewey. He wasn't even here to defend himself.

No one in the room spoke for a long, awkward moment. Even the dogs grew quiet. The soft, gentle sound of snoring came from Milo as he lay sleeping by my feet.

"I'm so sorry." Aunt Constance sniffed as her eyes moistened. "I can't deal with all of this. I've been saying and doing things that aren't normal for me. Why, just this morning, I snapped at a delivery man because he'd placed a package inside my screen door. I panicked, thinking someone was breaking in." She shook her head. "I swear on my husband's grave, I'll have a nervous breakdown if this situation with Viola doesn't end soon."

Mom stood and came around the table to give Aunt Constance a hug. "We're here for you. Anything you need, just ask."

"I only w-want my life b-back." Aunt Constance sobbed into Mom's shoulder. Her chest heaved as she broke down.

"Why don't I make you a cup of tea? We'll sit outside on the patio and enjoy the sunshine and chat about pleasant memories. That should calm you. Okay?" Mom patted her shoulder and Aunt Constance nodded.

I waited until Mom and Aunt Constance disappeared outside, and then got up from my chair. Carrying our plates and utensils to the sink, I rinsed while Izzie loaded them into the dishwasher.

Dad came up behind us and squeezed our shoulders. "You girls should get out of here before your mom decides we should all take a trip down memory lane. Unless that's how you want to spend the rest of your morning?"

"As pleasant as that sounds, we have tons to do at the shop," Izzie said.

"Tons." I tossed the dishtowel into the sink. Even if we didn't have so much to do, I wasn't in the mood for a family reel of past Christmas holidays or Thanksgiving dinners. Rather than sentimental or nostalgic, I was feeling determined to help find whoever had killed Viola and end the torment Aunt Constance was experiencing. That's how I wanted to help her.

After a quick change of clothes, I met Izzie downstairs. She was playing tug-of-war with the dogs and their chew toys. My heart swelled. "I don't know who will miss him more when his owner is found. Me or Max."

"Count me in that equation too." She stood up straight and slipped into her jacket. "What if we don't find his owner? Would you want to keep him? Taking care of two dogs is a lot of work. I'm not even sure Mom and Dad would approve."

I sighed. I didn't want to get my hopes up. I had called to make an appointment with the vet to check Milo for a microchip. If he had one, Milo would be back to his home before the day ended.

"I already spoke with them. They're okay with the idea. I had to smile when Mom made the comment that all God's creatures are welcome in our home. I teased her and asked if that included Mr. Bixby's pet iguana."

Izzie laughed. "I can picture her face now. Eyes bugging out while the color drains from her face."

"Exactly." I hefted the strap of my bag over one shoulder. "You two pooches behave while we're gone." I gave them each a hug and followed Izzie outside.

"What's your take on Dewey? You think he's Viola's killer?" Izzie slid into the passenger seat of my car. She'd called Marino's Auto Repair first thing this morning to tow her car to the shop.

"Not quite." I shifted into gear and steered onto the road. "Everything that makes him look guilty seems too convenient."

"Like someone is framing him." Izzie pulled down the vanity mirror and swiped on lip gloss.

"Yep. And how about those peppermint candies? No way would Dewey choose that kind of candy. You know how much he hates peppermint."

Izzie gasped and poked my arm. "Unless it wasn't the killer who delivered the trick-or-treat message."

"You're right. Maybe the candygram came from a person who wants Aunt Constance to worry." I turned into the parking lot and let the car idle.

"Could be that person really believes Aunt Constance is the killer and hopes to get her to confess."

"Like a citizen fighting for justice. Yeah, I get that, but why not go to the authorities and tell them why she should be arrested? Seems a more effective way to get it done." I exited the car and popped open the trunk. Removing bags of supplies, I handed some of them to Izzie.

"Maybe for a reason, like this person doesn't want attention or has something of his or her own to hide." Izzie's eyes widened. "Ooh. A mystery inside a mystery. The plot thickens."

I rolled my eyes. "You should be a writer instead of painting pictures. Speaking of painting, did you contact Wink about the ad for Trick Your Pumpkin?"

Izzie stepped up to the front porch. "No, because I have a much better idea." She turned to waggle her brows at me.

"Oh no. Not again." I groaned and nudged her with my elbow. "Please say this idea of yours has nothing to do with costumes."

"It absolutely does." She giggled. "Oh, come on! Quit acting so grumpy. It's Halloween, right? The perfect holiday for costumes. No one will judge or make fun. Besides, look what a great success it was the last time." She set the bags on the counter, then clasped her hands together underneath her chin. "I already have them picked out. We're dressing up as the Sanderson witches from *Hocus Pocus*."

I scowled. "There are three witches in that movie."

"I'm aware. Willow is joining us." Izzie smiled.

"Please don't say there are brooms involved, like in the movie. And I hope your creative muse doesn't go overboard and you don't try to add green makeup and warts on our noses." I pulled out rolls of paper towels from one bag and stashed a couple of them in the cupboard underneath the counter. Izzie's creativity sometimes did go overboard. We'd dressed as Mickey and Minnie Mouse this past summer to promote the shop. Standing on the street corner with a billboard hanging from my neck had made me wish I could crawl under the pavement. Still, Izzie had been right. The cartoon gig had been a hit, and we'd sold out tickets for several events.

"Ha. You are so funny. None of that. This will be fun, and everyone will enjoy it. You'll see Thursday evening."

"Wait. Thursday? The Trick Your Pumpkin event is Friday. Isn't that kind of late to promote it?" I glared. "Okay, what's going on?"

Izzie hiked herself onto one of the stools and patted the seat next to her. "True confession. We filled all but one seat yesterday. I have an ulterior motive."

I plopped down on the seat and sighed. "Of course you do."

"I thought we could multitask. Do some snooping. You know, listen in on folks and see if anyone says anything about Viola's murder." She squirmed in her seat. "Isn't that clever?"

My chin dropped while my eyes lifted. "You honestly believe that will work? Why would people talk about the murder, especially if what they say is incriminating, while they're in public, where others, like us, can hear?" I slapped my hand on the counter. "Because they wouldn't, Izzie."

She pulled back her shoulders. "Someone might. Or they might talk about other things that would end up being a clue to help us. Never know. Besides, we'll be promoting our business and establishing community goodwill by dressing up and handing out candy. So, that part's worth it," she argued.

"Fine. I agree with you about business promotion and goodwill. You know, I always wanted to dress up like a witch." I gave my best imitation of a witch's cackle.

"Great! Now, all you have to do is tell Willow." She hopped off the seat and took quick steps to the storage room.

"Oh no. Your idea means *you're* the messenger." I laughed and jogged to catch up to her. "Are you keeping the costumes back here?" I peeked inside the closet.

"No. They're at home in my bedroom. And I was kidding about you telling Willow."

"No, you weren't."

"Yeah, I had to try. You might've said yes." She winked. "You're such a pushover."

"Hello! Is anyone running this place?" The clip-clop of heels echoed and grew louder until Spencer appeared in the doorway. Both hands rested on her hips. "Here's some advice. If you decide to leave the front of your shop untended, at least lock the door."

I bit my lip. "Thanks, Spencer. We would've never thought of that."

"You're welcome." She brushed back her hair and surveyed the room. "Nice setup. You'll have to give me the name of who built your shelves and cupboards."

"The place came like this, along with the rent we pay. Sooo, . . . is there something you needed?" At least I kept the sarcasm out of my voice.

"Would you like something to drink, Spencer?" Izzie led the way to the front. "We have iced tea, soda, and water."

"No, thanks. I came by to ask if you can recommend a restaurant that serves great seafood. Someplace new and trendy? I'm meeting someone for dinner and want the place to be perfect. Like with ambience? I seem to recall Mom saying something about the Blue Whale, but that's more for old people, and it's ancient." She sat next to one of the tables.

"Ambience. Your date must be someone special. Gotta say, you work fast." I took my place on the stool and rested one arm on the counter.

"Nothing like that." Her eyes flashed. "I want to impress a potential investor."

"The Blue Whale would be perfect. The owner recently did some updates. We dine there all the time," Izzie said.

"Expensive?" Spencer asked.

"Somewhat. Worth every penny, though. Their chef is known internationally and studied at that famous culinary school in Hyde Park. What's it called?" Izzie tapped her lip and gave me a look.

I shrugged, then shifted my attention. "So, is this potential investor a local? Do we know him or her?"

"No, he lives in Manhattan." Glancing down, Spencer brushed her skirt with the back of her hand.

"And this person is staying in Whisper Cove?" My heart pumped with too much energy. Lots of people came to our town for a visit to see the sights. Even from Manhattan. However, after Ross's comment about his meeting someone last night, it didn't take much of a leap to guess the guy Spencer was talking about.

"For a short while, I guess." She tapped her manicured and polished fingernails on the table, rolled her eyes, and sighed. "Look, you know it's Ross. When we got together last night, we discussed Aunt Constance and my concerns, and then I casually brought up my plans to open a shop and how there always seem to be new expenses adding to my worries. That's when he commented that he was looking for new investments. I didn't bring it up—he did." She shrugged. "I gave him my proposal packet, which I happened to be carrying with me. He agreed to take a look. I figured you wouldn't mind."

"What Ross does or thinks is his business. Why should I care?" I tugged at my collar. Of all the women he could spend time with, why did it have to be Spencer?

"Anyway, I told him I had more questions about how he planned to defend Mom when she goes to court, so we're talking over dinner," she said.

"Ross is the best criminal attorney in the state. She's lucky to have him represent her. And who says she's going to court? She hasn't been charged with murder." I snapped out my words and immediately regretted them. "Sorry. What I mean is *if* Aunt Constance needs a defense, Ross is her best chance at winning."

Spencer stood and pulled on her jacket. "Well, I need to see for myself that he is. You two have a nice day. I'll let you know how it goes and whether Mom and I will keep Ross as her attorney. Bye." She swung open the door and took long, leggy strides down to the road.

My mouth flapped open, and I stared after her.

"Don't listen to her. Aunt Constance is the one who hired Ross, and she won't let Spencer interfere. You know that," Izzie said. "Besides, if she's confident that Ross will invest in her business, why risk a deal by firing him?"

"You're right." My breath eased out. "She staged one of her power plays to convince us she's in control."

"Or she really is looking out for Aunt Constance."

"I'd really like to believe that." I chewed my bottom lip and gave Izzie a lukewarm smile.

Izzie rested her knuckles against her lips for a second. "You can tell me. Does it bother you?"

"What?" I turned away and pulled more items out of the bags.

"You know. Spencer and Ross spending time together?" She laid a hand on my shoulder.

198

"The only thing that bothers me is how Spencer might give Ross a hard time." I swiveled around. "As for investments, I have a strong hunch Ross wouldn't be interested in any kind of craft shop. Heck, if he were, I would've asked him to invest in ours. Looks to me like they're both up to something and being total sneaks about it."

Izzie laughed. "Jealous *and* suspicious. What a lethal combination."

"Hey. I'm not jealous. If Spencer is up to something devious, or Ross is, that's their problem, not mine." I loaded my arms with cleanser, paper towels, and a sleeve of plastic cups before heading to the storage room.

"You keep saying that, but what I'm hearing is you're worried about Ross, which means you still care for him." Izzie followed close behind me.

"Only as a friend. That's what we are, you know. *Friends.*" I emphasized the last word.

"Great. Then you won't mind if they start seeing each other more often and in a more personal way." Izzie grabbed the cleanser bottles from my arms and set them in the cupboard.

"Oh my gosh. Will you stop? I don't care who he sees or dates." I dropped everything on the counter and left the room. "I'm going for a walk. Be back in ten minutes, maybe an hour." However long it took me to cool down.

"Chloe! I'm sorry. I went too far. Please, don't leave. I promise not to talk about it anymore," she called after me.

I kept going, out of the shop and straight into Hunter. "Holy word—Hunter! Where did you come from?" I backed up and took several deep breaths. Just the person I didn't needed to see while I was reeling with too many emotions that kept me off balance.

He hitched a thumb over his shoulder. "From that direction." He chuckled. "Which looks like where you're headed. Is something wrong? You look upset." The smile on his lips slipped a little.

"Me? Nah." I shook my head. "Just getting some fresh air. Thought I'd sit by the lake."

"Mind if I join you?" He hesitated and cleared his throat. "I need to talk about something."

I scratched the back of my neck. "Not sure I'll be great company, but yeah."

We walked over to sit on the nearest bench. The gentle lap and swish of water hit the shore, and the few Halloween decorations left hanging in the trees crinkled as they swayed in the breeze.

I sat at one end of the bench, as if hoping to keep a safe distance. I remembered times like this when I had felt down or out of sorts, and how all it took was a hug or even a pat on the back, and I'd crumble into a sobbing mess. Not the display I wanted Hunter to see.

As if reading my thoughts, Hunter took a place at the opposite end of the bench. "You want to talk about whatever is bothering you?"

I blinked. His eyes reflected genuine concern. "It's nothing. A sibling quarrel." I waved my arm. "Izzie isn't the easiest person to get along with at times."

He chuckled. "Oh, I know."

"I'm sure you do." I sniffed, with a slight smile lifting the corners of my lips. "She's working on it, though. She acted on

Mom's suggestion to take yoga classes and already had one session. I have hopes for her." Now, if I could only improve my attitude about Spencer. Maybe I'd join Izzie.

"A work in progress. I can respect that." He rubbed his jawline and leaned back against the bench. "What I came to say is, I hoped we could—" The jingle of his phone sounded. "Sorry—I need to answer this."

I stared out at the lake and let my mind drift. I didn't care if Ross moved on. The guy sitting next to me could be my chance at doing the same. However, Ross and I had a long history. We'd been close. Sure, the dedication he had to his job and career meant spending a lot of time at work, but I saw that behavior as having led to him neglecting our relationship. He'd taken it for granted, and that's what hurt. Living in New York with no family to comfort me and very few people I could call friends had left me feeling lonely. I couldn't expect him to change. Work was his life. Lots of people felt that way, but not me. I wanted a relationship with someone who was willing to put me first at least some of the time. Ross hadn't been that guy. I liked being friends, and friends cared about each other's feelings. I worried how Spencer would treat him because I didn't want him to get hurt. That's what I needed to tell Izzie and make her understand.

"Okay. Thanks. I'll take it from here." Hunter tucked his phone inside his jacket pocket, then turned to face me.

My chest grew tight. A pained look was reflected in his eyes and his jaw tensed. "What is it?"

"I'm sorry, Chloe. That was someone from the lab. They were able to lift a set of fingerprints from both Viola's bag and her glove. Your aunt's. Add that evidence to her sketchy alibi and the argument she had with the victim, and I'm afraid I'll have to bring her in. You might want to call Ross." He shook his head. "I have no choice. She's being charged with Viola Finnwinkle's murder."

Chapter Fourteen

I'd called Ross right after Hunter announced what he planned to do. Fortunately, he was able to arrive at Aunt Constance's house before Hunter. To his credit, he had managed to raise bail and convince the judge his client was not a flight risk. He'd even promised to take full responsibility. If she tried to run, the judge swore he'd put Ross in jail instead. I struggled not to laugh, hearing that. The light moment was cut short when he warned me not to get too hopeful because evidence was mounting against her.

Mom, Dad, Izzie, and I had rescued Aunt Constance from jail late that afternoon and took her home, where Mom fed her homemade butternut squash soup and sourdough biscuits, followed by apple pie for dessert. Despite her distressed mood, Aunt Constance certainly hadn't lost her appetite.

After dinner, Spencer arrived with a deep scowl and pursed lips to show her mood wasn't much better than her mother's. She wouldn't talk about whatever was bothering her, even when both Mom and Aunt Constance repeatedly asked. I had my suspicions, but I kept quiet and went to bed thankful for the close relationship I had with my parents.

* * *

"How about you take those two guys and the short blonde standing next to them? I can handle these other five." Izzie sighed. "I sure hope they have at least some artistic talent."

I stood with my arms crossed. The breeze off the lake was warmer than usual. This morning had brought sunshine and the promise of blue skies all day. I wore jean capris and a frayed, lightweight Henley top. We'd been recruited by the Sisterhood, aka Aunt Constance, to take charge of a group of teen volunteers to make new Halloween decorations, replacing those that had been destroyed by the storm. I was glad to help, but being forced to postpone our renewed efforts to do some more sleuthing and help keep Aunt Constance from going to jail again made me a grumpy volunteer. I studied the three teens and read their name tags—Ali, Travis, and Neal.

"Sure. Do you want your group to make the jack-o'-lanterns? I think my three can manage to weave streamers in the trees."

"Sounds good. And don't worry. We'll get the chance to put our sleuthing hats back on. Maybe starting with talking to them. I mean, look: the Sisterhood members and so many people from town are here helping out," Izzie said.

She was right. At least half the residents of Whisper Cove and members of the Sisterhood had come to the lake to help redecorate. In two days, many would return to set up the big fixtures, like craft booths, food kiosks, and games. All the loud chatter and laughter going on hinted everyone was excited for the upcoming celebration and not at all discouraged by what the storm had done. I picked up rolls of plastic streamers and tape and motioned to my group of three.

"Hey, cousins. I'm here to volunteer. Where do you want me?"

I glanced over my shoulder. Spencer stood there grinning at me, dressed in capris and a Henley that matched mine, only she looked glamorous and I looked like me. "Spencer. Why are you here?"

She scoffed. "Is that how you greet a volunteer? Since I'm soon to be a shop owner on Artisan Alley, I thought I should do my part. So, put me to work." The grin slipped back into place.

Izzie stepped closer. "Hi, Spencer. What a cute outfit. Why don't you go ask your mom? She's in charge and will know who needs help. Chloe and I are fine."

"Oh, okay." She shrugged and, after a second, walked away.

"What was that all about?" I whispered while our teen recruits stood off to the side talking.

"Maybe she's trying to make nice. You know, after what happened yesterday at the house?" Izzie lifted a box of supplies.

"Oh right. You mean after she accused me of sabotaging her date night with Ross? As if I planned for Aunt Constance to get arrested. Seriously, you'd think she would've been a little more concerned about her mom being behind bars than missing out on scoring Ross as an investor," I spouted off. Seeing the gawking stares from the teens, I snapped my mouth shut, then worked to recover the moment. "All right, Team Chloe. Come and get your materials, and we'll head over to that table."

"Teacher has a bad attitude. That's going in my report, Miss Abbington," Izzie teased with a laugh while she walked off toward the lake, her group trailing like a brood of ducklings.

"Ha! You are so hilarious," I shouted. "Come on, recruits. Let's decorate."

Oak trees spread across the grassy area from north to south along Artisan Alley and the lake. I instructed my group of three by giving a demonstration of how to twist and weave the plastic black and orange strips, then sent them off to decorate the trees. While hanging back to see what each could do on their own, I glanced at Izzie, who was giving her demonstration. I admired the swift moves of her talented hands as she created a jack-o'-lantern, complete with its own unique look, in minutes. No wonder her teens appeared dazed and confused.

"Slow down, Izzie," I whispered under my breath, and I chuckled as all five hands went up when she asked if they had any questions. Being a master at something didn't mean you could teach others those skills. Fortunately, since opening our shop, Izzie had learned a few tricks by observing Willow at work. One of her previous jobs had been teaching kids in making crafts of all kinds.

After ten minutes passed and no catastrophes or accidents had happened to my recruits, I strolled over to the far end, where the tall and lanky boy named Travis was chatting with a teen who wasn't one of the volunteers. Maybe someone needed a nudge to keep working, I thought.

"I'm telling you, Dewey Sawyer did it. I saw with my own eyes, man." The boy leaned closer to Travis, his back turned to me.

"That's bull. You were wasted that night and passed out. I know since I had to take you home later. We're lucky your mom and dad didn't catch us sneaking inside."

"This was before I passed out, dipwad. He was on the dock late at night, bent over and puking his guts out."

Travis shook his head. "Doesn't mean he killed that woman."

I cleared my throat and stepped closer.

Travis shoved the boy away, nearly causing him to fall. "Oh, hi, Miss Abbington. I was just getting back to work." He turned to glare at the boy. "And Branden was leaving."

I grabbed a hold of Branden's shirt sleeve as he sidestepped away from us. "Not so fast. What were you saying about Dewey Sawyer?"

Branden shrugged and stuffed both hands in his pockets. "Nothing. You must've heard wrong."

"I don't think so." I leveled my gaze. "When did you see Dewey at the dock, puking his guts out, as you put it?" When Branden shrugged again without comment, I shifted my attention to Travis. "What time did you take your friend home?"

Travis fumbled with the streamer in his hands. "Say around ten? I found my friend passed out on the lawn about twenty yards from the dock a little before that."

"Man, shut your mouth. You're making things worse," Branden said.

"You." I stabbed a finger in his direction. "You need to tell your story to the authorities, today. I mean like now. Or else I will. I'll tell them the *whole* story. By this afternoon, a detective will show up at your front door. I doubt you want your parents to know what you were up to that night, do you?" I only had to wait a couple of heartbeats.

"No, ma'am. That can't happen." Branden backed up. "I'll go right now. I have a car, and I can be there in no time." He kept walking in reverse, and reaching the road, he turned and sprinted toward the parking area.

"You think he means it?" I fixed my gaze on Branden until he steered onto Whisper Cove Lane and out of sight.

"Oh yeah. He's been in enough trouble lately with his parents."

I smiled. "He's lucky to have a friend like you. Just don't let his bad behavior become yours."

"Don't worry about that. My parents are scarier than his." He rolled his eyes.

I laughed. "Wise decision." Glancing up at the tree, I pointed. "Your streamers aren't balanced. Put more on this side." Without waiting for a response, I moved on to the next tree, where Ali had managed to pull a bench close and use it as a stepping stool. Short stature pushes you to be creative. I knew very well. Just like I knew Travis was right. Branden seeing Dewey at the dock sometime right before ten didn't mean our ferry pilot was guilty of murder. The teen's story only confirmed that Dewey had been in the area when Viola was murdered.

I came to an abrupt stop and gasped. Dewey had told us he'd been asleep in his shack all evening and hadn't waked until the next morning. Never once, not to Izzie and me, not to Hunter, did he mention waking up and puking his guts out, as Branden had so delicately worded it. I believed what Branden claimed he saw because the sight of it would be hard to forget. Dewey had lied, which meant he could've lied about everything else.

Anxious to tell Izzie about the latest discovery, I cheered on my three volunteers to finish as quickly as possible. Once

Izzie and I returned to the shop, I got on the phone to call Hunter and make sure Branden had made good on his promise. I heard the click of his phone and dove right in. "Have you heard any updates on Dewey's whereabouts?"

"How are you, Hunter? Oh, I'm fine, Chloe. Thanks for asking," he quipped.

"Sorry. It's this case and Aunt Constance being arrested. So many things are driving me over the edge." Not to mention Spencer coming to town and digging her manipulative claws into Ross to get what she wanted.

"I get it. Okay, as for Dewey, no one's seen or heard from him since he left town. I'm tracking down other family members to find out where this cabin is."

I paced the storage room. Izzie and Willow were out front talking to someone who'd dropped by for information about scheduling a private paint party. "What did you think of Branden's account of events? Do you believe him?"

"At first, I didn't. Then his friend showed up at the station. Travis? He told me you were the instructor at the volunteer mission this morning. Oh, and he said you were one scary lady."

"Yeah?" I lifted my chin. "Well, I can be pretty tough when needed."

"I'll keep that in mind." He chuckled. "I do have other good news."

"Oh?"

"I just got a call. Ross has managed to convince the judge that any charges against your aunt should be dropped. Seems he found a couple of witnesses who claimed that on the night of the event at Bellows Lodge, Viola dropped her bag, coat, and gloves into Aunt Constance's hands and told her to take care of them. That could explain her prints. Anyway, it puts our evidence in the case on shaky ground. Your aunt is lucky this time."

Relief flooded through me and I sank into a chair. "Thank goodness."

"Meantime, we need to find a match for the other set of prints found on the bag. Who knows? Maybe we'll soon put a name to the killer."

"Let's hope." I took a breath and tried to relax.

"Hey, I have to get back to work."

"Me too. Talk to you later." He hadn't mentioned finding out anything yet about the paddle, which was fine with me. Hearing the latest news about a legitimate reason for Aunt Constance's prints being on Viola's glove and bag was enough for my emotions to handle at one time.

Izzie and I had missed our chance to speak with any of the Sisterhood members volunteering this morning. Willow was covering the shop and had called with an emergency. A customer who insisted she'd signed up for an event in December but wasn't on our list was having a hysterical meltdown and demanded to speak with the owner. Turned out to be a glitch on the website, which hadn't updated the list of those attending. Willow fixed it within seconds and tried showing the customer, but she wasn't convinced. Izzie put her congeniality to good use and offered the woman a free ticket to Friday's Trick Your Pumpkin event, which filled that final open slot. It was a winning move for both sides.

As I moved to the front section of the shop, the door chimes tinkled, and Wink stepped inside. He looked unusually pleasant, with bright eyes and a large smile to prove it. I was curious to discover what had triggered his good mood. My bet was it had to do with Sarah Gilley.

"Afternoon, ladies," he bellowed, loud enough to resonate around the room. "It's that time." He tapped his watch.

"Time for what?" Izzie hopped up on a stool and twirled around. Facing him again, she pointed. "Your favorite game show is starting? Or wait. It has to be that soap opera. What's it called, Chloe?"

I played along and tapped my lip. "Hmm. Let me think." I snapped my fingers and dropped my jaw. "Could it be *Dark Shadows* has made a comeback? I've always been a sucker for gothic vampire stories, though I can't imagine who'd replace that actor who played Barnabas."

"Jonathan Frid. Right?" Willow clapped her hands and joined us.

Wink's smile grew into a rigid line, and his coloring turned deep red. "Very funny. Now, if you're through playing games, I'm here to collect the rent and payment for the ad. You agreed to fork over the cash today, remember?" He shoved an invoice into Izzie's hand.

Izzie cleared her throat and sobered. She opened her laptop and tapped a few keys. "There. Sent to your bank account." She closed the lid and leaned her elbows on top. "You could've just emailed or called about it."

"Yeah. Why are you really here, Wink?" I cozied my hip against the table and stared at him.

"I was taking a walk along the lake, and when I passed close to the ferry dock, I thought about your aunt. How is she, by the way?" Without being invited, he settled into a chair, and the smile returned.

"She's fine." I kept my answers short and avoided details that would prompt more questions. Knowing Wink, anything discussed would end up in the *Gazette*.

"Is she really?" His eyes widened while his head moved from side to side. "I find that hard to believe. Spending time in jail can't have been pleasant."

My shoulders sank. I shot a quick glance at Izzie and understood the message her pressed lips and ever so slight headshake conveyed to me. "She's fine, Wink. A total misunderstanding. No charges, no more jail."

Izzie shot me a puzzled frown, but I shook my head. There'd be time to explain later.

"Well, if you say so." He patted his thigh with the palm of his hand. "If there's anything I can do to help, please ask. She's a good woman and shouldn't be going through all of this."

I scratched the back of my neck and frowned. *What brought this on,* I wondered. The last time we had spoken, he'd seemed almost gleeful that Aunt Constance could be the killer. In less than five minutes, he'd had her tried and convicted with his theory of what had happened. Something underhanded was going on in that clever mind of his, but I had no clue what.

As if she were ten steps ahead of us, Willow smiled like a Cheshire cat. "Why don't you put an ad in the paper, asking for information that might lead to Viola's killer? Then, offer a sizable reward."

Wink sputtered and scowled. "Not sure about a sizable one. The paper is barely staying out of the red. I can't even pay myself a decent salary and—sizable isn't in our budget."

"Then how about a free six-month subscription to the *Gazette*?" Izzie suggested, but Wink shook his head. "Or three months," Izzie continued. "Some, or at least a few, people might like that sort of reward." Her voice trailed as Wink's scowl deepened.

"I might. Or I'll stop by her place for a visit to see how she's doing. Bring some flowers." He tugged at his collar. "I should go. I've got a paper to put together." With that, he hurried out of the shop.

I shifted to face Izzie and Willow. "That was weird. Right?"

"So weird." Willow jumped up to sit on the counter and crossed both legs. "Why was he acting like that? You know him better than I do."

"He's up to something," Izzie said. "Maybe Sarah put him up to asking about Aunt Constance."

"That's what I was thinking. He has some ulterior motive and is being sneaky about it." I scooted my chair closer to them. "Izzie, do you remember how he behaved the last time he came in?"

"Wink was convinced Aunt Constance was Viola's killer and talked like he was excited about it." Izzie nodded. "Now, he's acting like he cares about her feelings. Why?"

"He wants something. That's for sure." I twirled a strand of my hair thoughtfully, considering the possibilities, but nothing worthwhile came to mind.

"Say. What was that you said about no more jail for Aunt Constance?" Izzie said.

I explained Hunter's news. "Ross came through, after all. Aunt Constance should give him a bonus."

"Hey, ladies! Why all the gloomy looks?" Megan stepped through the doorway.

I noticed the bounce in her step that practically made her spring into the shop. The grin on her face and cheery voice hinted that something good had happened. Nice to see things had been going her way after all the trouble she'd been through this past summer.

"Wink stopped by a few minutes ago. Nothing to stress over, we hope." Izzie gave her friend a hug. "You, on the other hand, look ready to burst with good news. What's up?"

"You know that contact in Buffalo I mentioned, the one with the crafts gallery who invited me to join their program? Well . . ." She rose up on her tiptoes and clasped her hands. "He called to tell me the items I'd sent ahead to put on display caught the eye of a huge buyer for an international company. They're interested in contracting with me to create a line of candles to include in their catalog. Isn't that awesome?" She plopped down in a chair, suddenly losing steam.

"Oh my gosh! Megan, you've done it. Your dream is coming true." Izzie leaned down to wrap her arms around Megan's shoulders. "I'm so proud of you."

"That's wonderful news," both Willow and I chimed in.

"The only problem is, I'll have to make a lot of trips to Buffalo and New York City." She bit down on her lip.

"Why's that a problem? Sounds exciting to me," Izzie said.

"Mom can't cover the shop for long. She's having knee surgery next month. Looks like I'll have to close the shop during those trips. Losing sales isn't an option right now. Not with all the financial troubles I've had." Megan's shoulders slumped.

Izzie, Willow, and I gave each other a quick glance and nodded.

"We'll manage your shop so you won't have to close." Izzie pointed to herself, then to Willow and me. "We can take turns, and that way both our shops are covered. It's the perfect solution, Megs."

Megan blinked away her tears. "You'd do that for me?" Her chest heaved. "I swear. I have the best friends. You're all kind and loyal and—"

"Yeah, yeah, we're the most wonderful and all that." Izzie laughed. "Seriously, you'd do the same for us if we needed help. So, now that we've got that little glitch taken care of, I want your input." She quickly explained Wink's visit and his strange behavior.

"What do you think, Megs? You know him pretty well since he's been spending time at your parents' house," I said.

I'd heard from Mom that when Wink arrived in town to take over the *Gazette* a few months ago, the Hunts had volunteered to be the community welcome wagon and have him over for dinner once a week until he got settled in. Yet the dinner invitations had continued. I figured either the Hunts had taken a liking to Wink, or they felt sorry for him. Either way, Megan had a better take on him than we did. She had been living at home since losing her condo in July. What better way was there to get to know someone than during dinner conversations?

She straightened and her eyes gleamed. "Oh boy. This is such a coincidence, and after what you told me, it makes perfect sense. I'm not always at home for dinner since the shop keeps me busy, and late nights are becoming more common, I hate to say. Anyway, Mom told me Wink made an off-handed comment at dinner after complaining that the Gazette doesn't make enough. Just like he mentioned to you. He joked that he should look for a rich widow to marry, and then he could live out the rest of his days in comfort."

"Oh wow. That's—he really said that?" Willow shrugged. "What a tool."

"Yes, and there's more. Without skipping a beat, he asked if Mom or Dad had spoken to your aunt recently and said how sorry he felt for such a kind lady. Too obvious, right?" Megan shifted in her seat and stared at Willow. "You're spot on. He *is* a tool of the worst kind."

"A gold digger." I nodded.

"A gigolo." Izzie shuddered. "Chloe saw him with Sarah Gilley the other day. They were snuggling and kissing right outside Spill the Beans."

"What a conniving creep." Megan finished the round of adjectives for Wink. "He's never once mentioned Sarah to Mom and Dad. Mom would've told me if he had. Such a shame." She stood. "I'll let you know if Mom and Dad have any more news about Wink."

As I watched Megan walk outside, only one thought came to mind. Spencer and Wink might have a lot in common because it looked like both of them wanted a share of Aunt Constance's bank account.

Chapter Fifteen

I woke the next morning to sloppy kisses on both cheeks. Max and Milo cuddled like bookends, one on each side of me. Their tales wagged as I petted them and said good morning. "You two are the best morning wake-up. I think we should get out of bed and go downstairs for some kibble and maybe doggie treats. What do you say?" I laughed as they barked in unison.

I set them on the floor and peeked out the window to see frost on the ground. I hurried to slip into a pair of jeans and a heavy sweater, then skipped down the stairs. My phone jingled and vibrated in my hand. Seeing the familiar number, I smiled and answered. "Good morning, Hunter."

"Hi, Chloe. I'm glad you picked up right away. I have news." His voice was somber in tone.

I stiffened and my steps slowed. "What's wrong?"

"Why would you think—never mind. The lab report and the coroner's statement came in late last night. The blood on the paddle and Viola's are a match. No prints on the handle, which is no surprise, but I guess you could say lucky for your aunt. Again." He sighed. "Here's the unfortunate news. The coroner concluded Viola died from drowning."

I gasped and gripped the phone tighter. I understood or at least guessed what that meant. "You mean she could've survived the blow to the head. Poor Viola."

"Which means there's another take on this case I have to consider. If whoever hit her with the paddle didn't push her into the lake, that means we might be looking at a lesser charge. I'm not a criminal lawyer, so I can't say how this would play out in court. Your friend Ross has a line of defense he's used in these circumstances, I'm sure."

I sucked on my tongue. "You talk like Aunt Constance is guilty, and she'll be the one on trial. I hope you haven't given up on searching for other answers."

"Of course not. When the evidence adds up and every scenario's been looked at, then I'll have all the answers to my questions. Not before then, Chloe. Look, I have to go. I'll catch up with you later. Maybe stop by the shop."

"Sure. Thanks, Hunter." As I pushed the end call button, I tapped my free hand against my thigh and whistled. Max and Milo hurried to catch up. The case against Aunt Constance was stuck in a rut without a way out, words Granddad Abbington would use when he was frustrated. I wondered when or if we'd manage to get unstuck.

The dogs skidded into the kitchen and went straight for their water bowl. I dug into the bag of kibble and dished out portions for each of them.

Glancing at Izzie's glum face and noticing the lack of conversation from Mom and Dad, I frowned. "I'd say good morning, but from the look of things, I'm guessing that isn't a great idea. What's going on?" I poured a cup of coffee and sat at the table.

Izzie slid today's copy of the *Gazette* in front of me. "Looks like we got it wrong about Wink's motive."

I read the headline and gasped. "What the heck? Is he crazy? If Aunt Constance sees this . . . if Ross sees this, Wink might be looking at a liable suit." I skimmed through the article about Viola's murder, which included plenty of references to Aunt Constance and the evidence brought against her and ended with her arrest. "Wow. After writing all this, I'm surprised he didn't come right out and say she's guilty of murder."

"This reads like a gossip rag." Mom poked the paper.

"Yellow journalism isn't what the *Gazette* should be promoting. Wink should be ashamed," Dad added.

Izzie twisted her napkin. "I don't get it. He wanted to send flowers."

I straightened in my seat. "What if he did? Pay a visit and give her the flowers, I mean."

"Oh!" Izzie's eyes widened. "And Aunt Constance gave him the "thanks-but-no-thanks" brush-off and sent him out the door."

"Nothing like a suitor scorned and bitter enough to take out his feelings in a scandalous article." Anger and resentment fueled me with heat. "He can't get away with this."

"No, he can't," Izzie moaned, "but what can we do?"

We both shifted our attention to Mom and Dad, across the table, as if asking for help.

"Let's save any action we take for later, after we've cooled down and aren't so emotional," Dad suggested.

"He's right. Nothing done in anger comes to any good. If Chloe's hunch is correct, that article is a perfect example. By this afternoon, I bet Wink will be wishing he could take back his words." Mom sipped at her tea.

"Well, I'm about to add more bad news, or maybe both good and bad news, to your morning." I recapped my phone conversation with Hunter.

"Ah, that poor woman. What a tragedy." Knitted brows and pursed lips accompanied Mom's soft tone.

"This whole situation is a tragedy." Izzie threw up her arms. "For all of us, the ones who are living through this, especially Aunt Constance. I swear, she's not looking well."

"She's stronger than you think." Dad pushed his plate to the side and leaned back.

"Absolutely, she is." Mom glanced at Milo, who sat up and begged next to her. "Speaking of tragic or sad events, have you heard any news about his owner?"

She whispered her words, and I grinned. "I don't think he understands what you're saying, Mom. No, we haven't heard anything, and according to the vet, he's not microchipped. Looks like we're stuck with each other, pooch."

Milo cocked his head, then trotted over to sit up and place his paws on my leg.

I laughed. "Well, I take it back. Maybe you do understand." I scratched the top of his head. Turning to view Max, I laughed louder as he took the opportunity to finish up Milo's half-eaten breakfast. "You better learn to eat faster, Milo. Your buddy over there is a glutton."

"Okay, we should head to the shop. I need to go over the accounts, tally up sales, and take inventory of the stock. Willow is out until this evening. She's apartment hunting again."

"Too bad the previous place she rented wasn't available." I pushed away from the table and carried my plate and cup to the dishwasher.

"You mean too bad the building owner wouldn't keep it available until she came back to Whisper Cove." Izzie scoffed. "Not a nice move."

"She couldn't very well pay rent for two months while she was gone. Plus, why should the owner lose money on an empty apartment?" I argued.

"You're right. I just feel sorry for her. She's having no luck finding a place," Izzie said. "It was nice of Claire to offer her a spare bedroom in her house for the time being."

We left Mom and Dad while they discussed their day's agenda, which included instructing a painting class in Mayville, a trip to Cutter's Landing to arrange winter storage for their sailboat, and whatever else they could fit into their afternoon.

"You think we should give Aunt Constance a call? To see how she's doing?" Izzie chewed on her thumbnail as she walked outside.

I pressed my lips together to soften the smile beginning to surface. "And ask if Wink Lawrence happened to stop by yesterday?"

Izzie blushed. "Okay, yes, I'm curious, but I'm more concerned about how she reacts to that horrible article."

My jaw tensed. "I'm sure she's not happy about it. It's so frustrating. You'd think with deputies combing the area and asking questions, they'd have found Dewey by now. He needs to explain about that paddle and answer to Branden's story. He lied, Izzie. I think he's covering something up."

We headed for Artisan Alley in Izzie's Land Rover. Marino had called yesterday afternoon to say he'd replaced the battery, and the vehicle was ready for pickup. As we passed through the main intersection, I glanced over at the corner bench. Picasso the cat lay stretched out next to another furry friend, their tails swaying lazily while they basked in the sunlight. Felines knew how to relax and enjoy the moment. We could all use a little of that.

After parking, I exited the car and lifted my bag and jacket from the back seat.

"Wow. Would you look at that." Izzie pointed.

I followed her gaze, and her pointing finger, to examine the scene at the far end of Artisan Alley. A construction crew with their trucks and a bulldozer was busy at work, razing what was left of Sammy's shop. Spencer stood at a safe distance, waving her arms and moving her mouth as if she were spouting orders at everyone, which would be typical Spencer fashion.

"I guess it's really happening." I sighed.

"Spencer will be a craft shop owner and our new neighbor." Izzie smiled and nudged me with her elbow. "Hey, It won't be so bad. She'll have her hands full running the business and won't have time to pester us. You'll see."

"Pester *me*, you mean. You two get along fine." I tried to find something positive in the situation but came up with nothing.

"What is it you always tell me? Don't hold grudges, and let go of the problems you can't fix." Izzie gave me a wise look.

"No. I think you heard that in Mom's yoga class." I scrunched my nose. "Besides, Spencer is a special case. Making amends with her will take time, lots and lots of time."

"Only if you fight it." She waved her arms sideways. "Let it go, Chloe. Let it go. Whoooosahhh."

"Geesh. You are such a goofball quoting me *Bad Boys* and a Martin Lawrence line." I laughed.

"Well, it's true. My yoga instructor reminds me all the time." Izzie nodded as she unlocked the shop door.

"I'll bet he does," I teased. "Thanks for putting me in a better mood. Who needs whoosah to calm me when I've got you?"

"Aw, gee. I'm touched." She held a hand to her chest and batted her eyes.

"Silly you." I settled into a chair and opened the laptop, ready to punch in numbers. "Ready when you are."

Izzie opened the ledger she had brought along and pressed a finger to the page.

Before we could start, the door flew open. Spencer hurried inside, her cheeks puffed out in exasperation and her face red.

"I am so frustrated. Getting competent people to do work shouldn't be so hard. That unreasonable man in charge just told his crew to stop working." She skirted around me and behind the counter. Pulling open the fridge door, she grabbed a bottle of water and chugged down half. She pointed. "Just because the full payment wasn't in their bank account by this morning, they're refusing to do any more work. Isn't that ridiculous? The money will be there. I promised. They agreed, but there they sit, refusing to move an inch."

My brow lifted. I didn't hold back because this was Spencer. "How can you blame them? If you promised payment in full and that's what your contract says."

Spencer glared. "Not the point. There was a verbal agreement. The money will get to their account a few hours late. Doesn't mean we should waste a full day and have no work done."

I tapped my foot, impatient to find out why she was really here. Funny how she was so focused on her own problems and didn't say anything about Aunt Constance and the latest catastrophe, which was Wink Lawrence's article. She might not know, but my guess was even if she did, she wouldn't make it a priority of concern.

Izzie jumped in ahead of me. "Did you have your rescheduled dinner date with Ross?"

"Yes, and he turned down my proposal. Something about how his money was tied up and he couldn't invest right now." She glanced at her watch. "I should call the bank. The sooner these vultures get what they want, the quicker they'll get back to work."

Once the door slammed, Izzie gave me a nod. "Call Ross. There's got to be more to the story. Sounds to me like somebody has money problems."

"Oh yeah. She's desperate and hitting up anyone who can bail her out, I'll bet."

"Which would also mean Aunt Constance is a target." Izzie hopped off her stool. "I'll call to see if she's home and okay."

I watched Izzie walk to the back, until Ross picked up on the third ring.

"Hey, I was just about to call you," Ross said.

"Let me guess. It has something to do with the article in today's *Gazette*." I set aside the laptop, ready for his rant on how he hates people like Wink because all this article does is weigh down an already daunting case. Or something like that.

"What article? Never mind—tell me later. What I called about is your cousin." A moan resonated through the line. "She's a lot to handle. No wonder you never had a nice word to say about her."

"She's hard to take in large doses, but Izzie gets along with her. Go figure." I ventured outside in case Izzie was listening. "Spencer told us you were interested in her business."

"Not exactly true. I was being polite, but then the whole situation snowballed. She's been relentless and in an awful big hurry to get me to invest. It made me suspicious. So, I played along. The more questions I asked, the more I learned about her. That's when I got real curious."

"Let me guess. You did some digging and found dirt." I couldn't help doubting that Spencer's bio was squeaky clean.

"I checked with one of my financial contacts who has access to records. He did a soft inquiry into her credit record. She's defaulted on payments. And I'm guessing, after reading her work history, she has no experience running a craft shop."

"Yep. She closed business deals, but none that involve craft shops, I'm sure." I walked across the lawn to sit on one of the benches, hidden behind a thick oak, where hopefully Spencer wouldn't spot me. If she was still bickering with the work crew, that is.

"Which makes me wonder, how can Constance Abbington have so much money, but her daughter has nothing?"

"Long story. Let's just say the apple doesn't fall far from the tree. Like my aunt, Spencer is not very reliable when it comes to managing a budget, and her father knew it. Even if he couldn't change Aunt Constance, I guess he believed there was hope for Spencer. That's why she doesn't receive her trust fund until she turns thirty. I'm taking bets on how long the money will last."

"That's a bit harsh."

"Sorry. When it comes to Spencer, I have a trigger that won't quit shooting off negativity."

He let out a low whistle. "Lady with a loaded gun and an attitude. I feel sorry for Spencer."

"Are you kidding? She has a bigger and better trigger finger that can take me out along with anyone else she aims for. Don't underestimate her." I shuddered.

"I did call and ask her what other money was financing her business, but I got very vague answers. I have my suspicions, and I warned your aunt about Spencer's motives."

I scoffed. "I can imagine how Aunt Constance responded."

"She told me to mind my own business and concentrate on her case and keep her from going to jail again."

"Typical. She's always defended her, even when Spencer did something wrong." Like when Mom told her about Spencer locking me in the closet for over an hour. Aunt Constance's only response was that I must've done something to hurt Spencer's feelings in the first place.

"Anyway, I'm concerned for Constance. Maybe I'll dig further into Spencer's background when I get the chance. I got a call this morning, and one of my clients is facing more charges against him. I need to video-conference with the partners in New York later today, but I still want to see if there are other red flags about Spencer. My attorney instincts are telling me there's more to her story."

"Let me help. I'll do the digging. I'm sure I can find something." Spencer's footprint was all over social media. How hard could it be to gather information about her life?

"Thanks. Honestly, Spencer's business ventures are none of my concern, but I do care how her relationship impacts my client. Now, what article were you talking about?"

"Get a copy of today's *Whisper Cove Gazette*. You'll find it on page one. Have fun." I thanked him for calling, then quickly got off the phone, anxious to get back to the shop and hear what Izzie had to say.

As I crossed the lawn, I caught sight of Spencer. She had her phone slapped to one ear. Her mouth moved fast, and the volume carried down Artisan Alley. I guessed things weren't going well with the bank. It wouldn't surprise me if her loan was denied. Convincing Aunt Constance to ignore Spencer's plea for money seemed more urgent than ever. My worry was, if my aunt didn't give it to her willingly, Spencer would resort to some deceitful means to get her hands on the money.

I gritted my teeth. "It's time to find out what Spencer has been up to the past few years."

I entered the shop and could hear Izzie talking in the storage room. I put the "Closed" sign on the door and, grabbing the laptop, made my way to the back.

"Please, Aunt Constance. We know the article is bogus. By next week, people will have new stories to gossip about. And stop apologizing. You didn't know when you sent him away that he'd be such a jerk about it. Get some rest, and we'll stop by later." Izzie turned to face me as she hung up. "She's livid and scared. Wink only wanted to badger her with questions about the murder. He wasn't interested in her romantically.

She got so angry that she threatened to call the police and report him for trespassing. The poor woman says she'll never be able to face people again without feeling judged."

"So, we were right about him going to visit her. He definitely gives journalists a bad name." My cheeks puffed out as I drew in, then slowly released my breath. "I feel for her, and it is horrible, but once the killer is caught, everyone will forget she was a suspect, and all the nasty stuff in that article."

"I told her as much, but I don't think she heard me. Did Ross say anything about it?" Izzie straddled the back of a chair and rested her chin on top.

"He hasn't seen the article. We talked about Spencer, though." I gave her the highlights of our conversation.

"I have to admit, I'm thinking the way you would. Why did she turn up in Whisper Cove now? After all this time, she comes back when Aunt Constance is fighting for her freedom. Sounds suspicious." She glanced at the laptop in my hands. "What are you doing?"

"I'm digging for information." I typed the name of Spencer's employer, Jansen Tech Software, in the search bar and got on the website. "Hold on." I blinked, and my jaw dropped. "Izzie, the company Spencer works for went bankrupt and decided to close down permanently." I fixed my gaze on her. "Three months ago."

A queasiness spread through me. This story kept getting worse, underlining the question I couldn't get out of my head. What was Spencer planning? I had every suspicious thought possible circling inside my brain. Not the ideal time right now, since I needed to focus on how to clear Aunt Constance's name and lead the way to who killed Viola. Or at least help find that person. I didn't intend to step on Hunter's investigative toes, but in this circumstance I'd do whatever it took to save Aunt Constance and the Abbington name from being dragged through the gossip dirt.

"Wow. What do you think she's been doing for the past three months? Hanging out at some California café, sipping Appletinis?" Izzie drummed her fingers on the chairback. "I'm truly at a loss to defend her, which is a shame because I always got along with Spencer."

"Yeah, I'll admit, even though we have our differences, I'm surprised she'd keep something as serious as losing her job a secret. Do you think Aunt Constance knows?" I wasn't sure why I asked, because I already had the answer in mind.

"Of course. She can count on her mother's support, no matter how bad things are," Izzie said.

"Do you think we should confront Spencer?" I tipped my head, giving the suggestion some serious thought.

"She'd know we were snooping." Izzie bit her nail. "But how else will we get answers?"

"The thing is, we don't want to take too much time away from Viola's case. That's where our efforts should be going." I sighed, then refocused on the laptop and scrolled through any other information I could find about Spencer's now defunct employer. I shot out of my seat as a sudden notion hit me. "Why didn't I think of that before?" I snapped my fingers. "Sammy."

"Sammy?" Izzie tilted her head to the side.

"The property belonged to her. She'll have all the details of the sale to Spencer." I rummaged in my bag. "I'll give her a call and ask."

I drummed my fingers on the counter in quick tempo, waiting for someone to pick up. Three rings later, she answered. "Hey, Sammy! How are things in Altoona?" I pushed the speaker button. Izzie and I listened to a frenzied recap of Sammy's family happenings and her news of starting up a business with her cousins.

"Me partnering with them wouldn't have happened, but I got lucky when someone offered to buy the Artisan Alley property. Neat, huh?"

"Good for you." I paused a second. "I'm sure you know the buyer is related to us. Spencer is our cousin."

"Yes, I asked the realtor representing her. I never talked to your cousin directly. The deal went like a dream. I had no problems or complaints, if that's what you're getting at."

I glimpsed Izzie for a second. "No, that's not it. Do you know how the purchase was paid for?"

"Why are you asking? Is something wrong? Like I said, the deal went through. I got my money, and my cousins and I are excited to open Accessory Imports." Her voice pitched higher.

"Nothing's wrong, Sammy. Not for you, anyway." I tugged on my ear, working through how much to tell her. "We're just worried about Spencer's mother, and we're trying to gather as much information as we can. Do you know if the money you received came from a bank loan or was paid in cash? Not exactly the kind of thing sellers are aware of, but I thought there was a chance you—"

"Hold on. You don't need to explain. Just so happens one of my cousins works at a bank. This wasn't exactly what you'd call ethical, but we did a little digging to make sure the buyer was legit. We didn't want any problems to botch up our plans. Anyway, through my cousin's connections, we learned the buyer, your cousin, was approved for a loan from First National Bank of New York with twenty percent down. Does that help?"

My breath quickened, and I returned Izzie's high-five gesture. "Absolutely. Thanks, Sammy." I hung up and, with a trembling hand, laid the phone on the counter.

"Wow. First National Bank is where Aunt Constance keeps her money. Dad and Mom too. You know what that means." Izzie's eyes grew bright. "If she didn't help Spencer get that loan, and maybe even dish out the twenty percent down, I'll eat Mom's quinoa recipes for a month without complaining."

"I'll second your bet, and I like those quinoa dishes less than you do."

"How do we handle this? Confront Aunt Constance? Have Dad do some snooping behind her back? He's the appointed financial advisor of the Abbington money."

"Out of respect for her, I think we should ask Aunt Constance."

"What if she denies it?" Izzie chewed on her ragged thumbnail.

"Then we ask Dad to investigate."

"What about Spencer losing her job? If Aunt Constance doesn't know, and then finds out we knew but didn't tell her, she'll be plenty angry. Then again, I worry about what all this stress will do to her health. Maybe we should wait."

I rolled my shoulders to ease the tension. "I agree. She's stressed enough. Let's deal with one issue at a time."

Chapter Sixteen

I zzie took off early to open the shop and left me a note saying to come in when I could. She knew I'd had a rough night with Max and his tummy issues. It was nice having an understanding partner. I splashed cold water on my face, then sprinted downstairs to the kitchen.

Milo chomped on his food while Max stared longingly, then picked through his rice and chicken mix, his diet for the time being.

"Good morning. I hope there's some coffee left."

Milo hopped and danced around me, vying for my attention. I laughed at the sight of Max attempting to get at his canine buddy's breakfast.

Mom quickly snatched it away, then turned to me. "I made a second pot. Are you staying to eat? I can whip up an omelet," she said.

"No time. I'm late getting to the shop." I grabbed my coffee and a blueberry bagel. "See you at dinner. Love you." I gave her a quick peck on the cheek and peeked over her shoulder to view the backyard. "Where's Dad? I thought he planned to do some bulb planting today."

"Right now he's next door helping Mr. Bixby unload the firewood delivery. I'm heading out to my work shed to finish the painting I started. You have a good day."

After a steady rain had fallen throughout the night, this morning brought out the sun and blue skies. I inhaled the crisp, musky-sweet scent of dried leaves and the cool, pungent smell of pine sap. Smiling, I skipped down the porch steps and jogged to my car. I spotted Dad and Mr. Bixby standing by the pile of wood, chatting and drinking from the mugs they held, cupped in their hands. More than likely, that wood pile wouldn't be completely moved until late afternoon. Planting bulbs would be put off until tomorrow or whenever the weather cooperated. I loved the slow and easy pace of life around here. A pleasant difference from the hustle and bustle of Manhattan.

I turned toward Main Street to make a quick stop at For Sweet's Sake, to grab a muffin and coffee for Izzie, who probably hadn't bothered to eat before going to work. Stepping through the doorway, I froze. Spencer was at the counter, paying for her purchase. In her usual friendly fashion, she chattered on and on with Claire. "Morning, ladies. How are you?" I slid to a stop next to Spencer.

"Chloe. What a surprise seeing you here." Spencer smiled and tucked her credit card back inside her bag.

"It shouldn't be. I come here all the time, so no surprise." My tone grew edgy because all I could think about was how she'd lied, or at least hadn't told us the truth about her job, which was the same as a lie.

"Silly. I meant surprised because I figured you'd be at work by now." Spencer flipped her hand in a dismissive gesture.

"Well, I'm off. Thank you, Claire. Bye, Chloe," she called as she made her exit.

Claire's shoulders shook as she bellowed a laugh. "That woman is sure about drama."

"What do you mean?" I frowned.

"Every time I've run into her, she's got a new story to tell. Always loaded with the drama. What a life she must have."

I tugged my wallet out of my bag. "You mean she's stopped here before?"

"Well, twice at the bakery, but I also met her in Buffalo at the bus depot. I was coming back on the train from Chicago after visiting my sister, and then took the bus the rest of the way home. Your cousin was on that ride, but when was that? It's been a while. Hmm, let me think." Claire tapped her lip with one finger and stared at the ceiling.

"Wait. What?" My mind raced to count back. Megan had spotted Spencer a week ago. What was Claire implying?

Claire snapped her fingers. "I can't believe it's been two weeks. Of course, my sister and I talk on the phone almost every day, but yes. The trip when I saw your cousin was two weeks ago. I remember she told me she was going to Mayville to see her mother—that's your aunt Constance, right? After that, on to Whisper Cove about business."

"Yeah, Aunt Constance is Spencer's mom." My voice grew flat. Two weeks ago would have been right before Viola's murder. Spencer was in Mayville at the time. Or at least, that's where she'd told Claire she was going. That could've been another lie, but what worried me was the possibility that Aunt Constance had lied too.

"Is something wrong, Chloe?" Claire's brow creased.

I forced my lips into a smile. "No, everything's perfect. I'll take a coffee and a bran muffin to go."

I sped down Whisper Cove Boulevard. I couldn't wrap my brain around what Claire had told me. Why would Spencer have led us to believe she'd arrived home this past Friday and not two weeks ago? Of course, I hadn't asked what day she got here, but still, that detail bothered me. Sometimes people covered up their stories with lies when they had something to hide, didn't they? On impulse, I hit the voice command button. "Call Laurel Bay Hotel." The hotel was tucked away in the wooded lakeside town of Laurel Bay, east of here. It was the perfect place for Spencer to hide out for several days, but why would she?

"Laurel Bay Hotel, how may I help you?"

"Yes, this is Spencer Abbington. I was thinking of paying my tab, but I can't remember how many days I've been here. Silly me." I tapped the steering wheel as I sat at the red light.

"Miss Abbington, you have fourteen days on your bill so far. Are you planning to check out today? If so, I can—"

"Never mind. I just remembered I have an appointment in town tomorrow and another the day after that. Seems my brain is frazzled with everything on my agenda. Sorry to bother you." I stabbed the end call button and released my breath. "This is insane. How many lies has she told?"

I parked and sprang out of the car. With my bag and Izzie's breakfast in hand, I hurried inside the shop. "Izzie." I clutched my chest and waited until my heartbeat slowed.

"Are you okay? You look ready to pass out." Izzie came from behind the counter and took everything I was carrying out of my hands, then pushed me into a chair.

"Sorry." Giving myself another few seconds to relax, I nodded. "Spencer lied about how long she's been in town. She's been here for two weeks."

She sat across from me. "What? How do you know? Oh boy, why would she lie about that?"

"Think, Izzie. Two weeks ago? That's right before Viola's murder. She checked into the Laurel Bay Hotel."

"No." Izzie shook her head slowly. "I don't like where you're going with this."

"I'm not going anywhere with it. I'm saying she lied about when she arrived. I called the hotel, pretending to be her, and asked how many nights I'd been charged for so far. Fourteen. She lied, Izzie. I worry what else she could be hiding."

I bent over to rest my elbows on my thighs and cradled my chin. Izzie's hunch was right. I was "going there" but thought it wise to keep that scenario to myself. Spencer had been in the area the night of our painting event at Bellows Lodge and of Viola's unfortunate demise. Totally irrelevant to the murder case, but I was uncomfortable with coincidences.

"You're right. She's been sneaky and secretive this whole time." Izzie slouched in her seat. "Maybe we should skip the costume gig this afternoon. Too much is going on. Besides, dressed like that, we'd be too conspicuous. I mean, who's going to say anything about the murder when three witches are lurking close by?"

"That's what I've been saying. Why don't we save the costumes for the Hallows Eve celebration on Saturday?" I relaxed as relief washed over me. Parading around town in costume wasn't in my comfort zone, but on Hallows Eve, all the merchants and plenty of locals would be dressed up as their favorite characters, with plenty of ghosts, goblins, and witches joining in the fun.

"For a moment, I thought of us dressing up tomorrow evening for the Trick Your Pumpkin event, but let's not take the chance of getting paint stains on our costumes." She scrunched her nose.

"How about a more direct approach? For starters, a conversation with Wink might be useful." I held up two fingers. "And Sarah. Whatever's going on between them is sketchy. Too bad Dewey went into hiding."

"Hunter will find him. Oh, and we need to add Marilyn to the list. She reminds me of a crazy groupie with a fatal attraction. If she turned out to be the killer, I wouldn't be at all surprised," Izzie added.

"Then it's settled. Now, all we have to do is track them down to talk and hope we learn something useful." I tapped my chin. "Marilyn and Sarah should be helping to set up kiosks and game booths. We'll go out there this evening after dinner. As for Wink, we can always catch him later at the *Gazette*." That queasy feeling in the pit of my stomach hinted the odds were stacked against us learning much, but we had to try.

"Don't forget Aunt Constance and Spencer. We need to have a conversation with them too." Izzie winced. "Won't be easy getting to the truth."

"After we deal with Marilyn, Sarah, and Wink. Okay?" I groaned. If it weren't for Aunt Constance being in the middle of this tragedy, I'd gladly take a back seat to Hunter and his investigation.

We busied ourselves with last-minute prep for tomorrow evening's event. Izzie and I finally got around to carving our pumpkin for the contest while Willow painted faces on a few to display in our window. She'd already finished her stage paintings for the event, showing the steps of our instructions. By mid-afternoon, everything on our to-do list had been checked off.

The jingle of door chimes alerted us to a visitor. I brushed off my jeans and walked to the front of the shop. Marilyn stood at the entrance. I smiled. Nothing easier than having a suspect come to your doorstep. I glanced over my shoulder. Izzie stood in the doorway and gave me a thumbs-up. Marilyn was all mine to question. "Hi, Marilyn. What brings you here?"

"I wanted to pay my admission for tomorrow evening's event." She turned her gaze away from me, to scan the room. "This place is wonderful. All the paintings and decorations, and the way you've set up the room for events—it's all perfect. I will have to come more often. I love painting. I'm only a novice, but I try and make my best effort to improve." She slapped her hand with her leather gloves. "My late husband turned one of our guest rooms into a studio, bless his heart." She sniffed and lifted her chin. "He was a saint. Anyway, how much do I owe you?"

"It's thirty-five, but you don't have to pay. The Sisterhood donated money to cover all of our guests. Their way of apologizing, I guess."

"Um. You mean for trying to sue you after Viola's death? Yes, I figured that's the way it would end up. Such a cheap move on their part. Anything to take the focus off the Sisterhood being involved in the tragedy of murder. They can be shady in that way. Just like they were when they closed our chapter and fired Constance." Her eyes narrowed as her voice and tone grew angry. "I'll never forgive them for that. Constance and our group deserve better."

I smoothed the creases in my apron with both hands. "It's nice how you take such great care of my aunt. She talks about you all the time."

I didn't add specifics, especially the negative comments Aunt Constance spouted off. That wouldn't be wise. Izzie might have it right in calling Marilyn a crazy groupie with a fatal attraction, maybe like the intense and dangerous kind. I had to tread carefully with my words.

She patted her hair. "Yes, well, she deserves the best. I saw you there earlier this week."

"Sunday." I nodded. "You drive a blue convertible, right? I spotted you pulling into the driveway as we drove down the street. Poor Aunt Constance wasn't feeling well that day. Having to answer questions about Viola's glove being found in her car and so close to being arrested—it nearly made her faint again. Your note seemed to perk her up, which was fortunate after finding the nasty trick-or-treat message with its warning." I shuddered and rubbed my arms.

Marilyn blinked and her jaw dropped. In the next instant, her mouth snapped shut and she tried for a smile that didn't quite form.

"Oh? You didn't know about that?," I continued. "Well, let me tell you, Aunt Constance is so brave. She insists it's just some child's prank. Probably neighbor kids having a little fun. I'm not so sure, though."

"That's . . . how horrible. I should give her a call." Her eyes fluttered as she rummaged in her bag. "Where is that phone?"

"Marilyn, she's probably right outside, helping with the Hallows Eve setup. Wouldn't you think?" I might have gone too far with my comments, but before I could offer her something to drink or suggest she sit for a while, she disappeared outside.

"Well, that was disturbing." Izzie came from behind me and planted one fist on her side.

"It's almost like she idolizes Aunt Constance." I peered through the picture window. Marilyn waved both arms as she took hurried strides toward a group of ladies. Aunt Constance was in the center, pointing at one of the kiosks and shaking her head.

"What a challenge. We have Marilyn, who loves and supports Aunt Constance to a fault. On the other end, there's Sarah Gilley, who appears to hold a grudge against both our aunt and Viola."

"That's true. She threw out a lot of criticism about them but stopped short of suggesting Aunt Constance had murdered Viola."

"No, but her comments were almost as damaging." Izzie nudged me. "We should have a talk with Sarah, and soon."

"Yep." By now, Marilyn was following Aunt Constance around the lawn, her mouth moving and, I gathered, filling my aunt with plenty about how worried she was.

"Let me go. She might open up to someone who's a stranger. I can pretend to dislike your aunt, which should make Sarah comfortable to talk." Willow approached, wiping her hands with a wet cloth.

"Good idea. I'll have to point her out. If she's out there, that is." I walked to the window and scanned the grounds.

The tall, white-haired figure should be easy to spot. However, lots of Sisterhood members were older and had the same hair color. "There." I pointed next to the boat dock. "She's standing next to—awe sheesh. She's with Wink. You might have a hard time getting any information with the two of them together."

"I've got an idea." Izzie grinned and grabbed her phone. "I'll call to tell him I was passing by his building and there's a line outside with people holding protests signs about the *Gazette* publishing biased news. He'll be running to town in seconds."

"And when he sees there's no one there?" I tipped my head to one side. "You don't think he'll be at our doorstep, fuming mad that you sent him on a wild chase?"

"Maybe they needed a break. Or the authorities told them to leave because they didn't have a permit to protest. Seriously, I can come up with a dozen excuses. I'm not worried." Izzie nodded at Willow. "Just be ready to go out there when he leaves."

"Are you sure you can handle this?" I clenched my teeth and winced. "Maybe I—"

Willow laid her hand on my arm. "You've told me in detail about Sarah, a play-by-play of your conversations, your aunt's opinion, and anything else. I feel like she's a member of my family. You know, the grouchy cousin who comes to dinner and puts everyone in a bad mood. I have several like her on my mom's side. Trust me, I can deal."

I tousled her pink and purple hair, which made her laugh. "All right, then."

"Hi, Wink. It's Izzie. There's something you might want to take care of." Izzie waved her arm after she finished the conversation and motioned Willow toward the door.

"Good luck!" I waved as Willow slipped outside. "She'll be fine, right?" I turned to Izzie.

She shrugged. "Heck if I know."

"Great." I tossed the balled paper towel I'd been holding into the trash can.

* * *

Nothing came out of Willow's talk with Sarah. Wink had returned within five minutes, since all the "protesters" had vanished. The sum total of what Willow had learned was Sarah professing her love for Wink and how they had plans to marry. Willow couldn't get a word into the conversation about Marilyn or Aunt Constance or Viola. Sarah was gushing with her news. Then Wink pulled her away. Forget marriage plans. The shocker was believing Sarah could turn on the happily ever after charm.

I headed on foot to Millie's Diner for our takeout. The dinner crowd filled every table available. Millie's crew of servers bustled from guest to guest, taking orders and delivering meals. The noise of laughter and chatter was almost deafening. I had to shout at Stevie, who was manning the counter.

"Hi, Stevie. I'm here for my order."

He nodded and held up his finger, then turned to check the trail of bags sitting behind him on a shelf.

I tapped my fingers against my thigh and looked around the room. A high-pitched laugh that sounded like the rat-a-tat-tat of a machine gun rang in my ear. I recognized that laugh. Gwen had to be enjoying herself, probably on a date with Winston. Leaning sideways, I peered through an opening in the wicker trellis that divided us, and my jaw dropped.

Not only were Gwen and Winston in my view, but I also spotted Spencer sitting across a table from Ross.

"Hey, Chloe. Here's your order," Stevie shouted.

"Shh." I flapped my arm and glared a warning.

Stevie set the bag on the counter and held up both arms in surrender.

Satisfied and relieved neither of them had heard Stevie, I put my ear as close to the trellis as I could without getting pricked by wood splinters.

"I don't get you. In fact, I think you should be ashamed. First, you were all for me representing your mom's case. Now, you're asking me to help declare her unfit and in need of psychiatric care? And I asked myself why you would even consider doing something so cruel to your mother." Ross smacked the table. "Then, it hit me." He stabbed a finger at her. "If the court declares her unfit and sends her for a psych eval, you could get control of her money."

"No, no, you don't understand, Ross." Spencer sobbed. "I'm doing what's best for my mom. She's not well and needs help. I can't—"

"Stop. Would you stop? I've heard enough. My answer is no, I won't do what you're asking. And no, I won't step down as your mom's attorney, not unless she wants me to. I think we're done, Spencer." Ross pushed away from the table.

Heat flushed through me. I stormed around the partition and stopped in front of Spencer. "You are—I knew you were up to no good. I told Izzie that I didn't trust you, and I'm sorry to say I was right. You should be ashamed of yourself, Spencer Abbington. Aunt Constance deserves so much better."

Spencer's eyes widened. For an instant, she braced her shoulders and lifted her chin as if to put up a defense. Yet, just as quickly, she dropped her head in both hands, and her whole body shook as she sobbed.

I reached down to stroke her arm. Despite all my complaints about her, she was still my cousin. "Hey, I'm sorry. I didn't mean—look. I'm worried about your mom, and since you've been away, it's kind of been our job to watch out for her. Bottom line is we're family, and secrets will only pull us apart." I knelt down. "Why don't you tell me what's really going on?" My voice softened to a whisper as the customers around us had begun to stare. "Maybe we should take the conversation outside?"

Ross nodded and called to the server. "You two go on ahead. I'll take care of this."

I wrapped an arm around Spencer and led her through the diner to the exit door. Spotting the bench on the corner, I steered her in that direction. "Now, let's start with why you lied about when you got to town, because I know for a fact that you've been staying at the hotel in Laurel Bay for two weeks. I checked."

She sniffed and dabbed her nose with a tissue. "Mom made me promise not to tell and to keep out of sight for a few days. She said it was better for her if no one found out when I arrived. Chloe, it was frightening to see her that way. She pleaded and cried and begged me to go back to L.A., but I couldn't leave her like that."

"Why? I don't understand." I gripped my end of the bench. Ross hadn't appeared, which made me think he was giving us time to talk alone.

Spencer grabbed my arm and squeezed. "This is between you and me. Only you and me. Understand?"

I blinked. What was going on? Dread inched through me and left a sour taste in my mouth. I couldn't be right about my hunch, could I? Spencer might be mean and insensitive sometimes, but she didn't have it in her to kill someone. *Right?*

I nodded slowly. "Okay."

"I was at home that horrible night when Viola was murdered. I saw the look on Mom's face when she came home from your event. She was talking to herself, saying she shouldn't have left her alone. She made me promise not to tell anyone about that evening because of how it would make her look. I shouldn't have listened, but she worried if I got involved, I'd have to answer all those questions the authorities would ask." She squeezed harder and shook her head. "We have to do something. Unless you have a better idea, the only way I can think to keep her out of jail is to put her in a psychiatrist's care."

"What are you saying, Spencer?" My heartbeat skipped as she looked away for a second. When she turned to face me, I froze. I could count on one hand the number of times she'd looked frightened. This was one of them.

Her tongue ran along her upper lip. "Chloe, I think, I mean, I *know* Mom killed Viola Finnwinkle."

Chapter Seventeen

I dragged the rake to gather more leaves into a pile along the front edge of our property, where the trucks would drive by to suck them up with their machines. I took a deep breath. The ground released a musky scent where it had been uncovered and laid bare. Despite the busywork, my mind kept looping through what Spencer had said. I couldn't accept the idea that Aunt Constance was guilty of hurting anyone, no matter how strong her words might be at times.

Peeking around the side of the house, I spotted Mom and Dad raking near the back of our lot. Early this morning, they'd recruited Izzie and me to help before we'd had much of a chance to talk. We decided to keep quiet about the startling information Spencer had told me. Mom and Dad didn't need any unnecessary worries.

Last night, Ross and I had taken charge and delivered Spencer back to her hotel room, where she took a sedative and went straight to bed. I'd called Izzie to give her a quick version of the story and told her to order something else for dinner. I'd left Millie's in such a hurry, I'd forgotten our takeout. As it turned out, Millie, being the sweetheart we all loved, had sent

Stevie to the shop to deliver the meal. By the time I returned, Izzie and Willow were finishing up their food, and mine was tucked away in the fridge.

I leaned my rake against the nearby tree and walked to where Izzie stood. "We need to talk, to plan, to figure out what to do next." I shoved both hands in my pockets to take off the chill.

Izzie sighed. "And do what? Spencer says Aunt Constance killed Viola. She *claims* Aunt Constance acted and talked like she was guilty of the crime. She says a lot of things, but she doesn't have proof."

"But she heard Aunt Constance talk to herself. 'I shouldn't have left her alone.' What if she meant Viola? I'm not agreeing with Spencer. I don't really think Aunt Constance killed Viola, but she might have seen something and is afraid to tell anyone. Right? It's possible. You know she hasn't really explained that missing hour, the one she has no alibi for." I leaned closer and lowered my voice. "What if she was there when Viola was murdered?"

Izzie threw up her arms. "Please, Chloe. We don't know who Aunt Constance was referring to when she said that. As far as acting upset and panicky, she'd just learned the bad news about the Sisterhood chapter and her job. Who wouldn't be upset about that? Spencer got it wrong. She's overreacting."

"Maybe. At least I'm pretty sure Ross and I talked her out of that ridiculous plan."

"Committing Aunt Constance to a loony bin? Totally wrong." Izzie leaned her cheek against the rake handle.

"Loony bin?" I scoffed. "Nice choice of words."

Izzie rolled her eyes. "You know what I meant. Okay, she suggested a psych eval and some treatment to keep her out of jail. Still, not a smart plan."

"Right again. All the more reason to concentrate on our suspect list. We need to learn more about Marilyn and Sarah, for starters. Maybe follow them around and see if it leads to something useful. Or . . ." I tapped my lip, and all at once my eyes popped wide open.

"Or what?" Izzie leveled her gaze. "I'm worried already, and you haven't even told me what devious plan is circling around in your brain."

"A game of hearts. We flush out the queen—or in this case, the killer." Heat warmed my cheeks as my confidence grew. "We send notes, anonymously of course, to each of them. Something like, 'I know you killed Viola Finnwinkle. If you don't meet me at the ferry dock this evening at nine and bring ten thousand dollars, I'll go to the authorities.' What do you think?"

She reared back her head. "Scary but impressive. My cautious self is saying it's too risky. Don't shake your head. Your impulsive side is taking charge. I get it, but what if one of them brings a gun and tries to shoot us? Or here's a thought: maybe neither one is the killer. We've wasted an evening playing blackmail when we could've been out doing some real investigating."

"Yeah, all of that's true." I wrinkled my nose, but a slight grin surfaced. "So, are you in? We can go upstairs and write those blackmail letters. Oh—wait! A quicker way would be to call, disguise our voices, and give them the message. What do you think? Yeah, much better."

"They'll recognize our phone numbers, Chloe." She sighed.

"Burner phone." I grinned. "We can buy a disposable one at the gas station, ditch it when we're through. Easy peasy."

"This could go so wrong, and if Hunter finds out, he'll never forgive us."

"Stop worrying about Hunter. We're desperate. Spencer could change her mind and go through with her plan. Can you see Aunt Constance surviving in a funny farm?" I demanded.

"Funny farm?" Izzie tsked as she slowly shook her head. "And you criticize me for being insensitive. Okay, so we're desperate and time's ticking."

"You're with me, then?" I winked. "Don't worry. If guns start firing, I'll jump in front of you and take the hit."

"You're not funny." She grabbed her rake and walked to the shed.

"A little funny," I shouted while jogging over to where I'd left mine.

"Not even."

I laughed, and with rake in hand, I ran to catch up. Sparks of enthusiasm surged through me. Sure, the plan could be risky, but we were running out of options and needed to eliminate suspects. I hadn't given up on Dewey being the guilty one. Time and place fit, and if his prints were on the paddle, not to mention on the bag, Hunter would think so too. However, since he was MIA, we couldn't do anything about him until he surfaced from his hiding place.

"Operation Flush the Queen is about to go down, Aunt Constance," I whispered.

* * *

"Welcome, everyone. Chloe, Willow, and I are so glad you came out this evening for our Trick Your Pumpkin event. We have paints, glitter, rhinestones, and even stick-on decorations for those who are super enthused about glamming up their pumpkins." Izzie beamed with a mile-wide grin.

"You'll find apple cider and donuts from For Sweet's Sake along the back counter. Help yourselves. We'll get started in a few minutes," I added.

"We can still back out, you know. If we don't show up at the dock, no harm done," Izzie whispered.

"We've taken it this far. If you've changed your mind, it's fine. I've got my baseball bat and police whistle." I kept facing the doorway, where Willow stood greeting our guests, and waited for a couple of them, in particular, to appear. The burner phone had worked perfectly. Both Marilyn and Sarah had answered on the first ring. Since Izzie was too nervous, I had handled the calls. I quickly gave the message, then hung up before either one could say a word.

"Do you really think I'd let you go alone?" Her voice squeaked. When the guests sitting near us stared, Izzie burbled out a hiccup and gave them an apologetic smile. Her head snapped around, and she cupped one hand around her mouth. "Sisters shouldn't desert each other. Wasn't that what you told me this past summer? And you're right. If you go, I go, even if I think it's dangerous."

I sighed. "We'll be fine. We can hide in the car, or behind something, and wait for one of them to show up, if you want." I eyed Aunt Constance as she walked in, followed closely by Marilyn. In another minute, Sarah entered the shop.

The clock inched closer to six thirty. We had decided to schedule this event a little earlier, since most everyone had plans to sit by the lake with their binoculars and cameras this evening, hoping to catch a glimpse of the Chautauqua ghost, Abigail Bellows. Even though the legend claimed she wouldn't appear until Hallows Eve, folks were hopeful. And after Rita had spread the rumors that she'd seen the ghost lady floating across the lake on the day of our Autumn Sizzle painting event, the excitement had grown.

I joined Izzie and Willow to circulate around the room and personally greet everyone. The three of us agreed to do our best to keep eyes on Marilyn and Sarah, in case either acted or did something suspicious. I doubted they would with so many people in the room, but considering the phone calls we'd made, they might be nervous and not able to keep their emotions in check.

I stepped nearer to where Sarah stood talking to another sister member. She was extending her hand to show off the engagement ring on her finger.

"Wink is such a generous man. I mean, would you look at the size of this rock? I couldn't be luckier." As if someone had suddenly turned off her happy button, she scowled when Marilyn walked by with Aunt Constance. "Would you look at those two? The queen of our now defunct Sisterhood and her shadow. How pathetic."

I rolled my eyes and stepped up to the stage once more. I'd keep my focus on Marilyn instead—or, I should say, on Aunt Constance and Marilyn, because Sarah was right. They were practically glued together. From the look of her pinched lips and narrowed eyes, I doubted Aunt Constance was happy about the situation. Marilyn seemed clueless as she handed her idol a cup of apple cider and a donut. Then, glancing side to side, as if to see no one was watching, she popped something in her mouth and chewed slowly. My brow creased. What was that about?

Izzie returned to the stage and tapped her paint brush. "Ladies and gentlemen, if you would please take your seats, we'll get started."

I held up the sketching pencil. "We're going to use the sketching pencils to lightly outline our pumpkins on canvas. Like this." I drew the round shape while Izzie and Willow visited each guest to assist where needed.

With each step, the pumpkin paintings took form, and each had its own unique style, bedazzled with a choice of preferred trimmings. The clock inched closer to eight and the time to wrap up the event. "Before you leave, be sure to use one of the blow-dryers on your works of art. You won't want to decorate your car seats with all that glitter and paint." I stepped down from the stage and grabbed a couple of wet wipes to clean my hands, then took a sip of apple cider. I choked and sprayed some on my apron. Sarah had approached Aunt Constance, who was engaged in conversation with Willow. However, Marilyn stepped in to block Sarah's way. Each bobbed from side to side. Like an offensive lineman and a defensive tackle, Marilyn blocked and Sarah tried to get past her. In the next second, Marilyn and Sarah were nose to nose, their faces red as beets and mouths moving faster than I'd ever seen anyone talk. Before I could approach, Aunt Constance turned and her jaw dropped. She stepped between them, her hands splaying to force them apart, until Sarah stomped out of the shop.

"Hey! You want to get started on cleanup?" Izzie called out from behind me.

I waited until Marilyn and Aunt Constance, trailing behind all the others, finally left. "Sure." I picked up one of the trash cans and walked down each row, disposing of water cups and make-shift paper-plate palettes.

Willow approached as she collected brushes and placed them in the wash bin. "That Marilyn is such a snoot. I heard her say that most of the sisters are unfaithful and show no respect for your aunt, especially Sarah. No wonder most of them don't like her."

"They all might be jealous of her too. The way she keeps so close to Aunt Constance and cuts her off from anyone else." I pivoted on my heel and pointed. "At least we know Sarah has issues with their relationship. Did you hear anything when the two of them were arguing? You were close by."

Willow's brows lifted. "Doesn't sound like the Marilyn you described, right? I'm not sure why she would cause such a public scene. The only thing I heard was Marilyn telling Sarah to make an appointment and that this wasn't the place or time for a gripe session. Sarah's words were muffled by your aunt's laugh until, the next thing I knew, she spun around and stopped what could've gotten ugly."

I shuddered and glanced at the clock. "I don't have time to figure it out. Maybe Marilyn's outburst was triggered by whatever she popped in her mouth. Probably some kind of meds."

"What meds? All I saw her munching on were peppermint candies." Willow shrugged.

I stiffened. "Peppermint?"

"Yep. Say, didn't you tell me the bag of candy delivered to your aunt was filled with peppermints?" Willow sat in one of the chairs.

I nodded. Marilyn didn't fit the profile. Why would she send Aunt Constance a threatening message? She cared for her, admired her, and claimed she'd always protect her. I gasped and nearly dropped the cups and plates I held. Shoving them into the trash, I cringed as my head exploded with a possible scenario. Marilyn wanted to be needed. Aunt Constance had been targeted as a murder suspect and had been a hysterical mess ever since. Marilyn was by her side almost every minute, to comfort and help her. In that way, Marilyn felt needed.

"What if Marilyn sent the candygram so Aunt Constance would stay afraid?" I blinked, wide-eyed, at Willow.

"I thought she liked your aunt. Why would she want her to keep being afraid?"

I shook my head and shrugged. "Some sort of sick obsession to be needed? I don't know. Either she's way too bold or totally oblivious, but engaging Sarah in an argument like that sure got my attention and my curiosity piqued."

"Curiosity in thinking she sent the candygram? Or committed murder?"

"Maybe both, but we can't forget Sarah is part of this equation." I shuddered. Something bothered me. Something that didn't add up. Marilyn didn't seem the bold and reckless type. She was prim, proper, and precise. The message had smudge marks, like someone with dirty fingers had handled it. At the bakery, she'd pulled out a wet wipe to clean her hands before and after our meeting over coffee. Would someone like her leave a smudge-marked message?

As for the argument, Sarah seemed more like the type to instigate. Maybe she'd said something cruel to taunt Marilyn. What if she'd wanted to cause a scene to make us think Marilyn could have had an out-of-control moment and been angry enough to defend Aunt Constance by killing Viola? My head was spinning. If that's the mood we were facing this evening, Izzie might be right. Maybe going to the dock was a risk.

Turning, I studied Willow's puzzled face. "I want you to do something for me, okay?"

"Sure." She frowned. "Why?"

"Just listen." I lowered my voice. "I want you to go to the back room and then call for Izzie. Say you need help. That will give me a chance to sneak out."

"But why? I thought you two were going to the ferry together." Willow tilted her head. "Doesn't sound safe, Chloe."

I squeezed her arm. "Please, Willow. I can handle this, but I don't want to take a chance of Izzie getting hurt. I couldn't live with that. This is my plan and my risk. Now, will you do what I say?" My words and tone edged upward.

"Fine." She sprang out of her seat. "Izzie will be so angry with you when she finds out, and with me too, most likely." She threw up her arms. "Seriously, I get it. I mean after what happened with my brother this past summer, who am I to judge?"

"Thanks, Willow. You're the best. One more thing. When she notices I'm gone, tell her I went out to the lake to give our parents and the Bixbys some of those leftover donuts and that I'll be back in a few minutes."

Willow sighed. "Guess if I'm going to lie for you, it doesn't matter if I tell more than one."

I waited until she called for Izzie, then I tiptoed to the front, grabbed my jacket from behind the counter, and quietly slipped outside. The cooler night air bit my cheeks. I zipped my jacket and tucked both hands in my pockets to keep warm. Animated chatter echoed across the lawn as dozens of people anchored themselves to their chairs and gazed out at the lake. I spotted Mom, Dad, and the Bixbys sitting nearer the shore and huddled around the large propane heater Dad had purchased for such occasions. No campfires were allowed on this section of the lake.

I jogged up Whisper Lane and made a right turn onto the boulevard. A few hundred yards ahead, the ferry dock sustained its shadowy form, cloaked in the foggy night. The clocktower read ten minutes before nine. I sprinted the rest of the distance and tucked myself behind an oak tree to wait. The minutes ticked by, and I saw no sign of Marilyn or Sarah. I slouched against the tree trunk and moaned. The moment was turning into a boring police stakeout, not the dangerous situation Izzie or I had imagined. I stuck the flashlight back in my pocket. I'd been in such a hurry that I'd forgotten to bring the baseball bat, which remained leaning in the corner of the shop, next to the mini fridge behind the counter. So much for my intended defense, but in a good way, it looked like none was needed.

I turned to walk back to the shop and hitched my breath. Izzie rushed up, panting like she'd run all the way. The baseball bat I'd left behind was in her hand. "Izzie." I braced myself, ready for the lecture. "Before you say what I figure you probably have a right to say, you should know neither one showed."

She twisted her mouth and wagged her finger. "That was not fair. You left without me and I . . ." She hiccupped. "We were supposed to be in this together. Sisters united."

"I'm sorry. It's just—did Willow tell you about Marilyn? She's more than a little disturbing. I can't figure out whether she's guilty, but she worries me. A lot. And then there's Sarah. She probably started the argument with Marilyn, and I don't trust her either." I swallowed hard.

"I would put my bets on Sarah. Now that woman is the scary one." Izzie seemed to relax.

"Sarah does have a mean streak. I'm not sure Wink realizes what he's in for." I chuckled. "I guess we might as well leave. Nothing happening here."

"Or is there?" Izzie pointed a trembling hand behind me.

I turned to see a figure moving across the deck. Stocky and tall, which hinted that the person was a man. On the other hand, it could be a woman. Both Marilyn and Sarah were tall and thick through the middle. Both had worn pants to the painting event this evening. I gripped my flashlight and stepped toward the deck.

"Chloe, don't you dare." Izzie caught the bottom of my jacket and tugged. "It's not safe."

I pulled out of her grasp and glanced at the bat leaning against her leg. Quick as a wink, I took it from her and moved forward. "Maybe it's Dewey, and he needs help. Just let me get a closer look. I won't go too far."

"Then why do you need the bat?" she hissed. "Chloe!"

I ignored her and tiptoed onto the deck. The shadowy figure disappeared. My comment to Izzie about Dewey being the one moving across the deck wasn't just an excuse. He could have left his cabin hiding place and returned to Whisper Cove, but waited until night because he was still afraid of being arrested for Viola's murder. I clenched the bat in both hands. There could be another reason he came back. Maybe he'd left a clue behind, some evidence that would convince Hunter that Dewey was indeed the killer.

Footsteps pounded off to my right. My head snapped around, and I fumbled to pull out my flashlight and turn it on. Nothing moved across the deck. No sign of Dewey or anyone else. I tiptoed over to the entrance of the shack structure and peered inside. This was where my brave moment came to a stop. If someone was hiding in there, I wasn't about to let him or her ambush me.

"Chloe? If you don't answer me, I'm coming after you. Just as soon as I pull my shoe out of this hole in the deck. Boy, will Dewey be mad when he sees the damage."

I gasped at the sudden break in silence. The sound of Izzie's voice, despite its throaty, whispered tone, carried through the air. I waved my flashlight at her. "Don't bother." There was no point in staying. We were done, and nothing had been accomplished. My shoulders slumped. It felt like Aunt Constance was doomed, and I couldn't prevent it.

"Ouch!"

I froze. The mumbled cry had come from behind me and on the other side of the shack. I winced but took only a second to decide, then pivoted on my heel and sprinted toward the sound. Rounding Dewey's hideaway, I viewed the deck, panning the area with my flashlight.

"What the—is anyone there? Dewey?"

At once, something warm and fuzzy covered my head. The bat in my hand dropped to the floor with a thud. I squirmed side to side as arms wrapped around my shoulders and held tight. With one hand pulled free, I yanked at the arms keeping me in their viselike grip and envisioned a kung fu move where I'd flip my captor and claim victory. The thought was short-lived when my legs seemed to roll forward as a forceful kick to the back sent me tumbling to the deck floor and landing on my face. Steps pounded as whoever had held me escaped. I sat up and threw off the covering to breathe the cool air. Blinking, I stared into Izzie's terrified face and scowled.

"Please tell me you got a look at whoever did this." I held up the wool blanket that had held me captive.

She huffed and crossed her arms while her foot tapped. "No. And what were you thinking? You could've been clobbered with something a lot worse than a blanket." She blinked away tears and pulled me up into a fierce hug. "Thank goodness you're okay. I can't survive without my big sister." She gave my arm a playful pat. "Don't ever take a chance like that again. Okay?"

I brushed off my pants and nodded. "I'll try not to."

"Did you get a look at whoever was on the deck?"

"Nope, but it's someone who's good at playing hide-and-seek." Frustrated and a little angry with myself for not being quick enough to catch my attacker put me in a foul mood. "Let's go home. Willow can lock up the shop. I need a hot shower and a cup of cocoa before I collapse into bed."

She squeezed my arm. "I'll make the cocoa while you take your shower."

We stepped off the deck and walked straight into Hunter. He was leaning against his vehicle, with arms crossed and wearing an angry face that looked scarier than those jack-o'-lanterns we'd carved.

I gasped. "Oh boy."

Izzie anchored her hand on her hip. "H-hey, Hunter."

"Ladies, why don't you stick around so we can have a chat and catch up?"

Chapter Eighteen

Anyone surviving a long-winded lecture from an angry detective deserved a medal, especially when that detective had the name Hunter Barrett. Izzie and I kept quiet the whole time, or at least until he asked us what we'd found while carrying out our reckless plan. I took the full blame and insisted that Izzie had only come to the dock because she was worried about me. No points for Willow, who'd caved under pressure and spilled the details of what, who, when, and where. She couldn't defend the why part—how we thought it was a great idea to catch the killer.

None of the talk with Hunter was pleasant, and that was on top of the fact that we'd gathered zero evidence. My recap of being attacked by a fuzzy blanket made me angry and embarrassed. I only wanted to put the whole incident behind me, but in a small town like Whisper Cove, any chance of that was nonexistent. I couldn't rule out the possibility that someone had passed by and near the dock on their way home from an evening out. We would've been too caught up in our plan to catch a killer to have noticed. Besides that, Marilyn and Sarah might've talked to others about the "crazy person" who called and threatened them with blackmail. If it turned out they had nothing to do with Viola's murder, why wouldn't they talk? No doubt, our Hallows Eve celebration the next evening would bring whispered stares in our direction. I dreaded the idea of facing everyone, but we had to attend. Tradition trumped humiliation.

* * *

Without ruining my face paint, I wiggled my nose to satisfy an itch. Adjusting my wig of blonde curls, I leaned over to Izzie. "Did we have to add face paint to our costumes? I feel more like the Wicked Witch of the West from *The Wizard of Oz* than a Sanderson sister. And are you sure this paint you bought doesn't have latex in it? You know I'm allergic." I was a nervous, agitated mess. After last night's debacle, I just wanted to curl up in a ball and sleep for days.

"You gave me the idea. Remember? Besides, there's nothing wrong with using a little creative license. And for the tenth time, no. There isn't latex or any other sort of irritant. Stop fidgeting. That might help." She tugged at my sleeve and winked. "You look adorable, Miss Sanderson. Witch becomes you. Ha. Get it? *Witch* puns are the best."

"I appreciate you trying to cheer me up, but it's not working. Also for the tenth time, I'm sorry I got you caught in the middle."

I walked down the line to straighten the ghost paintings the sisters had brought to the event for our display. After all, a promise was a promise, even if it had only been a ploy to gather information.

"Aw, come on. You took the blame, and that's more than I deserve. Remember, I did agree to your . . . um . . . brave scheme to catch a killer."

I lowered my painted face and curled my lips. "Sarcasm noted, but there's still someone running free who thinks it's okay to use a paddle for batting practice on someone's head. Meanwhile, Aunt Constance could be packing her bags for her trip to Chautauqua County Jail. Even if witnesses at the event had explained how her prints got on the bag and glove, a prosecutor could argue she'd also handled those things at the crime scene and murdered Viola." I threw up my arms. "Izzie, how did things go so wrong?"

"Look." She stood next to me. "You're the strong, rational sister. Stop freaking out, will you? Let's have a little more faith in Hunter. He's the 'evidence is everything' guy. Isn't that what you told me? If he believed Aunt Constance was guilty, she'd be arrested again and back in jail. He doesn't have what he needs yet to build a solid conviction."

"You're right." I snapped to attention. "In fact, there is just as much evidence pointing a finger at Dewey." I lifted my chin. "Back on track, that's what I am. Snoop sisters are reunited and back in business." I grinned and gave her a high five.

Hundreds of people filled the grounds outside. Every merchant from town and along Artisan Alley was taking advantage of the opportunity to sell products while engaging in self-promotion. Adding to the fun, we were all dressed up in costumes ranging from the classic *Star Wars* Chewbacca to *Avatar* and *Mortal Kombat* heroes—and of course, the traditional ghosts, goblins, and witches, like us.

Smells of barbecue from Bob's smoker grill permeated the air while the long line of anxious and hungry people snaked around chairs and booths. As promised, plenty of apple fritters, donuts, pie, dumplings, cider, and every possible dessert containing pumpkin were available at each booth. Cameras by the dozens flanked the shoreline, set up for the real show, which was the ghost lady of Chautauqua Lake. Wink promised that anyone who captured a shot of Abigail that could be authenticated would get two free tickets to the *House of Hauntings* stage show being performed at a theater in Mayville.

I heard a high-pitched yip and smiled. Max, in his fireman's suit, trotted up to me and licked my leg. Bounding across the yard and close behind was Milo, dressed in a blue policeman's uniform. "Hey, look at you. Paw Patrol to the rescue." I gave them each a hug.

Mom and Dad stood in the distance, stopping to talk to Ross and Spencer. I rolled my eyes. Ross and Spencer. I couldn't get over saying those two names together. However, Ross had a soft heart for females in distress. Spencer's story had touched his compassionate side, but only as a friend, he assured me. I wasn't jealous, but friends watched out for friends, and Spencer was a woman with emotional baggage. Probably none of that mattered. Ross was leaving tomorrow for New York, something about a client emergency that no one else could handle. He'd promised to return if Aunt Constance needed further help, meaning if she was arrested for Viola's murder, I gathered. In brighter news, at least for me, Spencer had announced her plans to return to Los Angeles, where she claimed to have contacts that might help her get a job.

Mom and Dad waved goodbye and walked toward us. They wore sixties retro hippie garb, complete with tie-dyed shirts and fringed vests, as well as bandanas with peace signs wrapped around their heads.

I waved and whistled to get their attention. "Do you think they've heard about last night?" I asked Izzie. When we had gotten home, they hadn't yet returned from their outing at the lake with the Bixbys.

Izzie snorted. "Heads buried in the sand would know by now. Tibetan monks living high up in the Himalayan Mountains would've heard. Astronauts—"

"Stop," I snapped. "How about we think of this logically and lose the sarcasm. Just because neither of our suspects showed up last night doesn't mean neither of them is the killer. A person who had the guts to murder someone would be bold enough to call our bluff. *Or* one of them did show up and stayed hidden to see who the blackmailer is." I shuddered. "Making us perfect targets."

"Yeah. Think of your blanket-toting attacker. That attempt, though lame, could've been meant to hurt you." Izzie scowled. "Okay, enough. This conversation is scaring me and messing with my happy mood. It's Hallows Eve. Time to celebrate all that's good in Whisper Cove."

"Hello, girls. Looks like a great turnout," Dad said.

"Yep. Aunt Constance was here a few minutes ago to say she was leaving one of the sister members in charge so she could go home to nurse a migraine. Under too much stress, I imagine. Anyway, she says we'll make plenty for charities and the new town hall project. Maybe even have a chance to compete with Mayville in returning the floating amphitheater back where it belongs in Whisper Cove." I grinned. The amphitheater had been an attraction in our town for twenty years, until Mayville outbid us and the theater was moved north to its new location.

"That would be nice. I miss those concerts," Mom added. She turned around in a circle. "Now, where did those furry pals run off to? They were here just a second ago."

"They're probably at Bob's booth, begging for some barbecue meat." I whistled and clapped. "Max! Milo!" When neither came running back, I lifted my skirt off the ground and stepped from behind our booth. "I'll find them."

"You want me to come with you? Maybe Mom and Dad could cover for us," Izzie suggested.

"No need." I waved an arm and skirted around people, chairs, and booths to reach Bob's. What I didn't tell Izzie is that I'd be multitasking—searching for the dogs *and* for Marilyn and Sarah, to have a talk. Even if neither was the killer, both of them knew more about the other sister members than I could ever find out in a short amount of time. Focusing on details of the painting event at Bellows Lodge where all this had started seemed logical. Viola's announcement could have triggered any one of those who had heard it. Maybe one of the members had followed Viola out of the lodge, intending to have a talk with her and convince her that dissolving the chapter would be counterproductive, but then things got out of hand. Other than Dewey and Aunt Constance, no one had known that Viola had left her car parked at the ferry dock. I winced. Why did Aunt Constance have to end up as a character in every murder scenario?

"Not very helpful, are you?" I told myself as I trudged across the lawn.

Max and Milo were nowhere in sight, but I did spot Sarah Gilley, standing alone, dressed in blue, head to toe, as one of the Blue Meanies from *Yellow Submarine*, which seemed appropriate. Her eyebrows pinched together as she held a phone to one ear. I straightened, clenched my fists, and marched toward her with determined steps. Without Wink lingering to catch our every word, I had the perfect opportunity to find out why she and Marilyn had argued and where she'd gone after leaving our shop last night. If she answered those questions to my satisfaction, I could ask more, about who she believed had murdered Viola, because I didn't buy the theory she'd given me at the memorial. My gut told me her suggestion that Viola had died by accident was a total ruse, but why?

Rounding the last booth, I skidded to a stop, frustrated as Sarah left her food stand and, with her arms swinging from side to side, hurried toward the ferry dock.

"Oh no, you don't. You're not getting away this time," I mumbled under my breath. Hiking my skirt higher, I sprinted to catch up, nearly colliding with Claire, who balanced a huge tray of apple fritters in her hands while crossing my path. I skipped sideways and kept moving. "Sorry," I shouted.

The yip and growl of one pint-sized canine sounded off to my left. I groaned as Max and Milo played tug-o-war with a large chunk of barbecue while Bob shooed them away. With finger and thumb, I whistled sharply, which got their attention after they gobbled up the barbecue. Both scurried to join me while I picked up speed to reach Sarah. Whatever she was up to had to be urgent. Maybe something to do with that phone call, or she might have spotted me and wanted to avoid a confrontation. Boy, if that didn't show guilt of some kind, what did?

The neon blue of her costume flashed as Sarah tiptoed underneath the motion detector spotlight attached to the storage shed. Hugging the wall, she inched closer to the door and disappeared inside.

Max and Milo stood panting next to me. I stared down at them. "That looks suspicious, doesn't it? Guess we should check it out." Nothing better than two furry, four-footed pals to give me some protection. Even if they were lightweights, they had sharp teeth. I chewed my lip, contemplating the risk. I didn't want a repeat performance of last night's attack. We were at least a hundred yards from any booth or group of people, and it was dark enough for someone to sneak up on me. If I had to guess, Sarah had gone to the storage shed to get the paddle—which had previously been moved, but she couldn't know that—so she could dispose of it. That meant she was most likely the killer.

"I don't know, guys. Do we really want to tangle with a killer? Maybe we should call for backup."

Max woofed as if to agree, and Milo patted my leg with his paw.

"Happy you're with me." I nodded. Before I could pull out my phone, Sarah stomped out of the shed, slammed the door, and headed the hundred or so yards toward the ferry dock, probably angrier than ever since she hadn't found the paddle. I leaped across the last stretch of lawn.

What is she up to, now? I couldn't imagine why she'd go in that direction instead of returning to her food kiosk. Maybe because she figured the paddle could've been moved from the storage shed back to the dock.

"Hey! Chloe, wait up." Pounding footsteps grew louder while Max barked.

I turned. "Ross?"

Bending over, he locked both hands on his knees, then held up one arm with his finger pointing. "Hold on." His chest heaved again as he slowly straightened. "I should walk to work more often."

I raised an eyebrow. "Maybe you should. Why are you here and not with—never mind. Why are you here?"

"I saw you running this way and caught up to say bye. I've decided to leave this evening and drive through the night. I won't get much sleep, but this way I can meet my client earlier tomorrow." He glanced around us. "Why are *you* here? Shouldn't you be at your booth, selling paints and stuff?"

As if I needed his reminder. I gasped and took off toward the dock, with Max and Milo sprinting close behind. "Have a safe trip," I called out with an arm wave, and nearly tripped over the hem of my skirt. Bunching it in my hands, I hurried the rest of the distance, only to find nothing but clouds and darkness ahead of me. My heart sank and my optimism fizzled. Sarah had disappeared. I cursed myself for stopping to talk to Ross. Yet I would've been hurt if he'd left without a goodbye.

"Whatever you're up to—and it's probably something you shouldn't be—I can't let you go alone."

Spinning around, I lifted my chin. "Who says I'm up to anything, and if I am, who says I need help?"

Ross sighed and threw up both arms. "You're impossible."

"I'm not arguing with you this time," I huffed.

"Fine by me. Now, who are you after, and why?"

"I don't have time to explain. Just follow me, and please stop talking." Even Max and Milo got the message as all of us approached the ferry dock in silence. I gasped as the figure of Sarah appeared in the moonlight.

The woman in neon blue walked to the far end of the deck, where Viola had either fallen or been pushed into the lake. With one hand shading her eyes, she leaned forward, peering at the far shore, when a loud scream came from the other side of the dock. Sarah's arms waved like propellers, and she lost her balance, taking a nosedive into the water.

"Oh my goodness." I clutched the hem of my skirt. "That's . . ." I squinted to get a clearer look and dropped my jaw. "Dewey?"

The cry for help and the words "I can't swim" pushed all of us into motion. Max and Milo barked and ran to the dock as fast as their little legs could carry them, while Ross and I hurried to follow.

As we reached the dock, Dewey hopped in circles as he pulled off his shoes, and then, with a running start, jumped into the lake. My eyes widened as Max and Milo took Dewey's cue and dove into the water, splashing as they paddled in circles. I laughed at the comedy of the canines, then gasped. Far in the background, a billowy white image floated across the lake. As the clouds passed by, and the full moon brightened the evening, the silhouette of a woman grew clearer. Trails of white fluttered in the breeze like sails on a boat, while in the distance, someone cried out, "It's Abigail Bellows. The ghost of Chautauqua Lake is here to haunt us."

* * *

Dewey handed me a towel from a barrel full of them, for the passengers to use, then stepped back, wringing his hands. "I'm so sorry I screamed. You looked like that woman." His eyes darted from Sarah to me and back to Sarah. With one heave of his chest, he dropped his shoulders. "I have something I should say. I'm ashamed. Yes, I am, but the truth is better than me holding onto this lie. I can't do it. I just can't, you know?" He rubbed the back of his neck. "I'm weak. I keep telling myself alcohol is the devil because it gets me in trouble. I don't ask for it, but there it is, like a demon woman seducing me."

I scrunched my face and passed the towel to Sarah, who handed me the soaked items she pulled from her pockets. I grabbed another towel from the barrel and dried off all of her stuff as best I could.

"Dewey, please. Let's not talk about demon women and seducing, okay? How about you tell us what you mean by lying." I had a general idea from his comments that Dewey might know more about the night Viola died, but he needed to fill in all those blanks. Meanwhile, my call to Hunter had gone to voicemail. Not feeling in a patient mood, I decided to piece together as much information as I could, despite the disapproving looks Ross kept sending me.

Dewey pointed at Sarah. "She looks like the one who stood on the ferry dock that night."

Sarah shivered and crossed her arms. "I don't know what you're talking about."

"I'm right." I narrowed my eyes and stabbed a finger. "You went inside the storage shed, hoping to dispose of the weapon because you killed Viola. Didn't you?"

Sarah blinked her eyes and sputtered her words. "This is insane. You must be loopy from inhaling too many paint fumes. I got a call from Marilyn. She didn't sound like her usual self, which is all businesslike, if you know what I mean. Anyway, she rambled on about going to the ferry dock and getting evidence out of that storage shed. Like I said, not herself. So, I was worried about her and wanted to help."

The white billowy figure deflated as the boat carrying four teens rowed into shore, flanked by two others from the Chautauqua Navigation Division. The romantic side of me was disappointed. This Abigail Bellows was no more than a teenage prank that had failed. At least the so-called haunting had been fun while it lasted. My eyes widened as I recognized one of the teens. Branden, along with the other boys, got out of the boat. I said a silent prayer that Travis hadn't joined in, and the kinder side of me also said one for Branden. I recalled Travis's comment about how much trouble Branden had gotten into lately. When his parents found out about this, they might not be too happy. Maybe I was way off, but considering the materials they might have used to make their ghost, I wouldn't be surprised if this prank and the stolen items from Gwen's shop and the general store were connected.

My attention snapped back. Thinking about pranks moved my thoughts in another direction. "Where were you around nine o'clock last night?"

She raised her chin and sniffed. "Cuddling with Wink, and not at the ferry dock to meet you. Yes, I heard all about it, which means you and your sister were the ones who made those blackmail calls. First impressions can't always be true, I guess, because you turned out not to be as nice as I'd thought."

I bit down on my tongue to keep from snapping. She was holding back part of her story. "I don't get it. You aren't a fan of Marilyn, but you came running to help her? Why?" I tapped my foot while Ross worked to calm Dewey, who was acting more nervous than usual.

"I told you. She asked for my help." Sarah finally stood and walked over to stare out at the lake.

"No. No, *you* wanted to help. You never said she asked. So, which is it? What are you hiding, Sarah?" My heart pumped with an adrenalin rush. I was close to finding out the truth, whatever it was.

"I mixed up what she told me. She wanted my help. That's it." She bobbed her head up and down while rubbing her shoulders with the towel.

I snapped my fingers. "The evidence in the storage shed! You were worried she found something that would implicate you in all this. That's it, isn't it?"

"I'm telling you. She was with that woman who died. They were arguing," Dewey yelled.

Sarah threw up her arms and spun around to face me. "Fine. I was there that night. I offered Viola a ride to the dock to pick up her car because I thought maybe I could convince her to keep our chapter and pick a different one to give the heave-ho. Like that piddly one up near the Finger Lakes in some town I can't remember the name of because it's so tiny." She grimaced with tight lips and clenched her hands. After a deep breath, she smiled. "Sorry. I promised Wink I'd go to therapy and work on my anger issues. So far, not great, but I'll keep at it. Where was I?"

"Trying to convince Viola?" I suggested with a calm voice.

"Yes, well, it didn't work. I kept talking, and she kept moving away from me and stepped on the deck. I don't know. She looked upset, maybe a teensy bit scared? Anyway, I'm ashamed to admit, I left her there and drove home. I swear on my Grandma Gilley's grave, she was alive and well when I left her." With that, Sarah dropped to the ground and sobbed.

Dewey sprang to his feet. "She might be telling the truth. I remember seeing her walk off the deck, but then I passed out again right after." He rubbed his jaw. "Come to think of it, I was passed out most of the time that evening. Sorry to say."

I exhaled loudly in exasperation. If Dewey was right, I was happy for Sarah, but disappointed that filling in this part of the events of that evening didn't bring us closer to identifying the killer. And if Sarah was in the clear, that left Dewey and Marilyn. I stared at our ferry pilot and groaned. If he was telling the truth, no way had he been awake to commit the crime.

At once, a thought occurred to me. "Dewey, when did you come back to town?"

His face reddened, and he rubbed a towel across the back of his neck. "Last night. Now, I know what you're thinking. I should confess that particular detail too. Sorry to say, I got spooked when I seen you on the deck. I apologize if I hurt you any. I didn't intend to. Honest I didn't."

"You were the one I heard. You're my blanket-toting attacker." I sighed and shook my head. "Dewey."

"It's true. I didn't want anyone to know I'd come back, not until that woman's killer was found, but my cousin kicked me out of the cabin. Said I overstayed my welcome." Dewey's head hung as he avoided my gaze. "I only came to the dock to grab my jacket and some other items. Being in such a hurry to leave before, I forgot to take them. Anyway, I planned to get my things and go hide someplace else where nobody would look for me. Again, I apologize."

I didn't know whether to believe his story, but if I did, that left only one person to blame. Marilyn Pervis. "There's one more thing you need to be honest about, Dewey. Did you hide Viola's bag in your shack?" I steadied my gaze on him.

He shuffled his feet, staring at the ground. With a sigh, he looked up. "I suppose you won't believe me, but I thought one of the passengers on the ferry left it behind. I told you how they're always forgetting things. I have a box full of those. Anyway, I found that bag snagged on a nail and hanging off the far side of the deck. It was after you and your sister and the detective with all his men left. They must've failed to notice it when they searched the area. I remembered hearing you say that poor woman's bag was missing. It got me thinking, so I searched inside it." He rubbed a hand across his neck. "I'll admit, I panicked. I didn't know what to do. That's when I hid the bag. I needed time to think. Then you found it. I know it was wrong, but that's what I did."

My pocket buzzed with a phone call. Turning away from the scene of confusion, I answered. "Hello?"

"Oh, thank God you picked up. I called emergency, but when it comes to the authorities, who knows when they'll show up?" Aunt Constance panted as the words flew out of her mouth.

"Aunt Constance." I let her name drag out. I remembered the last time she'd called 911 to complain about her neighbor's spotlights blinding her view outside the front window. Not at all an emergency. Who knew what trivial issue had prompted her this time? "Why would you call emergency?"

"Why?" Her voice shrieked. "I'm in trouble and afraid for my life. That's why." Someone screamed in the background followed by the sound of pounding on a door. "There's an insane woman outside my bathroom. I'm hiding in here, but she's threatening to break in. I seriously believe she can do it." She sobbed into the phone. "Please come quick. I need you."

"What insane woman, Aunt Constance?" I paced back and forth across the ferry deck. I asked the question but was ninety percent sure who we were talking about. Or at least eighty percent sure. From the parking lot, I spotted Izzie, Mom, and Dad hurrying my way. "Aunt Constance, talk fast. Who's outside your door?"

"Marilyn Pervis. She's outside my door, yelling and screaming, and I'm pretty sure she killed Viola."

Chapter Nineteen

"Chloe, are you all right? We heard screams." Mom took hold of my shoulders and turned me to face her. Her gaze traveled from my head to my black leather shoes. With a satisfied nod, she stepped away.

"Thank goodness. For a moment, I thought the killer might have, er, you know?" Izzie tapped her head, then shot our parents a tentative glance.

"Oh, you mean like last night when you two decided to meet with a possible killer because you believed you could do what? Make a citizen's arrest." Dad shook his head. "You should've called the authorities."

"Sorry, but there's no time to discuss what we should or shouldn't have done." I stabbed a number on my phone and then waited while the call kept ringing. "Hunter! Thank goodness you answered. Aunt Constance is in trouble." I rushed to explain. "And Marilyn Pervis is at her house, acting strange and upset, maybe threatening her. I'm not sure because Aunt Constance is frantic and afraid. She called emergency, but can you please go there? A familiar face might help keep her calm." I gripped the phone and swallowed the lump in my throat.

"I'm on my way. Probably be there in ten minutes. I shouldn't have to say this, but maybe it's safer if you don't show up? I'm guessing that's what you're thinking."

"I'm sure you can handle the situation." I winced when Izzie gave me that stare.

"I hope you mean that. I'll call to make sure officers are on their way."

I managed a thank-you, then hung up. Still gripping the phone, I shoved it in my fanny pack. He was right. Marilyn could be carrying a gun. Or what about that tiny pink and purple pistol that Aunt Constance kept in her nightstand? It wasn't loaded. Still, with everything going on in the past couple of weeks, maybe she was desperate enough to arm herself for real. I stared at Izzie, opened my mouth, then snapped it shut.

"She'll be fine. We don't need to worry. Right?" Izzie blinked.

"Unless she has one of her episodes or does something crazy." I raised my shoulders. "Never know."

"And faints. That would be bad. She'd need someone she trusts to care for her." Izzie nodded.

"We should go. I'll drive." I glanced over her shoulder at Mom and Dad, who'd taken over the task of drying off Max and Milo.

"Don't worry about me." Sarah shouted and waved. "I'm fine. I'll just stay here until Wink comes. I know he cares."

I winced and turned to face her. "Sorry. Maybe Dewey . . ." I turned to see he'd disappeared, then settled my gaze on Ross.

"I'll stay with her." Ross stepped close. "You go and take care of your aunt."

I smiled. Caring about others was one wonderful quality in him I couldn't deny. "Thank you. Would you mind telling our parents where Izzie and I are going, and ask them to take care of Max and Milo? I don't want to waste any more time."

"Done. I'll call you after I get back to New York." He leaned in but then hesitated.

I wrapped my arms around him and squeezed. "You're a good friend. The best I could possibly have." My voice hitched for an instant, then I laughed. "Bye, Ross." I grabbed Izzie's hand. "Let's hurry. Aunt Constance will be in panic mode by now."

My anxiety had grown worse. I was genuinely concerned for her. Aunt Constance could be many things, but she was a decent person and the best aunt, who'd doted on us since birth, or at least as far back as my memories would take me.

Izzie hopped in the passenger side of her Land Rover and pulled out the spare key from the glove compartment. She set it in the cup holder. "Glad you're driving. I can't get my hands to stop shaking."

Without skipping a beat, I got in, took the key, and fired up the engine. Hunter was probably there by now. I struggled to restrain myself from calling. Without taking my focus off the road, I used one hand to dig through my fanny pack and pull out my phone, and I tossed it in Izzie's lap. "Call Hunter. I want to know how things are going."

Izzie reared back her head and sniffed. "You want me to call so he can be angry with me rather than you. Not nice, but I will because I'm anxious to know too." She lifted the phone. "Say, when did you change your cover? I like the purple."

My head snapped around for a quick second. "That's not mine." I blinked, and when my mind caught up to speed, I sighed. "The phone belongs to Sarah. She handed me her stuff to dry off after the dump in the lake. In all the chaos, I must've thought it was mine." I pulled out my phone and tossed it to her. "On second thought, maybe it would be safer to call Aunt Constance. If she answers, just make it brief. Ask her if Hunter and the officers arrived."

"In that case, I'll connect your phone to my car, and we'll listen over the speakers. If Marilyn is already handcuffed and sitting in the back seat of a squad car, that would be nice to know." Izzie pressed buttons on the console, then sat back while the phone rang.

After the tenth ring, the call went to voicemail. Izzie disconnected the line. "She probably left her phone in the bathroom."

I rubbed the back of my neck. *He said he'd call.* "We should be there in about twenty-five minutes." I moved my hand back to the steering wheel and tapped out a quick drumbeat.

"Hey. I know. Since we have time to kill, why don't you catch me up and explain what happened at the ferry dock? Let's start with Sarah looking drenched and more sour-faced than normal. There has to be a story behind that." Izzie nodded.

I stopped drumming and was grateful for the distraction. "Well, in a quick recap, I followed her to the storage shed, where she popped inside to search for what I figured was the paddle, then stormed out, looking like she wanted to kill somebody. Instead of returning to her booth, she walked onto the ferry deck, where Dewey spotted her. He screamed because he recognized her from the night Viola was murdered. Sarah was startled by his scream and fell in the lake. Dewey jumped in to save her, even though the water isn't that deep near the shore, which is kind of funny—but not really, considering the circumstances. Anyway, Sarah explained she had gotten a call from Marilyn, claiming she planned to move evidence out of the storage shed. Sarah was worried about Marilyn and went to look for her there." I took a deep breath. "Of course that made perfect sense because she's the one who drove Viola to the ferry, hoping to convince her to save their chapter and dump a different one, from up near the Finger Lakes in a town named . . . something or other. Can't remember. But when Viola refused, Sarah claimed she drove off and left Viola, alive and healthy."

"Wow." Izzie blinked. "All that happened in a matter of minutes. Who says Whisper Cove is a quiet town?"

I steered through the back streets of Aunt Constance's neighborhood. Slowing to a crawl, I turned onto her street and could see the lights of Aunt Constance's house as we drew near. It seemed almost every window was lit, and there was also the spinning red bulb of a cruiser sitting in the drive.

"So, if Dewey isn't the killer and Sarah appears to be in the clear, then Marilyn must be the guilty one?"

"Why do you sound so unsure? It's a textbook case. Just like Uncle Seymour, only in this instance she really carried the protect and defend idea too far."

"I don't know. It's almost too easy, but hey, sometimes the case turns out exactly like that." Izzie reached inside the center console and pulled out a pack of gum. "You want a stick?"

I shook my head. "Maybe we should park at a safe distance to keep the car out of sight."

"Ha. Someone's regretting our decision to come here." Izzie popped the gum in her mouth and chewed.

I ignored the dig. "Then we take a casual walk past the house and see what's going on."

"You mean like a recon mission where we spy to assess the situation? That's so cool. I feel like James Bond." She chewed faster.

"Yeah, sure," I muttered and pulled to the curb. We were three houses away from Aunt Constance's, but with a clear view of the front. I made out Hunter standing next to an officer. They were obviously carrying on a conversation. The EMTs weren't parked in the drive, which meant nobody was hurt. Still, Aunt Constance had to be frantic by now. We needed to be with her. "New plan. We're going straight up to Hunter and demanding to see Aunt Constance."

"Do you think that's wise?" Izzie moved alongside me.

"I'll tell him Aunt Constance called and begged us to come." I also needed to know the ending to this story. Was it Marilyn who had killed Viola Finnwinkle? Or was the killer running free and Aunt Constance still a suspect?

Walking up the drive, I could see Hunter's face transform from smiling to jaw clenching. I puffed my cheeks and straightened my shoulders. "Before you say anything, Aunt Constance called and begged us to come."

"Yes. Yes, she did. Poor woman is panic stricken." Izzie sniffed and swiped her brow with one hand. "She needs family."

Hunter rolled back on his heels. "You mean called you with this?" He snapped his fingers at the officer, who handed him a bag. Inside was a phone with a familiar yellow and green design.

I cleared my throat. "She . . . um."

"She has a landline," Izzie rushed to say.

"No, she doesn't. Come on, ladies. Let's not play games. You want to see her? I'm not stopping you. Officer Daniels is inside with the two of them. Neither one is saying much. Let's go." He waved an arm for us to lead the way.

Once inside, I ran over to Aunt Constance, Izzie close behind me. "Are you okay?" I rubbed her arm.

"We were so worried." Izzie hugged her, then narrowed her eyes at Marilyn. "She didn't hurt you, did she?"

"No. She didn't have the chance." Aunt Constance sniffed and dabbed her nose with a tissue. "These wonderful officers came right away and saved me. Thank you." She blinked at the man with a name plate that read "Daniels." Despite the compliment, he only gave a slight nod at her.

"I'm telling you. It was the painting. I figured it out. When I asked her and she told me she'd destroyed it, I should have known. The answer was right in front of me. The painting had to be hers. I'm such a fool."

Marilyn lowered her head. "I only came to warn Constance that she might be in danger. I would never hurt her," Marilyn cried and squirmed in her chair. "I had nothing to do with Viola's death. Believe me."

Hunter leaned toward me. "Marilyn keeps rambling on about that painting you found left behind at the lodge. I can't make sense of what she's saying. Only that the person who painted the picture means to kill again. But she can't or won't tell me who. Just keeps mumbling that she should've known." He shook his head. "Maybe she was crazy enough to kill Viola."

I frowned. Nothing in that painting hinted to me that the killer would strike again. Unless Marilyn was referring to the ghost image and the legend. However, that was purely make-believe. "Wait. How did she see the painting?"

"According to one of our guys working the front desk, Marilyn came into the precinct earlier today to lodge a complaint about her neighbor's tree dropping too many leaves on her side of the property." Hunter nodded at the officer standing next to Marilyn. "Deputy Daniels informs me that at that time, my crime team members were moving evidence, including that painting, to another room. She must've gotten a look at it then because she became upset and hurried out of the building without finishing her complaint form."

"What a shame." Aunt Constance clucked her tongue. "You of all people? Loyal, honest, always offering to help me, and all the while you were trying to frame me for the murder you committed." She smacked the chair and stood up. Her finger pointed. "Well, that's all over now. You Judas."

With cuffed wrists clinking as she raised her hands, Marilyn tried lifting herself from the chair. "It wasn't me. I followed you to the dock, then kept driving because I felt guilty and ashamed. I returned to the lodge, Constance. I didn't hurt Viola."

"You admit it. You followed me, and then you must've returned to the dock and killed Viola because . . . because—*you*! You sent me that candygram with that scary message warning me to confess, didn't you? Why? You are one sick woman, Marilyn Pervis. I heard you. You stood outside my bathroom and said you'd been so angry with Viola, you wanted to kill her for destroying my career. How could you do something so horrible?" Aunt Constance fanned her face. "Oh my. I don't feel very well."

Hunter stepped close to Aunt Constance and laid one hand on her shoulder. "You've had a rough evening. Why don't you rest, and I'll take your statement tomorrow?"

The hall clock chimed ten times. "It's late, Aunt Constance. Let's get you ready for bed."

"I'll take care of her." Spencer walked into the room and pulled off her coat and gloves. "You and Izzie should go home and get some rest. You both look like you need it."

I glanced wearily at Spencer, then at Aunt Constance. "Are you okay with that?"

"Yes. My daughter and I have some things to discuss. Thank you, again, officers. Detective, I'll see you tomorrow."

As they went upstairs, I walked through what Marilyn had said. She had followed Aunt Constance to the dock that night. Hunter caught the words too. I noticed the glint in his eye and that slight twitch of his chin. One thing Marilyn hadn't lied about was returning to the lodge. I remembered seeing her walk out at the end of the event with her painting. However, she would've had plenty of time to commit the murder and get back to the paint party event well before it ended. I had no memory of her until everyone was leaving. Also, that missing hour was beginning to take form, and a piece of the puzzle had to do with Aunt Constance stopping at the ferry dock. Spencer had heard her say she shouldn't have left her alone, meaning Viola. Spencer had also said how upset and out of sorts her mom had seemed when she came home. Why didn't Hunter make her explain right now, I wondered? I needed to know the story. I wanted reassurances that my aunt was innocent because something nagged at me, some tiny detail that didn't make sense or add up, but what?

"Daniels, please escort Miss Pervis to the squad car and take her to the station. We'll talk there. For starters, Miss Pervis, you've broken into a private residence, and that's a crime. I shouldn't have to tell you that you're in serious trouble. If you have a lawyer, I'd advise you to call him or her."

"I didn't break in." Marilyn struggled to pull out of Officer Daniels's grasp. "Constance gave me a key to her house. She likes how I look after her, you know. Why would I hurt her?"

"Come on, Miss." Daniels led her to the hall.

"I came to warn her. That's all. She needs me. You can't arrest me."

"Don't forget to read Miss Pervis her rights, Daniels," Hunter said.

"Will do, Detective." Daniels continued with Marilyn in tow and reached the front door.

"Do you have enough proof to charge her with Viola's murder?" I asked after I heard the door click shut.

"Not really. Or at least, not yet. The lab will check to see if her prints and DNA match any found on the evidence and on the victim's body. We'll find something." Hunter tapped his phone against the palm of his hand.

"Uh-oh. Not you too. You don't look like you're sure about any of this. Please tell me you're not still considering Aunt Constance as the killer?"

He ran his tongue over his upper lip. "I'm not. I just . . . this is too neat and tidy. Marilyn, Aunt Constance's loyal servant, protecting her from anyone who harms her, kills Viola because she presents a threat? Too easy."

"Just what I said." Izzie's eyes widened. "How about that? I'm thinking like a detective." She nodded decisively.

"You also said sometimes that's exactly how a case turns out. Neat and easy." An inward groan vibrated through me. Why couldn't this be over? Why did Aunt Constance have to lie about where she'd gone that night? "Say, why didn't you ask Aunt Constance about her going to the dock? Maybe she's ready to tell the whole truth, now that we know she stopped at the ferry dock that night."

"I want to wait until after my talk with Marilyn. Then if your aunt says anything that doesn't match the story, I'll know one of them is lying."

"Huh. I'd think you'd give Aunt Constance the benefit of the doubt and question her first." I crossed my arms.

"Remember, your aunt is the one who lied in the first place."

"No, now wait." I wagged my finger. "She never said anything about where she went for a drive, so that's not lying."

"Intentionally leaving something that important out of the conversation is the same as lying." He threw up his arms. "Why am I arguing with you?"

My phone rang and saved the moment. I cocked my head and stared at Hunter, who hadn't moved. "I thought you were in a hurry?"

"I'll wait." He hitched his thumbs in his pants pockets.

"Fine." I slapped the phone to my ear. "Hi, Ross. How's your babysitting gig?"

"Uh, not so great."

"Meaning?" I held my breath. Could the evening be filled with any more drama?

"Well, I sat with Sarah and we chatted. Did you know she used to sing in a rock band? Crazy to imagine. Anyway, she asked if I could get her a hot chocolate to take the chill off. I'm a gentleman, so I did, but when I got back, she was gone."

"Oh." My brow lifted. "Maybe Wink came for her, and she left with him. That would make sense." I covered the receiver and whispered. "Sarah's gone missing."

"Yeah, it would, but then your mom and dad returned. With Wink."

"Wow. Is Wink mad? I bet he is." I shrugged at Hunter and Izzie. "But it's not your fault. You had no idea she'd leave like that," I hurried to add.

A shaky laugh came through the receiver. "Oh, it gets better."

"Great." I sank down in a chair. Not giving it a thought, I pressed the button to put him on speaker. I couldn't imagine where he was taking this story, but I had a gut feeling I wouldn't like it much.

"Dewey is panic stricken. He claims Sarah tore apart his shack and scattered everything on the deck. He says she was screaming about her phone going missing. Anyway, he's upset. She's upset and gone off somewhere."

"Is that all? I have her phone." I explained what had happened and felt a sense of relief.

"But she's still missing."

"She probably went someplace else to look for her phone. Did anyone check her booth and the surrounding area? If she thought she dropped the phone there, maybe that's where she is."

"Chloe, we've looked everywhere. Who gets so worked up over a missing phone? It's like she went ballistic, screaming at Dewey and throwing things around."

"Yeah." My face scrunched as I puzzled over what he said. Nobody obsesses over their phone that much. Well, except teenagers—it's like they're attached to their phones by umbilical cords. I unzipped my fanny pack and removed the purple-covered device.

"What are you thinking?" Izzie whispered, even though Hunter and Ross could easily hear her.

"She's too upset, and it must be for a reason." I tapped the phone but couldn't get in. "Great. It's password protected." I looked up at Hunter. "I don't suppose you guys have some sort of master password to break into phones, do you?"

"That would be illegal," both Ross and Hunter said at once.

"I had to ask." I set Sarah's phone in my lap. "Well, whatever she's hiding, I guess we'll never know." Suddenly, the phone buzzed and a message popped up on the screen. *Thank goodness for iPhones and the new waterproof feature.* Sarah had set her phone to show and send messages even when it was locked. I read the short sentence. "It's from Wink. 'Whoever you are, my fiancé wants her phone returned pronto.'"

"Well, at least we know she's okay." Izzie nodded.

"Hey, Ross. Sarah's fine. She obviously caught up with Wink."

"That's a relief," Ross said.

"Thanks for calling, and have a safe trip home. Talk to you soon." In my mind, I played back everything that had happened this evening. Something about Sarah's behavior didn't add up, but I couldn't put a finger on exactly what. Not yet anyway. As for Marilyn, she had seemed genuinely concerned about Aunt Constance's safety, even though Hunter could be right that she was crazy enough to kill Viola. I turned to Izzie. "We should get back to town. You ready?"

"Yep. It's late. Bye, Hunter. Thanks for taking care of things. You'll let us know what happens, right?" Izzie put on her shiniest smile of encouragement.

"I will. Have a safe drive home. There are traffic checkpoints scheduled this evening. Don't want you to get a ticket."

"Aw, you're looking out for us. Thanks, Detective." I gave his shoulder a playful punch.

Izzie and I walked down the drive. The moon and stars shined to brighten the evening. I snapped my fingers. "I almost forgot something. I'll be right back." Sprinting across the lawn to the house, I caught Hunter just as he came outside.

"Can you wait? I need to run something by you." We talked for a couple of minutes, and then I returned to the sidewalk and caught up with Izzie.

"What was that about? I saw you talking to Hunter." Izzie waggled her finger and smiled. "You're up to something, aren't you?"

"Not at all. Just wanted to make sure Hunter would keep his promise and let us know if he gets more out of Marilyn." I couldn't give her a smile in return. My nerves were frayed, leaving me too tense. I couldn't shake the gut feeling that told me something was still very wrong. This case of Viola's murder had too many loose ends. It was time to tie them up and send someone to jail.

We made it to Whisper Cove and home by eleven. Noise coming from the lake hinted that the celebration was going strong, with no indication that folks would be leaving soon. From the looks of our house, where only the porch lights and one window lamp were on, my guess was that Mom and Dad were celebrating with the rest of them.

"I am so exhausted." Izzie threw up her arms and let them flop down at her sides. "I can't believe our parents have more energy than we do."

"They aren't the ones running their tails off, trying to find a killer," I quipped.

"And at the same time working day and night to make Paint with a View a success," she added.

"True." I unlocked the front door and stepped into the foyer. Max and Milo skidded across the floor and collided with me. "Hey, guys! Look at you. All bathed and brushed like you came out of a salon. So handsome." I bent down and was treated to dozens of kisses. I bit down on my lip, thinking quick. "Um, Izzie, why don't you go on up to bed? I think I'll take these guys out across the road for a bathroom break."

"You're the best." She yawned, her arms stretched wide, and climbed the stairs.

"I do try." I waited until I heard the bedroom door shut. "Okay, you two. I told a little fib. You're staying here while I take a walk. How about some treats? I have peanut butter–flavored biscuits ready and waiting."

Max danced around in circles on his hind legs while Milo sat up and pawed the air.

"Glad you're on board with the plan." I hurried to the kitchen and gave them each two treats, then walked through the back doorway and into the yard. Hugging the side of the house, I inched my way toward the front. My plan could turn out to be a total zero, but I had to try. After receiving several text messages from Wink's number, saying, *I want my phone back, whoever you are,* I texted back to arrange a meeting at the dock. Chances were, Sarah didn't know I was the one who had her phone. Then again, chances were, she did. She'd handed me her things after getting out of the lake. Still, she hadn't directly addressed me in her texts—a small detail, yet worth thinking about.

I skirted around the house and crossed the road to walk along the lakeshore. Another possibility was that Izzie could be on the right track. Maybe Sarah had something on her phone that was too embarrassing and private for anyone to see. Like photos or who knew what. Whatever the reason, I was taking the risk to meet her. I had to find out the truth.

Twenty or so yards ahead, a tall woman with a bob of snow white hair stood on the ferry deck. Sarah shoved both hands in her pockets and tucked her chin under the coat collar. She hadn't spotted me yet. I scanned the area around her and saw no movement of anyone else near. At least Wink hadn't tagged along. This wouldn't work unless Sarah and I were alone. A sudden thought caused me to peer at Dewey's hideaway. No light or movement came from in there.

Nearing the dock, I waved both arms to get Sarah's attention. Seeing her reaction wasn't possible at this distance and in the dark. As if my thought triggered it, the post light next to the dock turned on, bathing a startled Sarah in a yellow glow. She blinked and then scowled.

"You. I thought maybe you had my phone, but I wasn't sure." She snapped her fingers while I stepped onto the deck. "Give it here."

I stopped, keeping a six- to eight-foot distance between us. I held up the device and waved it in front of her. "It's funny, but did you know the police have a special password, kind of like a master key, to unlock any phone? Yeah, I wasn't aware either. After getting a call from Ross, telling me how upset you were that you'd lost your phone, I checked my fanny pack. I remembered that you handed me your stuff to dry off. Somehow I must've pocketed your phone. Sorry." I shrugged.

"You're forgiven—now hand it over." She thrust her hand out, palm up, to receive it. A nervous tic surfaced, causing her left eye to wink.

I tapped the phone against my hand. "I would, but . . ."

"Chloe. That's my property. So, please." Her fingers wiggled while her feet shifted side to side. "I'm kind of in a hurry. Wink is waiting, and he's an impatient man."

"Didn't you say Marilyn called you about moving evidence out of the storage shed? Yeah, I think those were your exact words." I took a step back as she stepped forward. My gaze darted across the parking lot and beyond to the grassy area.

"I don't remember. Now, hand over the phone, girlie. Before I lose my temper."

I took a breath to calm myself, but my heartbeat hammered against my chest. "Your recent calls show none from Marilyn. In fact, in the past week, you two had no phone conversations. Don't you find that odd?"

She took several steps toward me, and I hopped off the deck. "I don't have to explain myself to you or anyone else," she said, and lunged toward me.

I jumped to one side, and she flew by me, landing flat on her face with a thud. "Oh no. Are you okay?" I reached for her arm to pull her up, not thinking of anything but how she might have hurt herself—broken a bone or gotten a concussion.

She slapped my arm away and sobbed into the grass. "My wedding plans are ruined. I'll spend the rest of my days in jail. All because of her." Sarah rolled over but remained flat on the ground. "I could've been happy without the presidency. I could. Not without the chapter, though. At least that's what I thought until I met Wink." The tears flowed. "He makes me feel so beautiful. *Me.* Can you believe it?"

I knelt down to sit beside her. "You are beautiful, Sarah. Just a little angry most of the time, but that's okay. He loves you. Is that why he tried to convince everyone that Aunt Constance was the killer, and not you?"

She nodded and sniffed, then frantically shook her head. "Oh no, you don't. You're trying to trick me, but it won't work." She stabbed at me with her finger. "I'm not saying another word. So if you'll hand over my phone, I'll be on my way." She sat up and brushed off her lap.

"I can't let you do that, Miss Gilley." Hunter walked over and hoisted Sarah to her feet. He looked at me. "Just heard from Daniels. He checked Marilyn's phone like I asked him to. No calls were made this evening. However, the missing security footage from the Whisper Cove Casino was finally turned over to the station. Good thing the casino is close by and the camera pans the ferry." Hunter cuffed Sarah while nodding at me. "The owner, Mr. Mackleroy, sent his apologies for taking so long. He just got back from the Bahamas and is the only one who seemed to know where to find the tape we needed. Lucky for us, it shows this lady hitting the victim over the head. The blow was forceful enough to make Viola stumble off the deck and fall into the lake. Miss Gilley walked away without so much as a glance to see if her victim was still alive. I can't say for certain she went to the shed, because it's out of camera range, but after a minute or so, she came back into view, got in her car, and drove away."

"It's not me. It had to be someone who looks like me," Sarah sputtered. Her eyes widened. "Marilyn! We have a similar build. It was dark at the time, and she's the one who probably swung that paddle and clobbered Viola."

I caught my breath. "How did you know the weapon used was a paddle?"

"I, I—you told me! When you accused me of killing Viola, you said I must've gone to the shed to get rid of the paddle so no one would find out." She glared.

"No." I slowly tilted my head to one side. "I said weapon. I never mentioned a paddle, and neither did Detective Barrett."

"Sarah Gilley, you are under arrest for the death of Viola Finnwinkle. You have the right to remain silent . . ."

I stayed by the dock while Hunter led Sarah to the cruiser, where Officer Daniels stood next to the opened rear door. I was surprised, but not too much, in finding out my hunch had been right. Before this evening—the incident at the storage shed and dock, and seeing how Sarah had behaved—I would've put all my money on Marilyn being the killer. Turned out, she was guilty of only one thing, and that was being too protective of her icon, Aunt Constance. Anyone could see she needed some serious therapy and maybe a few yoga classes to calm her. I grinned at that thought, then walked along the lakeshore to return home. It was closing in on midnight, and the noise from the Hallows Eve celebration had quieted to a dull murmur. At least I'd get a peaceful night's sleep, knowing Viola's murder had been solved, and justice would be served.

Chapter Twenty

"I can't believe this is over." Aunt Constance sipped her tea and smiled. "My life is back to normal, and I have a new opportunity to look forward to."

We sat on the back patio of Aunt Constance's house, overlooking the lake. I raised my glass of wine. "Here's to normal. Even if it lasts for only a short while, we'll take it."

Aunt Constance had finally opened up to admit that she'd gone to the ferry dock in hopes of making amends with Viola. However, when she opened her car door, she spotted both Sarah and Viola shouting and arguing. As Sarah had stomped away, and Viola continued her screaming tirade from the deck, Aunt Constance decided it might not be the best time for their discussion. So she'd hurried out of the parking lot, which was most likely when she had dropped her hat, she said.

"You thought Sarah had left, when actually, she hadn't. Hunter told me she admitted to turning around because Viola had triggered her when she called Sarah a pathetic loser who nobody liked. Sarah spotted the paddle a passenger had left behind on the ferry. She grabbed it and clobbered Viola, then hid the paddle in the storage shed. Hard to believe she had the forethought to return to the painting event, so as not to be missed."

"The creepy part is how she painted that horrible scene with Viola facedown in the lake and bragged about it to Hunter. If you ask me, she's the one who needs a psychiatrist," Izzie said.

Creepy or not, all I could think of at the moment was how the tragedy could've easily been avoided. If Viola and Sarah had held their tempers and let the matter go, no one would've ended up dead or charged with murder.

"Yes, well, Hunter told me Sarah insisted she didn't mean for Viola to die and doesn't even remember finishing the painting. It's almost as if she was in some sort of fugue-like state, probably in shock over what had happened," I said.

"Or having a guilty conscience. Who knows?" Izzie sighed. "At least it's over."

"Marilyn admitted when she stopped by Sarah's to discuss some paperwork about the chapter, she asked to see her painting. She knew Sarah had talent and was curious to take a look. Marilyn was surprised how agitated Sarah got. She snapped that she'd thrown the painting in the trash because she didn't like the way it had turned out. Marilyn told Hunter she thought it was odd behavior, but then she forgot about the incident until she saw the painting at the police precinct when she visited to file a complaint about her neighbor's tree. She suspected it belonged to Sarah and worried when she noticed the image of the body floating in the water," I said.

"She really couldn't have known Sarah would come after Aunt Constance," Izzie argued.

"Yes, but she didn't want to take any chances." I nodded at Aunt Constance. "You know how overly protective she is of you. But Izzie is right. At least it's over now."

Everyone clinked their glasses while Aunt Constance nestled in her chair and sipped her tea, spiked with just a touch of brandy, I imagined. She was right. With Sarah Gilley behind bars and Marilyn starting her mandatory visits with a psychiatrist, we all felt relief. Except maybe for Wink. He'd hung a sign on the door of the *Gazette* office to announce he was taking a few days off to go fishing. His glum mood hinted that he had truly loved Sarah. He'd had no clue Sarah had committed the murder until her arrest. That old adage about how love is blind fit in this situation. I hoped the prison Sarah wound up in allowed plenty of visitation hours.

"I couldn't live with myself if I filed harassment charges against Marilyn. Her heart has always been in the right place, even if she's a bit too passionate in her actions. Poor woman isn't taking it well. She's embarrassed to see a doctor, who I'm sure will point out her problems." Aunt Constance set down her cup.

I chugged my wine to keep from responding. Aunt Constance had given Marilyn a key to her home. The judge had ruled that her actions didn't constitute a break-and-enter charge. However, he was concerned that Marilyn lacked control. To my way of thinking, that was a polite way of saying she acted like an obsessed stalker. With three months of probation, depending on the psychiatrist's evaluation, she'd get off easy.

"I'm glad Sarah finally broke down and confessed. Maybe that will earn her at least a few points with the court," Dad said.

"What about the candygram? Did she admit to sending it?" Mom asked.

I nodded. "She did. She knew Marilyn loved peppermint candy. She had a hunch someone would draw conclusions and think Marilyn sent it. My guess is Sarah wanted to take the attention off herself in case Hunter still considered her one of his suspects."

"You mean like we did?" Izzie groaned. "The snoop sisters nearly bumbled and got it wrong."

"But we got it right in the end." I tipped my glass in her direction.

"You mean *you* got it right. You're the one with a detective's brain. Who would've thought that Sarah's misplacing her phone would lead you to suspect she was the killer? You risked your life with that crazy scheme to catch her in a lie." Izzie shook her head. "That took guts."

"Not when I got Hunter to go along with the plan. I knew he'd step in if things got dangerous," I said. Of course, he could've come a minute sooner, before Sarah leaped to tackle me. Thank goodness for quick reflexes.

"Say! I just thought of something that hasn't been explained. What about Viola's glove underneath your back seat, Aunt Constance?" Izzie leaned forward in her chair.

She waved her arm. "Oh, that. Detective Hunter doubted my story about Viola placing her bag in the back seat and the glove dropping out, but that's exactly what happened. I remembered Viola mumbling under her breath when she opened the car door to retrieve the bag. It had fallen off the seat and onto the floor. Somehow the glove must've been shoved underneath, and she didn't notice. At least that's the only explanation I could come up with, and Detective Hunter agreed."

"Gotta say, I'm not surprised Dewey panicked and kept her bag after he found it hanging off the deck. He knew possessing evidence would make him look like Viola's killer." Izzie flipped through her phone, then turned it to face us, displaying a photo with a screaming jack-o'-lantern held in the arms of its creator. "Chloe was right. Mrs. Bixby won the pumpkin carving contest. Look how happy she is. The committee just posted the photo on the town's Facebook page."

"I hope you aren't too disappointed," Mom said.

"Are you kidding? She promised me when she does her interview with the *Gazette* to give Paint with a View credit for inspiring her with ideas. Neat, right?" Izzie bounced in her seat and grinned.

"Always an angle." I chuckled. Hearing a sharp bark, I looked toward the lake. Max and Milo ran after a squirrel that scurried up the oak tree. Max hopped as if he could catch it while Milo barked and circled the tree. I laughed, envying them in some ways. The only thing they worried about was when their next meal was coming and who would take them for a walk along the lake so they could chase the ducks.

"Any word yet about Milo?" Izzie asked.

"Nope. Although Hunter did say now that Viola's case is closed, he would check with the other precincts in neighboring towns."

Secretly, I hoped we could keep him a little longer, or maybe forever. Max loved his playmate. He would be sad if Milo had to leave.

"Where's Spencer, by the way? Did she leave town without saying goodbye?" Mom asked.

"She's gone." Aunt Constance flipped her hand dismissively. "She got a job offer back in L.A. It's only temporary, but it has the possibility of becoming permanent, depending on her performance. We had a heart-to-heart talk beforehand, though. We needed to clear the air."

"You mean about how she tried to have you put away in the loony bin?" Izzie commented.

"Izzie." I scowled and poked her arm.

"Ouch. Well, she did, didn't she?" Izzie rubbed her arm, then turned to Aunt Constance. "But it was only because she was desperate. She thought you really might have killed Viola, and that was the only way she could keep you from going to jail."

I groaned. She kept digging that hole, but at least Aunt Constance laughed it off.

"In true Spencer form. I love my daughter with all my heart, even when she schemes to get her way." Aunt Constance braced her hands on the arms of her chair and stood. "I don't mean to rush you, but I have a meeting with the contractor who's building my shop. Isn't it wonderful, girls? We'll be neighbors on Artisan Alley. You know, after I lost my position as president of our Sisterhood chapter, I thought I had nothing to look forward to." She shrugged. "Life can certainly be funny that way."

"Yes, it can." I stepped in to give her a hug.

To be honest, I was relieved to hear that Spencer had handed over her pet project, and all the expenses that came with it, to Aunt Constance, without a second's hesitation. After all, our aunt was the one who had financed the whole deal in the first place. Despite our differences, I hoped Spencer would be happy with her decision to take the new position back in L.A.

"I told Spencer this was an opportunity to become more responsible with her money. If that job doesn't go well, she'll be begging for the next handout. Well, I'm putting my foot down next time. I can't coddle her any longer." Aunt Constance sniffed.

I pressed my lips together while Izzie coughed. Neither one of us believed she could hold to that promise. I patted my leg. "Come on, pooches. We need to get back to the house for some lunch."

Izzie, the dogs, and I rode home in my car while Mom and Dad drove in a different direction, north to the Finger Lakes. They had plans to visit a few wineries before their gig instructing a group of seniors on how to paint with watercolors. I admired how they always kept busy despite their comfy, worry-free lifestyle, where they didn't really need the extra income. For that reason, the check from this paying job, along with any other, went to charities. They had a long list of them.

"Speaking of gigs, what's our event schedule look like for the next couple of months?" I asked.

Izzie's brows inched together. "We weren't speaking about gigs, but our schedule is packed, at least three or four events every week through December. Why? Are you planning to leave town? Maybe some romantic getaway with your honey, Hunter?" She giggled.

A flush of warmth rose up to my ears. "What romance? Hunter and I aren't anything. We're friends who like spending time together and—why am I explaining myself to you?

Can we go back to talking about the business, as in our paint shop?" I jutted my chin and pressed harder on the gas pedal.

"Someone's a bit touchy. I think it would be fantastic if you two became a couple. Don't you?" This time her voice sobered.

I glimpsed her face, which had turned sincere. "Maybe. Probably. Yeah, it would be nice." I chuckled.

As if he'd heard us by way of some telepathic waves, my phone rang through the car speaker, and Hunter's name displayed on the screen. Pausing for a heartbeat or two, I pressed the answer call button. "Hey, how are you? Happy the case is closed, I bet."

"Happy and relieved. Turns out those kids had taken a practice run to see if their ghost prank would work on the same day you had your group painting by the lake."

"Ha. Rita should hear about this, though I'm not sure it will convince her that what she saw wasn't a real ghost."

"Oh, and I spoke to Gwen, your shop neighbor. She's happy the judge ordered those teens to do fifty hours of volunteer work at her business and at the general store they broke into."

"I'm glad too. Branden might be a rebellious teen, but spending time with Gwen should soften his rough edges. As for the others, they probably went along with the plan because they wanted to be a part of something, even if it got them in trouble," I said.

"Where are you? Sounds like you're in a car."

"Izzie and I are driving back from Aunt Constance's place. She's glad to have her life back and is making plans for the future. Life after the Sisterhood, I guess you'd call it. So, what are you up to today?" My fingers rubbed up and down the leather steering wheel. I knew Izzie couldn't help listening to our conversation, which made it awkward.

"Nothing much. Hi, Izzie. How are you?"

"I'm great. Don't mind me. I'm putting in my earbuds to catch some tunes." She winked at me, plugged in, and bobbed her head to whatever tune she was listening to.

"I thought, if you aren't too busy, we could have dinner together this evening. What do you say?"

Along with the soft tone of his voice coming through the line, I pictured his face. Those warm brown eyes, chiseled chin, and the tiny scar along the corner of one eye that added a touch of mystery to him caused me to smile. "Sure. I'd love that."

"Great. I'll pick you up around seven."

"Where are we going?" I checked my hair and makeup in the rearview mirror for a second.

"It's a surprise. No need to dress up. It's a casual spot. See you then."

I pressed the end call button and leaned back. The sign announcing Whisper Cove was a few hundred feet ahead. I tapped Izzie's arm, but her head rested against the door, and her eyes were shut. The soft hum of snoring vibrated from her lips.

As I waited at the traffic light to turn left onto Sail Shore Drive, I noticed Dewey standing far off on the ferry deck. He motioned to the waiting line of passengers to pull their vehicles on to the ferry. Good thing he was back in business. His job as ferry pilot was secure, but also his confidence had been restored. Learning about Sarah's arrest had assured him he hadn't been hallucinating about the evening Viola died. In fact, he was proud when Hunter asked if he'd testify at Sarah's trial as to what he'd seen that night. To me the best news was hearing he'd stopped drinking and had attended his first AA meeting yesterday.

Turning into our drive, I spotted a man standing on the front porch. He had a leash dangling from one hand. My heart lurched. Almost at once, Milo whimpered and clawed the back window with his paws. The lump in my throat grew, and I heaved several breaths to ease the tension. It didn't take much of a leap to guess what this scene meant.

"Okay. We can do this. Sorry, Max. A dog as great as Milo had to be missed." I nudged Izzie in the arm. "Hey, we're home, and we've got company."

She yawned and looked out the window. "Who's that?"

I unbuckled my seat belt. "From the sound of Milo, who's about ready to bust out of the car, I'd guess that man is his owner."

"Oh. Ohh. This stinks." Izzie slouched in her seat. "Milo was becoming part of the family. Max will be devastated."

"Well, he's not ours to keep." I exited the car. Staring straight ahead, I gave my head a shake and wiggled both arms, to relax, then opened the rear car door.

Milo bounded out and sprinted across the lawn to the porch. He jumped up and down, until his owner gathered him in his arms and laughed as Milo licked his face.

I reached them and extended my hand. "Hi. I take it you're Milo's owner. I'm Chloe."

"Milo?" His brow creased. "Oh! You mean Rex." His smile widened, showing dimples on both cheeks. "I'm Brody. Glad to meet you, and I'm really glad you found Rex. Looks like he's been in good hands."

I studied Brody while he stroked Rex and laughed at all the wet kisses he was receiving. By my guess, he was in his mid-twenties to early thirties, with blond hair cropped short and ocean-blue eyes. "So, how did you find out we had Rex?"

"Funny story. I live about fifteen minutes from here in Seneca. I left Rex with a close friend while I had to take a job out of town for a couple of weeks. When I found out Rex had run away, I couldn't leave to come home. My friend contacted the local police department in Jamestown—that's where he lives—but no one reported finding a stray dog looking like Rex. I can't believe he came down this far."

"Hmm. Maybe he was trying to find his way home? I mean, since you live close to Whisper Cove."

"Hey! Who do we have here? Milo, did you find your owner?" Izzie laughed as she stepped next to me, with Max close behind.

"Milo's name is actually Rex. This guy is Brody. Brody, meet my sister, Izzie."

"Nice to meet you." He stood and shook her hand. His gaze didn't leave her face, and his hand didn't let go of hers right away.

Izzie blushed. "Would you like to come in?" She turned, opened the front door, and waved her arm to usher him in. "We've got plenty of beverages, if you'd like something to drink. Oh, and I made a batch of chocolate chip cookies this morning."

"Sure. That sounds nice." Brody smiled while Rex trotted down the hall to follow them.

I chuckled and shook my head at Max, who lay at my feet, his chin resting on the porch floor. "Don't worry, buddy. I have a hunch that we can persuade Brody to bring Rex over for a few playdates. Now, let's get some doggie treats to cheer you up, and maybe some of those chocolate chip cookies for me."

He stood and wagged his tail. "Woof."

I threw back my head and laughed. "I love you, Max. Life is good, isn't it? As long as we've got each other, I won't complain." Life *was* good. The murder was solved, and Whisper Cove had returned to normal. And best of all, I had a date with a great guy.

Acknowledgments

F irst, I'd like to thank my agent Dawn Dowdle for guiding me, encouraging me, and being my advocate in this writing venture. I am blessed to have you in my corner. To my editor, Faith Black Ross, and all the other staff at Crooked Lane Books, thank you for continuing to support my Paint by Murder series so I have the opportunity to keep the story of Chloe and Izzie going. As always, you are a pleasure to work with.

To my husband who is always patient and willing to stop at Bemus Point whenever we travel up that way. And I mean countless visits because this lakeshore town is my inspiration for the setting of this series. He doesn't even mind when I ask the locals—total strangers, mind you—questions, so I can learn more about the area. Like the bartender who gave me the scoop about the floating amphitheater moving from Bemus Point, after twenty years, to Mayville because of money issues. Those little details are like gold nuggets when it comes to writing.

And to Max, my four-legged, twelve-pound bundle of fur. He's my muse when I need one, and great company when I'm

Acknowledgments

pounding those keys to bring you more stories about Whisper Cove and all the wonderful characters . . . including the cute, four-legged ones. In fact, I enjoy Max being in the stories so much, I decided to add another canine pal to this installment!

Of course, I'm so blessed to have a fantastic network of fellow authors. Our local chapter of Sisters in Crime and the author brainstorm group I belong to inspire me. Their knowledge and advice are priceless. I don't know what I'd do without their support. Probably shove my writing in a box and take up gardening or knitting to fill my days! Just kidding. I love the craft, struggles and all.

And finally, to all the people who read my work—both old and new followers who've come on this journey with me—I am eternally grateful because every author needs an audience, and you all are the best!